PRAISE FOR *The Blue Hour*

"Graced with characters so alive, so full of quirky humanity, you miss them when you've finished the book, and written in prose as clear and gorgeous as a mountain afternoon, *The Blue Hour* isn't just about the many ways love can end—it's about how connection jumpstarts when you least expect it, too."

—CAROLINE LEAVITT, author of *Cruel Beautiful World* and the *New York Times* bestsellers *Is This Tomorrow* and *Pictures of You*

"Laura Pritchett's exquisitely linked novel of short stories—Jhumpa Lahiri comes to mind—manages to be all at once poetic and funny, heartbreaking and true. And the theme of sex—its role as social bonder, marriage breaker— is so beautifully, rarely addressed. This is a snapshot of the new West, as seen from that most breathtaking perspective—the inside out."

—ALEXANDRA FULLER, author of *Don't Let's Go to the Dogs Tonight* and *Leaving Before the Rains*

"Laura Pritchett has taken on love in all its complexity. Reminiscent of Charles Baxter's *Feast of Love*, every chapter of this beautifully linked novel gives us a story of conjugal love, passionate love, unrequited love. Actually there are so many wonderful works that this novel made me think of—Alice Hoffman's *Turtle Moon* and the classic Sherwood Anderson's *Winesburg, Ohio*—yet Pritchett's work feels unique in its humor, its exquisite writing on sex, and in just how blue her world manages to be. I loved it in its parts and in its whole. A novel I'll hold on to in my heart for a long time."

—MARY MORRIS, award-winning author of *The Jazz Palace*

"In Laura Pritchett's new novel, women and men enter the crucible of fate and violence and desire, sex and the obscure reaches of near comprehension. They emerge as if bound in mist, walking the mountain they love, calling out across an abyss of loneliness and unrest. In this place charged with dusk, still held by light, *The Blue Hour* sets lightning on the sky."

—SHANN RAY, author of *Balefire* and *American Masculine*

"How many books does each of us come across in a year, a decade, a lifetime? No matter how many you've picked up before today, *The Blue Hour* is one you should disappear with into a quiet room right now. The terrifically talented

Laura Pritchett has written an immersive, sexy, singular novel, each of its characters beautifully drawn and direly infused with desire and sadness and joy. They are trying to find a way to love each other and the world and not be driven mad by their desires. This is the kind of book I'm always searching for and am very grateful to have found in the lyrical and heartbreaking pages of *The Blue Hour* —CHRISTINE SNEED, author of *The Virginity of Famous Men*

"I adore this community and the tender bonds among the characters. It is spiritual, sensual, emotional, erotic, all within a vivid landscape. Here, we have what it is to be a human in love: fear that love will end, unrequited love, violence in love, regret and loss, pain and mental illness, fantasy, perversion, swingin', the end of love, brand-new love, and responsibilities in love. Gorgeous and honest and profound. Gems of wisdom and beauty."

—LAURA RESAU, author of *The Queen of Water* and *Red Glass*

"Piercing . . . An original meditation on sex, love, and death."

—*Kirkus Reviews*

"Pritchett is boldly lyrical, whether she is writing about the eyes of archangels or the dawning of a new day, or especially the love lives of her diverse cast of characters, united in both a quest for love and residence around the beautiful Blue Moon Mountain . . . In this elegant book, there's an appealing verisimilitude in the way the characters are variously, tentatively connected."

—*Publishers Weekly*

"In delicately balancing concerns about love and sex with the real life—sick animals, dying brothers, work, children, the annual community bird count—Pritchett paints a remarkably realistic portrait of how the erotic and the ordinary constantly intertwine in most human lives. As in her previous work (fans will enjoy cameos by characters from other novels and stories), she also balances the human struggles with nature's astounding, abundant beauty, so powerful, yet so needful of protection . . . Sex and passion, mental illness and mourning, birds and bears, a couple dozen viewpoint characters—it's a lot to weave into a smooth, compelling tapestry, but Pritchett pulls it off beautifully."

—*Daily Camera*

# The Blue Hour

## ALSO BY LAURA PRITCHETT

FICTION

*Red Lightning*

*Stars Go Blue*

*Sky Bridge*

*Hell's Bottom, Colorado*

NONFICTION

*Great Colorado Bear Stories*

AS EDITOR

*Going Green: True Tales from Scavengers, Gleaners, and Dumpster Divers*

*Home Land*

*Pulse of the River*

# The Blue Hour

A NOVEL

*Laura Pritchett*

COUNTERPOINT
BERKELEY

Library of Congress Cataloging-in-Publication Data is Available

Cover design by Debbie Berne
Interior design by Sabrina Plomitallo-González

ISBN 978-1-61902-604-9

COUNTERPOINT
2560 Ninth Street, Suite 318
Berkeley, CA 94710
www.counterpointpress.com

Printed in the United States of America
Distributed by Publishers Group West

10 9 8 7 6 5 4 3 2 1

*Dedicated to the mountains,*
*the people who live among them,*
*and lovers of all kinds,*
*everywhere*

Smile O voluptuous cool-breath'd earth!

Earth of the slumbering and liquid trees!

Earth of departed sunset—earth of the mountains misty-topt!

Earth of the vitreous pour of the full moon just tinged with blue! . . .

Smile, for your lover comes . . .

O unspeakable passionate love.

—Walt Whitman, *Leaves of Grass*

# Contents

*Chapter One*

# Creature of Blue

Particular snowflakes fall on your head as you stand outside your home so as to see the sky darken and the first ones spiral down, and the snow that reminds you of the beauty and brevity of life, how much every person has in common, when measured against eternity.

If you turn away from the waves of blue mountains and look toward your house, you will see your wife. She is visible in the square light of the window, folding laundry in your bedroom, a singular woman who has the totality of all it is to be human flurrying around inside her.

Remarkable, the shallowness of love. You used to come up with grand hopes about probability and luck, health and good fortune. Meanwhile you forgot how ice-thin the space between love and not-love, fondness and irritation. You have lived with your wife in this small mountain town for nearly twenty years, and now your wife is disgusted by the sight of you, she is not in love with you, and you are not in love with her, and this fact has sent you outside to stand in the trees and to spiral alone in the dark valley. You see she is folding your stained undershirt, and you realize that the most popular story on earth is of falling in love, and the next most popular story is falling out.

There are many ways for love to end. For some, the lucky ones, there is an intense fight, an unresolvable issue. *Okay!* you shout at each other. *It's over!* For others, there is just a quiet dissolution, a slackening and weakening, hardly perceptible. Love most often dies by ice and not fire.

Still, you must take action, otherwise you could be rightly called a coward. You know that it is a great sin, perhaps the greatest, to spend your short life pretending anything, especially pretending to be in love.

When your daughter Zoë was five, she was sick with pneumonia, and as you held her fevered body, she whispered, I feel like a tooth that's dangling by one lousy thread.

You think of that now, because you're thinking that sometimes it is your job to orchestrate the last yank.

Anya, you tell your wife, when you stomp your feet at the door to your bedroom, knocking off snow in the square patterns found on the soles of your work boots, I'm so sorry, but I am no longer in love with life, and I am no longer in love with you. I need to leave. But before I go, I'd like to get down on my knees (and here, you get down on your knee, as you did when you proposed to her), and you say, Anya, I'd like to bow to your more complex, passionate, and authentic original, which I know is in there somewhere. And I'd like to ask you to remember my truest and best version too.

She has turned from the laundry to look down at you kneeling among chunks of patterned snow, a quiet expression on her face. Quit laughing, Sy. It's not funny. Nothing about this is funny.

I'm sorry, Anya. I don't mean to be cruel. Look at this snow, melting. I'm getting everything all wet.

She crouches beside you and takes your cold hands. She says, Get up, Sy. I *realize* you don't love me, Sy. You're not capable of it at this point in time. But you could be. Sy, you have two children. Don't you forget that. Please stop laughing. The kids will hear you.

While she's talking, you notice, out of the corner of your eye, the purple-blue blur, like sheer fabric that is dancing. This dancing creature—sent from whatever God is out there—has been following you for about a month now. Every time you see her, she whispers in your ear. She says: There are many ways for love to end.

The creature is floating above you now, and she reaches out her wings to help you rise to your feet. She is a bit like a firefly and she is murmuring phrases about the blue moon, the rose moon, the hungry moon, the harvest moon.

You bring your wife into focus. She is standing in front of you, only inches away, tucking her short blond hair behind her ear. In the past, she has been angry with you, angry with your selfishness, angry at your supposed mental illness, angry with your physical body and its pains, and she has also showed signs of pity and compassion and fear. In the process, she grieved your loss, she has had an affair. Now you are dead to each other, only she refuses to participate in the final yank.

You used to love her, of this you are certain. Then she became the receptacle of all your talk, saliva, sperm, slights. She has become ugly from it.

Anya, you say, let me just try to explain. You tell her you recall things, such as dates and events, the tie you wore to your wedding, you recall Zoë and her tooth, you recall the birth of your son, Michael, you recall finishing vet school, you recall touching hundreds of animals, you recall fixing the throat of a chicken who had its neck slashed open by a fox and you recall that the chicken lived. Then you tell her that you cannot, despite your best efforts, catch what any of that *felt* like.

There are many ways for love to end. You know it's gone for sure when you tuck your chin, look down at your own chest, and squint. It seems to be snowing in there and the snow has drifted into every watershed of your heart.

～

She grows gentle, seductive. She wants to bring you back. She changes from a clothes-folder to lover. She is on her knees with you in her mouth, and you are surprised, since neither of you have done this for so long, and she uses her teeth gently, her tongue in fluttering ways, so soft as to be nearly as transparent as firefly wings. For a moment you are imprisoned by her tenderness and you realize she is a different creature altogether, a life-form that is more fluid than substance, more energy than solid mass. This surprises you. It surprises you that in this moment you cannot escape the gentle sorcery of her touch, how she releases chemicals that soften and bind. Perhaps she is telling you good-bye.

Above you, the creature floats and laughs at your amazement, and her laugh is more of a golden sigh. She watches as you and your wife find yourselves on the bed, amid the laundry, and she sees how you glide your head between your wife's legs and slide your tongue into her as deep as it will go, how you hum and lick, how you hold your wife down, one palm to stomach, so that she cannot escape you until she comes. The purple-blue creature watches your wife climb on her hands and knees and you slide inside her, and when you become too gentle, how your wife rocks back into you, hard, how you both finish with a gasp and a ducking of the head, as if in fervent prayer.

Anya, you whisper in her ear, when you are resting, I chose you.

I didn't fall for you, or find you, or fall in love. I flew into it. It was so sweet and simple. I could trust what I felt. I knew my mind.

Shhhh, Sy, shhhhh, she says.

Enough, she says.

That bear earlier today scared me, she says. That bear could have killed our children. It's a good thing Gretchen saved them. I know you only worry about the mountain lions, but there was a *bear*, and it was *big* . . . and she starts to cry.

Outside, the coyotes yip, their cries sparkling through the air. You look up at the purple-blue creature floating above you and you ask her, Please? But she shakes her head. A golden purr escapes her mouth, like the beginning of a song.

Sy, we all get that way, as if we can't feel. Sometimes. Have you been taking your meds? Please tell me you've been taking your meds.

You tell her you have not.

Oh, Sy, she says, rolling away from you.

You tell her you wanted to feel again.

Oh, Sy, she says. For how long?

You tilt her chin toward you with your finger. Anya, you say, there are many ways for love to end, and I want to do it right.

I can't keep you, she says. You can't make someone stay. The quiet rhythm of her voice reminds you that she has learned to soothe you through calm inflection of voice. You also know that you have given her one other great gift, which is the courage to seek love. You have just discovered that she is having an affair with Sergio, for she rightly needed some form of love in her life, and since you were not able to give it, she found the strength to embrace it elsewhere. You gave her infidelity, you gave her that strength.

You can't make someone stay, she repeats, but I love you. The bear, Sy.

You nod.

I do love you, Sy, she says again. Sy, you can leave me later. You can divorce me when you're well. I wish you were taking your meds, she says, and again she is crying. We need to stay together for the kids. There's no such thing as a good divorce for a kid. There are *bears*. She hiccups with this last phrase, unable now to speak.

Anya, you say loudly, in the years that I was married to you, whenever I asked what you were thinking, your answer was never about death or the human condition or fear or joy or sorrow; it was about kids or house items or people on this mountain. Anya, I choose to believe you were lying to me. You never gazed into my eyes, or discussed your dreams. I used to think it was because you were not that kind of woman, but I choose now to believe I was simply the wrong man to do the asking.

Sy, she says, I do think of those things.

What a waste then, you say quite loudly, and even the purple-blue creature buzzes to the corner of the room, afraid. You should have tried to tell me! Did you think life would be more than this? I knew it wouldn't last, but I did think it would be bigger, that it would simply be more joyful.

The children, your wife says. They're a big thing. What are you looking at?

You are sitting up now, staring at the blur. Anya, you say, Anya, listen, I need to tell you this. At first, you think, I am out of love with life, but such thoughts are anomalies, quickly dispersed. Bad day, week, season. Or you notice the spiral of mountain mahogany seeds or the way a doe flicks her tail and picks up her hind leg at the exact same moment. Or the meadow beneath Blue Moon Mountain. Such information causes interference for a while. But the thoughts become more frequent until they are in your mind every day.

In fact, you realize, you are now thinking of this failed love as often as you used to think of love. You used to want to feel and see it all! You wanted to bury your nose in the fur of an animal you had just saved, you wanted to kiss your wife for a very long time, you wanted to see how light flies off water. But then one evening, such as this evening, you and your wife will tuck your kids into bed and it will be cold out, and just starting to snow, the season's first snow, the day after Halloween, and your wife sends you outside to watch the sky and then she makes herself tea in a blue mug and she goes to finish the laundry.

And during this time you will simply decide to tell the truth. You are thinking clearly tonight. Clear as the stars. You love the sky at this time of night. You are in the *l'huere bleue* of your life, the blue hour, the hour of dusk, the hour when everything changes. And you know you are out of love, in the quietest sort of way.

~

Your wife says you should sleep. Despite your lovemaking, she is still wearing some of her clothes, and she stands up to remove them and to put on red pajamas. A few fine strands of her blond hair stand up because of the dry weather. While she pulls on flannel pajama pants, you tell her that you believe now that you must do the very things that frighten you.

She goes into the bathroom. You hear the water running as your wife washes. You get up quickly and start to dress. As you are dressing, you hear your wife peeing. This makes you laugh and you can't stop and the purple-blue creature laughs with you, for she too is joyful and in awe at the dumb animalness of us all. You are nearly out of the house when your wife finds you, and she stands in front of the door until you pick her up and move her, and then she hangs on to your waist until you twist away. Then she shouts at you, she shouts your name, she tells you she loves you at the top of her lungs, and she asks you to kiss your children, and that is when you know that she knows, and you are impressed that she knows, and you love her for it, because you realize perhaps you have been wrong, it has only been a lack of good communication, and she has loved you all along.

When she picks up the phone, you go outside, start up your truck, which at first resists because of the cold, but comes to life with your coaxing, and then you drive. You would have liked to kiss your children's foreheads, that is true. But the purple-blue creature kisses *your* forehead instead, helps you conjure an image of their faces, and does this in a certain way as to bring you peace, not anguish.

You know you must hurry, that you must find your friend Joe, because he has the thing you need. It is starting to snow harder now, little tiny flakes that indicate how cold it is, and how much colder it is going to become.

Already all the wooden fence posts have little caps of white. You put in those fence posts yourself with post-hole diggers and a tamp bar and barbed wire; your hands still bear the scars. The purple-blue creature is floating next to you, nearly touching you—you can see her quite well now—the veins on her wings, the butterfly qualities about her. She is coming into focus, at last. She floats next to your face and helps you look for a particular truck. She has made it easy for you: There is Joe's pickup parked at the house nearest you, which belongs to Gretchen, your only neighbor on this quiet mountain road. Joe, your friend, is visiting his new lover. This lover, Gretchen, is your wife's best friend. Inside, Joe and Gretchen are exploring the crevices and peaks of their desire. Theirs is a love story.

In Joe's truck lies a Colt .45, wrapped in warm fleece, insulated, in a box that is locked, for which you have the key, having stolen it last week. Your own guns have been taken from you.

You leave your friend a scrawled note as a way of apology. The note does not get at the truer part of yourself that you're wishing you could show, but there is no time now; you had a lifetime to achieve that and you failed.

You drive up the mountain, for there is a particular meadow you're hoping for. The snow, it's beautiful, and silent, and purifying. The snow, it's disappearing into the black waters of the river beside the road. The snow, it's rhythmic and pulls you forward, beckons you ahead.

You know these thick-falling flakes will get worse and be a part of an unexpected blizzard. It is the first day of November, and this coming winter will be an unexpected time for everyone on the mountain. Difficult and yet full of change, full of fight, full of fury, full of love. They will move into a spiral of beauty, the way the snow spirals at you now. You think it a bit funny that the blizzard struck before your town of Blue Moon was ready. Salt for the roads has not yet been delivered; it has been so mild, the aspens still hang on to some gold, the bears are still out. But here is the snow. It will be a bad storm; that is evident by the way the wind is starting to swoop down off the mountain, angry and alive.

You drive farther up the canyon, careful on the turns, mesmerized by the points of white coming directly at your windshield, by the demons of swirling ghost-snow on the road.

At the base of the actual Blue Moon Mountain is a meadow. Nearby, you get out of the truck and the creature glides out behind you, floats around your head in calm circles. The snow is picking up, spiraling down one minute, blowing sideways the next, but silent. You think ahead: There will be one loud shot, and that shot will startle the birds and the animals, and even the falling snow, and even the moon, and for a fraction of a second, there will be the profound and deafening silence that is the same sort of silence that resides inside you. As you fall, there will be a moment in which you will finally feel all that has ever risen in your heart exploding into fine white dancing flakes.

## Chapter Two

# Under the Apple Tree

When Joe left me sitting under the apple tree and started to walk across the pasture, he looked back and waved, and then walked on, and then turned and waved, and then walked on, and then he did a complete circle with his arms out, like he was embracing the world. That made me laugh because we were both so happy and so willing to show it. I was leaning back against the tree, most of my clothes back on, wrapped in a blanket, and I watched him go in his spinning cheerful way, and I blew him kisses. Then he got near my trailer and dirt driveway, which is where he'd left his truck, and he climbed in, honked, honked again, and left.

We'd just made love and we'd both come twice, and my body was feeling full and complete and tired. The contrails from the flying sparks of orgasm were just starting to fade, and I felt them dissipate into the space of my body. As they did, I picked twigs out of my hair and wiped a smudge of dirt from my forearm and let my mind think things like, *the only thing grand enough for a human life is to love* and *this is where wild and gentle get sewn together*, and the sorts of things that make perfect sense at a time like that, and only at a time like that, and I just sat still and let them.

When he was gone, I considered the sharp rotting smell of apples, and the slant of cold sunlight on my bare feet, and the ache of my knees and inner thighs. After some time, I walked toward my trailer home, bundled up in my blanket, spinning around by myself, and once inside, I flopped on my bed, and I closed my eyes and replayed the whole thing—our lovemaking, and my orgasms, and his, and our mumblings. Then my mind wandered on to less romantic things, like the fact that my rear is dimpled with fat, but I like that position; and that perhaps I had said a stupid thing or two, which was too bad, but entirely predictable. I rubbed my head where it had hit the apple tree, and I brushed away the bits of earth still smashed against my spine.

Joe and I have the exact same hair color—so dark brown that it's almost black, only his is curly and mine hangs straight to my waist. Our hair is graying, Joe's near his temples and mine spread all throughout, and his is softer than mine, because the gray in mine has turned it less supple. I love it when he takes my hair up, suddenly, and starts to braid it, which is something he knows how to do from braiding harnesses, and I love pushing my hands up, through his hair, and feeling the soft place where scalp ends and hair begins.

I thought of our hair, and each other's hands in our hair, and I made myself come again. I was curious if I could accomplish three, which is something I hadn't done before. When my body stopped pulsing, I decided that orgasm is the greatest physical pleasure in life—greater than the feeling of being high, being drunk, feeling sunlight, touching water, catching a snowflake, or the taste of something sweet or salty or new, and that this had to be especially true if one was being held at the same time, and being kissed, and being loved.

I wondered how Joe saw the world, through what lens, filtered through what experience. I pretended to be him. I tried to be in his body, looking in the mirror at himself, touching his own stubbled jaw, seeing his graying curly hair and his own brown eyes, and how he might stare himself down, stare right at his own fears and hopes and hurts. I tried to feel how he might close his eyes and become aware of his whole body and perhaps be aroused, feel a spark, alert and alive.

Doing this made my heart hurt a little, but instead of evening out my feelings, or tempering them with those ongoing judgments the brain makes, instead of starting in with the *he-lacks-such-and-such-a-quality* and all those things the mind does so that it *likes* less and therefore *feels* less—those things, I did not do. I stared at the ceiling of the room, with my hand still between my legs, and *felt* Joe and *experienced* Joe as much as I could, and I let myself continue to do this, despite the very real danger.

I live too hard and I know it. Every once in a while I get myself into some trouble because of this but generally, over the course of my life, I have come to believe it's worth it. I drink too much, I smoke too much pot, I sleep around. That sort of thing. My body and heart are getting beat up faster than they should be, but I won't regret this life as much as some people will want me to.

I have one bias that I cannot rid myself of. Perhaps we all ought to be allowed to have just one, and mine is that I severely dislike stingy people. By this I mean not only in the cash sense, but in the people of the world who aren't generous with their *thank you*s or their *I'm sorry*s and most importantly, with the people who spend so little time thinking about others, so little energy loving. I do not like miserly hearts.

Which is probably why I like Joe so much, because he is, at the core, generous. He is, for example, willing to walk away from his new lover, and tell her good-bye in the most charitable way he can, by spinning and holding his arms out to the world. He is announcing: *Life is good, that was good, I love you.* That is something, really that is something.

I am a house cleaner. I sell pot on the side, even now that it's legal, because who wants to drive to town when they know I'm here, on the mountain, and a good grower? My goal here is to make a living as quickly as I can, so I can spend the rest of my day hiking, or snowshoeing, or reading, or getting high, and now, increasingly, with Joe and his body, or inside my brain, with Joe and his body. The only other interesting thing I can say about myself is that I've always been fascinated by sex; which is not to say that I've engaged in a huge amount of wondrous activity, but rather that I have paid attention to sex the way some people pay attention to race car drivers or sports teams. If there were a column in the paper, it would be the first I'd turn to, but since there isn't I follow this topic in other ways. I know about *The Hite Report* and *Deep Throat* and I know about Candida Royalle porn. I know what Freud and Foucault have to say, and I try to keep up with what's been said since, and I know the most basic truth about enjoying sex, which is that it's part instinct, but mostly, it's concentration, it's a learned activity.

It can't be learned with just anybody, though, and I'm beginning to think that's what's going on with Joe. That is why losing him scares me. He's going to open me right up, make me understand and feel, and then the loss will be one that I'm not strong enough to bear. He will get in his truck and drive out of my life, back to his horseshoeing and his mountain walks and his hunting and the things that do not include me. Or, more likely, I will do the same to him. I have always prized my freedom above all else.

I'm just hoping we can both be generous with each other for at least a while, at least long enough for my body to develop the neural pathways of this new feeling. I want to have the body-knowledge and the body-memory of what it is like to be this happy.

⤴

Anya's two kids are always coming over to my property to pick apples. Anya is my one friend, and she's also my only neighbor way up here in this mountain enclave. We have a remarkable friendship, really, and I love her. Anya has short blond hair, which she dyes, and she's married to the town vet, and she's a therapist, and she's got these two kids and she exercises and she eats right, and so in many ways, Anya is the opposite of me. That's why we're friends, at least in part, so that we can see the other life, the road not taken; we can bounce into that every once in a while without having to live it ourselves.

The apple tree sits right between our two houses, with about an acre on each side, and the tree lures her kids onto my place, which is more overgrown with raspberry bushes I planted, and the milkweed and mountain mahogany and grasses that nature did. I tell her kids to watch out because there's a bear. His scat is all over the place, big dumps of apple seed–laden piles. In fact, Joe and I had to work to find a place under the tree that was free of this stuff. I haven't actually seen the bear, but sometimes I can smell it, the vinegar smell of its urine, the rank smell of the body, and I imagine it's pretty fat by now and ready for winter. The kids need to be careful, and I tell them this, but they escape out of the house, right when Anya is trying to put bread in the oven, for instance—she is a great baker—and these kids were meant for the outdoors and I think that's great but I worry about the bear.

Anya's marriage is a regular marriage, which means, as she puts it, that sometimes it gets bad, then it gets better, then it gets bad again. As far as I can tell, there's not a lot of passion, but there is that nice blend of patience and knowledge and affection that marks long marriages, and except for the boredom part, it seems pretty nice. But the boredom thing is a big one; it's the thing that would kill me. It's probably more of an issue in her case, because Sy is sick, or used to be, at least, some say schizophrenia and others say bipolar and others say bipolar delusional, but in any case, the meds make Sy particularly dead-ish, dreamy-ish in a way that would make it difficult to be seen or known. I think that's why Anya's house is very organized, and she lines up cans in one cupboard and the plastic containers in another. She makes lists. Sometimes I envy the crisp edges of her desire, how it seems to be enough to hold her together.

Anya thinks I'm amusingly wild and I like regaling her with stories, and so when she came over for our five-o'clock whiskeys, which is something we do every other day, I told her about Joe. Anya's kids, who are now five and six, play at something or another, and mostly they are agreeable although sometimes they are irritating, and even though it's sometimes hard to like other people's kids, these kids I do like. So, while the kids were playing in the grass, near the apple tree, Anya and I sat wrapped up in blankets and drank and commented on how golden the aspens were this year, as if heralding a special winter, and I told her about how Joe's kisses had a certain pull to them, his hands had a certain knowledge, how his fingers listened. I told her that it was startling to suddenly, at this age, be experiencing such orgasms. Orgasms that came so easily, with the muscle contractions spreading through my body with unexpected lightness and force, great crashes of sparks that danced as they shot from my inner regions to my skin. But orgasms that, despite this force, were grounded in the most tender gentleness. I had never believed that a man, or the world, could seem so safe.

Anya stared at me a long time. She said, "Sy and I never have sex like that. Not anymore. Maybe we never did."

I could hear the waver in her voice, so I said, "Well, there's a lot of days when I wish I had one particular person. And that I had kids."

"Sy and I haven't really kissed in, well, about thirteen years," she said. "Since he got sick. Not a real kiss. Not full of love. Unbelievable."

"I don't have anyone to sleep with me at night," I said. "Not most nights."

"Well, Gretchen, we could all use more than one life." Then she said, "Are you ever scared at night? Noises and stuff?"

"Sometimes," I said.

"Sometimes I'm scared too, but for different reasons."

"But you feel physically safe, and that's something."

She nodded her agreement. We sat for a while and ate some of her homemade bread with Havarti cheese and the last of this year's raspberries, the sweeter kind that grow over by the edge of my property, in between my land and hers.

"Can I ask you something?" I finally said. "When you orgasm, during sex, you're telling yourself a story in your head, right? You're imagining another scene, other than the one that is occurring, right?"

Anya tilted her head and considered this. Then she chewed on her thumb and thought about it some more. "That's probably true."

"Can you orgasm without it? Without a story going on in your head?"

Her eyes moved across the pasture, as if the pasture was the landscape of her brain, and she was examining the horizon for memories and experience. "I don't think I can. I think I need the story. I'll pay attention to confirm that for sure." She stuffed some bread in her mouth and looked up at the sky.

"Because I couldn't. Without a story," I said. "But then, with Joe, I suddenly could. I mean, it's ridiculous! It sounds like a romance novel! It sounds like I'm one of those women doing a disservice to womankind by granting the man too much, by having too much pleasure, by exaggerating the possibilities. It also sounds like the beginning of a love, not the harder part that tests and tries you. I know that too. But I just want to be happy. I want to store these moments up for later."

"That's sounds smart. Have another drink."

"I've had bad sex before," I said. "Plenty of it. Bad sex, mediocre sex, standard sex. But suddenly this. It has to do with how *there* we are. Anya, it's a whole different way of being, really. And it's confusing my body, and I just didn't expect that kind of surprise."

She said, "Joe sounds better than any of your previous choices. By a long shot. Maybe you should figure out a way to make this work. Maybe you're really in love."

Anya chewed on her lip, which is something she does, and I could tell she was telling herself all the things she *didn't* like about my life, so she could confirm her choices. As part of her righting of herself, her eyes veered off to her kids, as if to say, *There, that's what you have, there they are.*

After she was done looking at them, I said, "Can I ask you one more thing? These stories, the ones we tell ourselves, they have violence in them, don't they? Spankings? Forced blow jobs? Being tied up? At least sometimes?"

Anya raised her eyebrows and then laughed. "Yes."

I said, "I think most women do. Link violence and arousal. What's that all about? Some buried remnant, some cultural leftover. It's true for me. Or it *was*, before Joe. But here's what I'm getting at. I was thinking about this while I was cleaning today. Humans are going to evolve. Someday, when you and me are long gone, you know, humans will be different, they'll change for the better. One, they're going to figure out how to communicate on a higher level. Two, they're going to be able to see another person better. Because three, they're going to be able to see inside themselves better, with some clarity. And four, this violence, it's going to disappear. For some women, it's just not going to be inside anymore."

She gave me an endearing look and said, "Gretchen, that's very optimistic of you."

"I know," I said.

"You're seeming very young today," she said.

"I know," I said.

"It's lovely. Your cheeks are flushed."

"It's ridiculous," I said.

⌖

Joe has one strange quirk, as I've come to find out, which is that he prefers to make love outdoors.

"I can't breathe inside," he told me.

"Winter is coming," I said. "It's comfortable inside. There are things like beds and blankets and heat."

He shrugged. "I can *do* it. I'm *capable* of it. I won't turn sex down. But I'm not going to like it, not as much."

So I immediately started thinking of ways to manage this particular request. Blankets I could pull from the shed and wash. Sleeping bags. Perhaps a little apple-tree shelter.

We were under the tree again a few days ago when we noticed that the bear had just clawed the tree. The bark had been shredded away, leaving long pale streaks of tenderness. What had happened, we surmised, is that the bear had gotten all the apples within reach and now he was climbing up for the ones at the top. He was getting desperate for calories; winter was coming.

"If we weren't outside right now," Joe said, "I wouldn't have seen the bear's claw marks. These leaves wouldn't be falling through the sky. And I couldn't watch the light and the way it hits your body. And they're all very beautiful."

That made me shy so I laughed. "Schoolkids, that's what we sound like."

This whole time, he had been inside me and rocking me gently—we had stopped to let our bodies catch up with the sensations—and then he really kissed me, and his hands went to my breasts, and his lips moved to my throat, which made my back arch, and then the pathways traveling between my mouth and breasts and pelvis were lit, and there was a very long period of feeling very good, so good that I had to hit the ground with my fist, and I could not help but moan and thrust my body into Joe's with a strength that would have scared me had it not been matched by a welling of tenderness. I was telling my body to come, come, and I was afraid I was going to numb-out, but then the *inside* of my body broke out in a sweat, that's what it felt like, and I heard myself making noises that seemed a little out of hand, but then an image flooded my mind, Joe walking with his arms out, embracing the world, and so I thought, oh yes, just let yourself do this, and he made his own animal noise as he came, and we both sounded like the wild creatures that humans can sometimes be.

For a long time, Joe ran his hands across my back, and front, and thighs. He told me about bears. That this time of year a bear will spend almost twenty hours a day foraging, and that the drive to collect food is very strong, and that now they've moved from the summer flowers and grasses to berries and apples, and they have to work hard to get the twenty thousand calories a day that they're going to need for winter. Bears mate in the spring but they have delayed implantation, which means the fertilized egg floats freely in the uterus, and the egg implants and develops now, in the autumn. And then Joe paused and said, black bears are solitary and intelligent and curious, just like you, and he kissed me. And he said, one of these days, we're going to see this bear.

When he was done talking about the bear, I talked about females and sex, since that's what was on my mind. I told him that the reason women could come more than once was that after orgasm there's an instantaneous refilling of certain chambers, meaning that orgasm doesn't return a woman physiologically to an unaroused state but rather to a pre-orgasmic level of arousal. Some women are not aware of their orgasmic capacity, including me, and that before him, I had thought I was unable to have more than one. I told him this was probably good for his male ego, but that wasn't why I was telling him. I told him I had my own selfish interest in the topic. I told him that orgasms made me feel strong, and also that they smoothed over all the hurt in the world. I told him that I had recently decided that good orgasms took some concentration, some imagination, and a little spark of craziness. They also relied heavily on a feeling of safety and generosity.

Joe sat there, head propped on his hand, touching my body. He seemed curious, in the best of ways, willing to listen without expectation or judgment.

I said, "Do you have to be somewhere? Do you need to go?"

"No," he said. "No."

"I don't believe you," I said. Then I added, "The more orgasms a woman has, the stronger they become. The more she has, the more she *can* have."

He said, "Gretchen, in certain ways, you remind me of a bear."

I said, "I just think you should know all this."

He leaned over to kiss my nose. I traced his body with my fingers, and when he buried his head into my shoulder I wrapped him in my arms. While we were resting this way, a gunshot sounded from somewhere in the valley. The geese took off slanting and honking into the sky, but I could sense that the rest of the world—the songbirds and mice and deer—stopped still.

"Hunting season," I said.

"Yes."

"Bear hunting is over."

"But not deer and elk."

Eventually, Joe had to go, he had an appointment to shoe horses, which was about the same time Anya would arrive home with her kids after school. Since the apple tree is in view of her house, we've had to take her schedule into consideration. We waited until the last minute, and then Joe and I gathered up our things and left, and when he climbed into his truck, he jumped right back out again to kiss me and he surprised me by saying, "You're holding my heart together right now," and I wanted to ask him about it, but he got in his truck, and he drove away.

∽

When I came home from cleaning today at noon, the kids were out by the apple tree, winging fallen apples around. I watched them as I unloaded my cleaning supplies: the bucket of rags, the containers full of chemicals, the vacuum. I'd cleaned three houses in record speed and it's amazing the sort of energy that love can give you. When I went inside, I wrote myself a note to buy a new can of WD-40 because that stuff is the best for taking off sticky substances, and I'd just used up the last of mine cleaning tape residue from a fridge door. I flopped on the couch and tamped some pot into my beautiful green pipe but didn't light it.

I was thinking now about the future for Joe and me. He'd left a few days ago, a short trip to Denver to see some family, due home tomorrow, and his immediate absence made me think of his future presence, or lack thereof. I tried to stop myself, but I couldn't resist going over the possibilities. Of course we would end, at some point in time. And we would end like most relationships end, in which one or both persons fade themselves out. It takes too much energy, too much bravery, really, to say good-bye, literally, with force, and usually there's just a silent withdrawal, hardly perceptible, until it becomes obvious. You quit being so generous—with yourself and the other person. Joe would quit going out of his way to stop by, and I wouldn't go out of my way to rearrange my cleaning schedule. And strangely enough, this lack of giving would make us feel trapped, like there was suddenly too much, and that there would then be conditions we would not agree to, and we would want again our freedom. Then we'd give each other a tired, sad smile, because somewhere inside, we'd know it was over.

One of the beautiful things Ovid wrote was, "If you seek a way out of love, be busy; you'll be safe then." So I sat on the couch and lectured myself about this: *Do not do that, do not get busy*. Instead, I decided, when we were over, I would sit around and smoke pot, and I'd let the great wilderness of the inner life take over, as it should.

Because it was a gloomy day, I knew Anya would be making brownies, for which she uses only Callebaut chocolate, because chocolate helps her get through gloom, and I knew she'd bring me some, because she's not stingy, and something about that made me want to walk out and see her kids. I stashed the pipe for later and went outside, and there they were, under the apple tree. They were wearing coats but no hats and gloves and Zoë had a clear line of snot running from her nose to her lip. They were crouched down, staring at two grasshoppers, who were, no joke, having sex. There was a bigger grasshopper and a smaller, greener one, and their tails were bent toward each other, connected at the end.

"Look, Gretchen!" Zoë squinted up at me. "These grasshoppers are wrestling!"

"Indeed they are," I said.

"Just like we wrestle!" said the boy, whose name is Michael.

"Sort of," I said.

"There's a lot of bear poop under your apple tree," said Zoë, as if I were responsible for it. "We poked at it with a stick. We think the bear ate ten million apples to have so much seed in its poop."

"That seems about right." Then I said, "Are you two happy?"

They looked up at me, red-cheeked. It looked like they were wondering if I was stupid. Michael didn't say anything but Zoë said, "Halloween was yesterday. I'm happy."

"Okay," I said. And that's when we heard it. A *huff, huff* and then another *huff, huff* and the first thing that hit me was the smell. A very bad smell, really, and I said, "Oh, kids," the same time that the bear appeared out of the raspberry bushes and regarded us. "Oh, kids," I said again, and I thought, *Damn, this bear was supposed to come when* Joe *was here*, but I said, very calmly, "Don't worry, kids. It will go away," and then I addressed the bear, "Bear, go away. Go away, Bear."

But it did not go away. It was moving from the raspberry bushes toward the apple tree, as if it had not seen us, although surely it had, because we were only thirty feet away. It seemed very calm. It was a dark brown, darker in the head, and its ears were round, and its nose curved upward just a bit. It took four steps and then it sat back on its butt and I realized it was a she because the nubs of her nipples ran down her belly.

Zoë let out a small animal noise, and Michael was frozen but I could tell he was about to scream or run and so I said, very fast, "Kids, don't move, do *not* move, stay right next to me, that's right, move right in behind me." I kept my eyes on the bear, who paused and seemed to be listening to me too. I shuffled them behind me. "Bear," I said, "we are not going to hurt you and you can have the apples. If you hurt us, I will hurt you back."

The kids were starting to cry and so I said, "Kids, I want you to know one thing. This bear will have to fight me before she gets to you. And let me tell you, I can put up a great fight." While I was talking the bear stared at me for a long time and then got bored and started walking in our direction, a little to the right. All she wanted was the apple tree.

I started backing up, kids behind me, and looking around for sticks but there weren't any, but there were a few bruised and wormy apples, scattered out where we were, so I bent over, slowly, and picked up three at my feet. I guessed that I could throw pretty hard and with pretty good aim, and no creature really wants to be pelted with apples, and so I believed the apples were going to save us, and then I felt calm and safe, which gave me enough time to pause and consider the bear.

She sat down, suddenly, and huffed. She seemed uncertain as to what to do herself. Her need to get to those apples was very strong. I decided I liked her because she was stubborn and perhaps lived too hard. If I did not have two kids behind me, grabbing so hard at my shirt that they were strangling me, I felt as if I might stand there and consider her for quite awhile.

"We're going to back up now," I whispered. "Are you ready? If she comes, I'll throw apples at her and punch her in the nose, and you two get to my house, no matter what. Hold hands. Okay?"

As we moved back, the bear got on all fours and lowered her head and then she moved forward, rapidly, right at us. She was angrier than I would have supposed. I heard myself say, "Oh god oh god oh god," and my arm cocked backward with the apple, ready to fast-pitch it at her face, and my other arm went backward and below, to shield the kids, and then I said, very loudly, "Bear! Your egg is implanting and you *will not* hurt us!" Suddenly I was very angry with her, and my mouth opened on its own and I made a very wild noise, a very wild noise for a very long time, a noise that basically meant *get the hell away from me and these kids.*

Joe came home a few hours later—he had returned early from Denver, due to a storm suddenly in the forecast, and he sure as hell didn't want to get stuck with relatives—and I told him about the bear. How she held her ground and watched us go. I told him that the kids and I watched her from my kitchen window, saw her stare after us and then climb up the apple tree, where she stayed for some time.

We were sitting up, near the apple tree, having dragged two chairs out there and having built a campfire in a rock-lined fire pit that Joe had quickly made for the express purpose of being able to be outside near the apple tree while he heard the story of the bear. It was just starting to snow, the first of the year, tiny flakes that reminded me of campfire ash, perhaps because they reflected the gray of the sky. The campfire itself started crackling in response and I pulled up the blanket around my chin—a thin one from my car—and said, "Let's go inside, this is ridiculous," and Joe kept saying, "It sure is," but we didn't move.

Joe pulled me into his lap and was hugging me tight because I was shaking. Perhaps it was the cold, perhaps it was the nervous energy, perhaps I had come to the point where I felt the need to unleash many words upon Joe because I needed someone to listen. I talked for a very long time. Perhaps more than I ever had to any other human. I told Joe that Anya had looked out her window and saw the bear gliding at us and that she'd dialed the fire department at the same time she started running for her kids, but then, when she saw the bear stop, changed her route so that she wouldn't have to run right by the bear. She came panting up to my trailer soon after we'd reached it. She promised me a lifetime supply of brownies. I told him that Anya's marriage had gotten to that place where imagination fails, and that she and her husband were each feeling like a prisoner. I told him we'd probably ramble through the same cycle, if we stuck it out. I told him that I loved him. I told him that when we broke up, I would think back as this being the Time of Joe, and that I believed a few good memories could sustain a person.

He held me to him, and listened and hugged me tighter now and then. Sometimes he said things back, little phrases to show his agreement, or simply to acknowledge he was listening, and, when I had wound down, he told me about the horseshoeing conference and about his cute blond niece and some elk he had seen a few days ago, including one female who kept rubbing her head against a tree. He told me he saw no need in forecasting the end of us, although he understood the impulse, and that he too had recently wondered what there was to live for, exactly, besides some form of love?

Our conversation wound around different topics and stopped-and-started and circled back and I felt like both our bodies and our words were like grapevines, and then I felt the foolishness of that, and then I let go of the feeling of feeling foolish.

It was during a lapse into silence that we heard the fall of feet. It was Anya, walking straight at us. She had in one arm a big two-toned brown blanket. Tucked in her other armpit was a silver thermos, and in this hand she also held a tinfoil-covered plate of whatever it was that she'd just baked. She was smiling, pleased for us. She handed the thermos and covered dish to Joe, and then, with both hands, she flung out the blanket in the air, where it hovered for a moment, and she guided it down on top of us.

"Joe," she said, "hello."

He reached up to shake her hand. "Good to see you, Anya."

"Have a brownie," she said. "Snowstorm is coming. You may not want to drive up the mountain tonight. Gretchen, thank you again for saving my kids." She brushed her hands together, as if she were now done with her job. "I'm off to have dinner with my family. Sy will be home soon." She brushed a thick strand of wet blond hair out of her face and turned on her heels and left.

"Joe," I said, as I watched her go. "Stay the night? Please. I need you next to me." I breathed out, releasing a long gust of air, and then my teeth began to chatter. We pressed our bodies together in the lawn chair and huddled inside the blanket and drank Anya's coffee and ate her brownies and watched as the snow moved sideways. The sky darkened and the snow picked up, and finally we stood, kicked the rocks into the fire, and ran for my trailer, our hands thrown out to the world.

## Chapter Three

# The Color of the Impression

To get past certain emotions, say love for example, it will take both effort and erosion. When the effort isn't working, despite a person's best attempts, and the erosion is taking too long despite her patience, this person will realize she is going to be required to hold certain feelings in her heart and continue on as if they're not there. She'll be struck by the knowledge that others are walking around doing the same thing, greeting her in this mountain town's tiny post office as if their hearts were not aching with melancholy, and even worse, that they'd prefer to keep the relevant words unspoken.

Well. That is what I learned from Ruben.

I was ice-skating on the pond, the new Australian shepherd pup bounding around next to me, leaping at my legs in adoration and joy, and it was this exuberance that caused us to collide, and I ran over her paw with the blade of my skate. Her yelp pierced the air as I plunged forward, right into the boat that I leave upside down next to the pond. My head hit the chine of the boat, the boat being a little plywood number I made myself. So many things happen in such a moment, of course, in the expanse of a meadow still filled with morning fog, and I thought *oh, this hurts* and tipped my head back so the blood in my nose would run backward, and my tongue felt out the cut on my lower lip, and my eyes sought out the puppy. She was limping over to me, leaving bloody footprints on the ice, including one red swipe where she slipped stepping over the push broom I'd used to clear away the snow.

I knew I was fine but that the puppy should get to the vet, if only because the prints were pure blood now, thick blood, like her foot was a brush sopped with red paint. I stood, sat again, stood, then sat, then stood and skated over to the edge of the pond, where I'd left my hiking boots. It took me some time to unlace the skates as my fingers were thick with cold and the laces were hard, but finally I gathered the pup in my arms and I carried her to my truck. I was dizzy, I wanted to collapse into the snow, but I told myself, as I do at such times, *oh, Lillie, shut up and wait it out,* because the pain would pass and I believed then that such fleeting moments shouldn't get much attention, though now I understand that they are in fact what make up my life.

There was an old towel under the pickup's seat. The last time I'd used it was to rub a newborn calf into life. He'd been plopped down, wet and slick, into the snow on a day that was ten below and his mama was doing a half-assed job of licking him warm. But the calf lived, and that's what I was thinking as I started the truck, the memory of me wrapping the calf in blue and the warmth of life underneath, just like when I put one hand on the pup's side to hold her down into the seat and apologized for the ways life can surprise you with pain.

That was several years ago. That was the last moment I remember of my old self, my self that had not yet met Ruben. The next moment I was in a train wreck, which is to say, I was in the wrong place at the wrong time in the wrong state of mind. I could not have avoided it, even if I'd tried, which I did not.

⤚

Ruben is not the vet. Ruben is the vet's technician, and judging from his looks you'd guess he's about thirty. A child. In comparison. To me. So perhaps I am crazy or worse. But Ruben looked at me as I told my story, looked at me for longer than one would expect. Ruben glanced at the puppy, and then looked back into my eyes, and again he held the gaze for some time. His eyes are very dark, liquid dark. The puppy was on the examining table and Ruben held the paw, and after I quit talking, Ruben started to sing a song under his breath, a country song I recognized but didn't know all the words to, and neither did Ruben, because he patched it together with *somethin somethin somethin*. Then Ruben said, "Name?" and tilted his head at the dog.

"Well. I don't know, I just got her. I call her Puppy."

Ruben's eyes moved from the pup's foot to my head. "Your forehead. You could use a stitch or two." But he said it without conviction, because we both knew I wouldn't be driving twenty more miles off the mountain into the sprawl of town for two stitches.

"I hit the *Far Side*. That's the name of my boat. Which is what I hit," I said. "Do you have any of that glue that sticks your skin together? It didn't hurt. Yes, actually, it did. But a passing sort of pain! Not the kind that sticks with you! You know that glue I'm talking about?"

In that moment, in Ruben's eyes was this thought: *We will be good friends.* That is a surprising thing for him to be thinking so soon, but nonetheless, that is what his eyes told me.

It might be too much to believe that's all it took. Although maybe not; maybe you can move from disinterest to interest to crush to heat to calm respect in a few moments. Perhaps it's uncommon to run into a new person on the mountain, one who has interests that closely align with yours—animals, outdoors, fragments of country music, tenderness in a world that is without—and then to have your breath taken away for no other reason than his searching eyes and some sort of quiet sadness buzzing about him. Perhaps, on top of this, you know you are a bit off-kilter, and that the outside world has a tendency to scowl at you since you cannot quite maneuver through life as they do, and perhaps you know that there are only a handful of people who are going to think that's fine and maybe even preferable. Perhaps all this can happen, and it is not love, at that particular instant, but it is the beginning of it, or at least contains the potential.

Ruben said, "Yes, glue, in a minute," like that was the conclusion he'd already come to. "Your pup has a deep laceration, but the tendon isn't severed. It's a full-skin thickness cut, though, so Sy will use skin staples, wrap it, antibiotic. Clean cut, though. Nice cut for a cut." He shrugged. "You're Lillie, right? The woman who helps out at the Vreeland Ranch? You're their ranch hand, right?"

"Yes."

"You have a lot of animals." This he said with a certain amount of admiration.

"Yes, lots of animals."

"Sy is fond of you," he said, referring to the vet. "It's odd I haven't met you before, considering."

"Well, I mostly stay at home. The Vreelands usually bring in their animals, and my animals, well, Sy usually stops by my home."

"You have bees, you sell honey."

"Yes, I do," I said. "People think I'm crazy. I know that. My neighbor, Wendell, calls my place a Damn Petting Zoo. I told him he had so much junk on his property that I could get tetanus just by looking."

Ruben chuckled, and of course there's nothing better than hearing someone laugh, especially when you cause that laugh. Then Ruben said, "The truth is, Sy is at home. Archangels are visiting him today." He looked at me to see if I understood, which I did. We all knew that Sy was schizophrenic or something, and on most days functional, but some days not. At this point in time, the community had voiced its complaints and compassion over Sy already, and I knew I had the option of driving all the way off the mountain for a real vet, or letting Ruben take over, this vet tech, this person whom I'd heard about but never actually met.

"Well," I ventured, "can you do it? Because town is pretty big and I get turned around. Usually I go only when my neighbor, Wendell, is with me because, well, Wendell and I are just friends, actually we don't like each other at all, so we're not even friends, but we do come in handy for each other, you know what I mean! Helping to fix a thing or going to town together because neither of us like crowds much. Neither do you, I bet."

"No, I don't," he said.

"Yes, true. I knew as much about you, although I don't know why I would. But then again, we can be aware of all sorts of things about people in our periphery. If you can fix my puppy, please just do it."

I pinched my lips together with my fingers, hard. That is a

funny thing about me; I spend most of my time alone and the silence of my body is more or less in equilibrium with the silence of the world, and it's only when I get with other people that I become this way, out of loneliness or nervousness or what I don't know—it's a little hard to clarify some things about yourself to yourself, even when you have long conversations with yourself about yourself in the silence.

"I can fix her paw. But I'm not a vet."

I kept my fingers over my lips and nodded. Our eyes met briefly and his eyes had something in them, not amusement or irritation, as you might think, but a *wish* for me to be comfortable around him, not so nervous, but perhaps that is something I imagined, because, of course, that is the sort of thing I would *want* to imagine. Here's something I've noticed, one of the greatest discoveries of my life: If you look carefully at people's eyes the first instant they look at you, the first instant in any glance, what they're really feeling will shine through before it flickers away, and what I saw was this compassionate wish. Then his eyes went hard because he was one person, and I was another, and our eyes must therefore mark that distance.

My own eyes went from his to a window, to the blue sky outside, where they stayed for some time, as if they were embarrassed for me. Ruben helped my puppy. I held the dog on the table and purred into her ear and scratched her neck and did not say, but certainly felt, how sorry I was, for already she occupied a large and intense place in my heart. I decided I should name her Ruby for that reason. I stayed quiet because I could tell Ruben needed me to; he was concentrating. He said only one thing: "A bee makes ten million trips to get enough nectar to make one pound of honey, I just read that." To which I said, "Yes," and I wanted to say,

*They'd break my heart with their work, except the gold sheen of pouring honey is so beautiful.*

But I didn't say that, or anything at all, because at the same time I was observing Ruben's hands with their thick fingers, and his palms seemed very soft although there were old scars and new cuts, dirt in the cuticles, blood blisters under two nails, and these were hands that knew something, and my heart was straining under it all. This sounds ridiculous, for I am not a teenager, not even close, and I'm supposed to be a steady elder, but I'm simply saying that from this point on, everything I felt had the embarrassing burning brightness and recklessness of a long-ago time. Perhaps I should not admit to such a thing, although I don't have much to lose since very few people care for me anyway. Although, as an aside, I believe that other people's opinions of us do in fact matter a great deal, because each other is all we have. Anyway, I wanted to reach out and touch his hand, but I did not. Because I did not, tears came to my eyes. Then I had to bite my lip very hard to keep from crying. This caused the inside of my lip to bleed, tangy salt. All this, and still my eyes stayed on his hands. Our hands in fact did touch one time, while he was fixing my dog's paw, and for some reason I said, "Oh, sorry about that," though I was not.

When Ruben was done, and the pup was standing on the floor, wagging her tail, holding her bandaged paw up, Ruben washed his hands and came to stand in front of me. He squinted at my forehead. Cleaned the wound with a cotton ball dipped in something. Dabbed on a bit of glue from his finger to my forehead. I tried (successfully I might add!) to breathe quietly and not let the tears slip, for suddenly my forehead hurt a lot, and I was feeling very alone, that kind of feeling that generally comes at night, that buzzing terror of a space when you recognize that you are alone, you are going to die, and you are going to die alone, and this was bad timing for such a moment to descend, but I managed under the weight of it all.

Ruben said, "You cut your lip." For a moment I thought that perhaps we both wanted him to kiss it. But such a thing is not allowed by the invisible forces that operate this world. These invisible forces have too much power. If only the world could be less influenced by them, then their potency would naturally decrease.

Ruben put on a Band-Aid. It seemed that his fingers stayed an extra moment on my head as he gently moved his hand over the plastic to push it down. He said, "It's nice to meet you, Lillie."

This is the moment that becomes slowed down in my mind. Because he said my name, because I am not a person who is ever touched. Then he directed me, with a wave of his arm, to the front of the clinic, where I paid my bill. Then I left.

That is the bulk of my story. By the time I got to my truck, with the pup in my arms, I was wondering what the best course of action is when one is in a train wreck. Run away from the wreckage? Or stay in the danger and heat?

≈

Please do not think I dreamed of us kissing, or our bodies coming together in rising desire, which is of course to say that I did indeed envision such things. But what I really wanted was to be in his presence. And that is what I yearned for during these past few years, which is how long I have fiercely loved him.

I've come to understand that I can be happy with very little, because I knew from the very beginning (though all my daydreams contradicted this, of course!) that it would be an unrequited love. I can be happy with very little, because I'd long ago ceased to believe that anyone could love me, and I do not say this to be coy or self-effacing, I say it because thus far it has proved to be the case, and because, to be frank, I have suffered from a touch or two of the bad forces of this world, and they have hurt me, and my recovery has sapped from me a certain energy that some humans have and project and which makes them noticeable, a little more human, and a little more alive.

Yes. I fell in love with Ruben. Maybe after all it wasn't love immediately, because at first it was probably gratitude, and then it was more about me than him, which is standard fare, I believe, but I believed it to be love when, at sudden times, it was more about him than me.

Several weeks later, my pup's foot had healed up, I went back. When I walked in the vet clinic, the puppy in my arms, a couple walked in right behind me, the man dressed in a denim jacket with white wooly stuff underneath, the woman in a slim-fitting jean jacket that was nowhere near enough to keep her warm, and we all shuffled up to the counter. As Ruben turned the corner, responding to the ding of the door, his eyes went from me to the couple, and I felt a tension rise and saw his face harden. He said to me, rather gently, "Can I help you?" but I did not want to be hurried, of course, I had many questions formed in my mind to keep him near me, and so I said, "Help them, first," and the man stepped in front of me and said, "Uh-huh, all we need is some tincture of iodine," and this seemed like a simple-enough request, so I was confused when Ruben hesitated, his eyes going back to me.

"A gallon," the man said during this pause. "For my horse's foot."

Ruben cleared his throat. "What's wrong with your horse's foot?"

"Thrush."

"We've got better products for that."

"I just need the iodine."

"I'm not sure we have any."

"I bet you do."

"I'm not sure."

By this time, I realized something was going on. My eyes were drifting back and forth and I could see both men knew something I did not. The girl was aware of it too, but she looked too exhausted to care, and, in fact, her tiredness looked as if it had nearly emptied her out. I also noticed that one of the lower buttons on this man's jacket was unbuttoned, and through this space, his right hand was placed, as if, for example, he was holding his stomach or something *to* his stomach, like a gun, and I noticed that because Ruben had noticed it too and then pretended he hadn't.

Ruben said, "I'll check in back." Then he said, "Lillie, why don't you come with me, I'll put you and the pup in the examining room."

"Okeydokey." I said it as if I were oblivious, and I followed Ruben back, but when he left me at the door of the room, I stepped just inside, right near the entrance, so I could still hear.

After some time, Ruben said to the man, "We've got a pint."

"That's all?"

"That's all."

"How about you order some more?"

"Do you want to leave your name and address?"

There was a pause. "Here's a phone number. Call when it comes in."

And then the ding of the door.

When Ruben came in the examining room, I caught his brown eyes and raised my eyebrows so that he knew I wanted to know. He hesitated. I raised my eyebrows higher. He smiled at me as he gave in. "Meth lab," he said. "A gallon of iodine lasts this clinic a long time. And you wouldn't use it for a horse's hooves, anyway. They'll boil the alcohol off and have the crystals."

"Oh," I said. "I don't know anything about it."

He told me about the vet in Wyoming who got held up last month, and about the traveling vet in Montana who had his truck hijacked. "I just applied for my concealed weapons permit," he said. "They're granting them to vets left and right. It's an odd thing, feeling vulnerable like that." He looked at me, and I knew what he was thinking, which most everyone around here thinks from time to time, which is whether or not a woman living alone in a trailer in the mountains ever feels that way, my answer to which is no, not really, or rather that I used to until I realized that you rarely notice an item, a tree for instance, that's been there a long time, and that the same was true for me, and there is a certain safety in being mostly invisible. For this reason it is mainly a comfort that I am minimally existent, because it means that I am safe and can watch the world.

"That guy had a gun," I said, but I asked it as a question.

"I thought so."

"I've got one, a .38 ACP." Now why I said this I don't know, because I knew that any such conversation could never present the truer version of myself that I wanted to show, and I was desperate to reveal something real, simply because I've spent my life constructing such conversations in my head, and I wanted to have one actually occur out loud. It is a fact that love turns you into a weird kind of salesperson about yourself, and this was not the best approach.

"Mine's a Colt. I don't like to shoot," he said.

"Me either, not really, too loud. If guns were quieter, maybe I'd like them more. Once every five years I take mine out and shoot, just to make sure that I can still hit the pop-can on the fence post."

"Exactly." Our eyes met, complicit in our understanding that this was not any sort of conversation that pierced anything but that perhaps it would have to do. But Ruben did an interesting thing then. It was a common thing; people do it all the time for one another. And it could be called a kind thing, although it did not feel like that at the time. He said, "I have a girlfriend."

I know this much about being blue, that if you give into it, it only gets worse, and that the same is true for love. But the fact is, it takes a lot of strength not to give in. So when someone clarifies for you that he is in no position to love you, or you to love him, and even when this is something you already know, because you have, for example, seen him and his girlfriend walking together, the best thing to do is not give in to the pain that suddenly shoots through your chest.

What you might do is this: You might tell yourself that you will no longer drive to town with the hopes of seeing him. You will not notice when he's at the vet clinic and when he's not. You will no longer bring him up in conversation at the post office, to see what others say about him, or simply to hear his name. That you will not hope, even, that one of your animals becomes ill enough to need vet care. Perhaps you will bow your head and think all these things. But when you raise your head up, still you will tell him to stop by next time he's in your area, because although it's not worth a trip up, your horse has developed an odd swelling in its chest and maybe ought to be looked at, and he will tell you, "It might be Pigeon disease, they get it from bacteria in the dirt," but then says that he might come by, because he needs to make some stops in the area anyway, and at the same time you are telling yourself to let him go, you are hoping that he will move toward you and you know that it will be exhausting, waiting for a thing that's never going to come.

While all this was going on, Ruben was writing something with a black marker on a piece of cardboard in sloppy handwriting, uneven-sized letters, some caps and some lowercase. Really, if I had not been so enamored, I would've been taken aback by such a sorry attempt at writing. When he was done, he turned it toward me so I could read it: WE Do NOt SeLL IodinE PrOducts. He said, "I saw a sign like this at another vet clinic. Actually, we *will* sell iodine products, but we'll keep them in the back. So if you need any."

I said, out of the blue, "Then it's like most everything else. You have to know whether or not it really exists, where it's hidden, and how to ask. And then some will get it and some will not." I didn't mean to sound bitter about this, although that's how it came out.

‿

I managed to stay away from town for quite a long time, going in only occasionally, and seasons passed, and then Sy shot himself. Perhaps the archangels had been in cahoots with God, and they were all busy playing tricks on Sy, or perhaps he was simply tired, or perhaps his brain chemistry was very very off, which is something I feel like I can extrapolate from my own life and understand, but in any case, Sy took Joe's Colt .45 and shot himself through the mouth. Joe felt horrible about it being his gun, but as I told him, along with many other people, Sy would have found a way no matter what, and that since Sy's guns had been taken away from him for exactly this reason, he was left with no choice, which is what Sy himself wrote to Joe in the note he left. In the note he also scribbled, *Archangels' eyes are blue, pure blue, no pupil; Jesus's are white, bright white light; and God's are black circles with a moon and stars, and they say that if I go now there won't be any more tricks to play on me. There is a beautiful blue firefly creature, and she is very kind, and she is telling me that the time is now. And it matters what light they cast on you so watch for the colors. I wish I could have shared my true self more with all of you. I never wanted to be a fake. It is harder than I realized to remain true. I am so very sorry for doing this to you all.*

I felt quite a bit of sympathy for Sy—did not blame him for being selfish like some people did—because I can simply picture moments when I too have wanted to walk out in a meadow beneath Blue Moon Mountain and shoot myself, and indeed, in my most off-kilter moments I have thought about doing just that.

On the day of the memorial, it was still spitting snow, and everything was covered in feet of snow, and the earth was still reeling from the blizzard, and the roads were slick and plowed only where the Vreelands and I had been able to get to in time.

To get to the service, I caught a ride down to the base of the canyon, to the grange, with my neighbor, Wendell, since my truck's ignition switch had gone out, and on the way Wendell and I conversed in such a way to confirm for each other that we really did not like each other; he thought I was a scattered and fragile woman, and I thought him a dull and stupid man, which in fact he is.

On the way down, I told him, "I was in love with a man once. Once in my life. I don't think I can forget about him. He's always with me."

This comment surprised Wendell, who, after some time, said, "I guess maybe you better try."

And then I got to say what I'd practiced. "For what? Then I'd remember trying, too."

I told Wendell this so I could get it out of my system and wouldn't have to tell Ruben. How many of us are going around telling the truth to the wrong person? Wendell took it as one more piece of evidence of my malformed character, which confirmed for him that he did not want a romantic relationship with me, which is something he wondered from time to time, because we were convenient, after all, and I took my confession as a needed relief to have voiced my love to someone, somewhere, at some point in time. So we were both of use to each other, as usual.

The person I hoped to see at the memorial, of course, was Ruben. I am honest enough to admit that even at a funeral of a fairly good acquaintance, of someone who had doctored my goats and peacock and cats and once, even, my rooster who'd had his throat ripped open by a fox but wasn't yet dead, even at this man's memorial, I was selfishly thinking of love, although it's also true that I was mourning, which is to say, simply, that I felt a very deep ache. Maybe they were related.

I noticed that Ruben was dressed in black jeans and roper boots and a dark blue sports jacket, and I had to avert my eyes so as to find some relief. What I did not realize then, but realized during the course of the after-funeral gathering, as I listened to people talk, was that I was possibly saying good-bye to Ruben as well. Because it is illegal for someone who does not have a degree and license to practice vet medicine, and now that Sy was gone, there was no way that Ruben could keep the vet clinic open, since after all there was no vet. I did hear it mentioned, however, that

Ruben, who, wisely enough, refused to go to school to prove what he already knew (and was thus refusing to give into those invisible forces that operate this world), might just drive around in his truck and doctor animals as a "friend who was helping out" and a person might pay Ruben for his help. At least for a few months. Who knows if such a plan would work, he was saying, and that's exactly what he was doing: testing this idea against the reaction of others. As I listened to a dozen conversations, I knew where Ruben was in the room, at all moments, which caused me to wonder if love is also simply keeping track of a person.

When Ruben came up to me, and asked about my puppy, now grown into a dog, it was not as I had hoped. Now there was nothing in his eyes that showed I was alive to him in some unique way. I kept looking for it, but it was not there. Maybe he saw my reaction to this because he tried to say something nice, then. He said, "I never asked you about ice-skating, long ago. But I imagined you, skating alone, on the Vreelands' pond. On that foggy day," and when I whispered yes, he continued, "It's pretty, the picture I have in my mind. Until the puppy got hurt, that is."

Ruben was looking at me, kindly enough, though in a tired way, and was starting to fumble for some words. So I shrugged and laughed, which was my way of mocking my own loneliness and desire, even as I presented it to him. I was saying, *Here I am, look what you've done to me, but please, ignore me all the same!* Of course, he had no idea of any of this; I understand that.

I wanted only for him to comfort me in my distress, even though he was the agent of my distress.

I touched his shoulder, then, and gave him what I could. Despite what I've said about lacking an essential energy, the truth is that sometimes I have some—a buzzing, golden thing—and when I need it, I summon it into being by closing my eyes and telling myself, *Find It, Create It.*

That's what I did then. I reached out to touch his shoulder, and I pushed my energy toward him, down the length of my arm, just in the hopes that it would enter his body, and as I touched his blue jacket, I pushed him gently away, toward the crowd of milling mourners, and I said, "Sy's death will change us all. It has already changed me. Take care now, Ruben. Good-bye!"

I watched his body move away from me, and took notice of my ache, and realized that quietness has a strange, buzzing hum that can nearly break you apart.

⟿

I think Sy knew this: The world goes on, goes on with great alacrity, and indeed it grows impatient with any sort of resistance to its spinning-forward force. During these last weeks since Sy's memorial, I have seen Ruben from time to time on the mountain. I try to leave the house occasionally, to prove to myself that I can. When I do, it seems that Ruben and I seek each other out in a vague way, or actually, he does not seek me out, but I seek him out in a way that appears vague but which is not.

When we meet up, we talk about the things that matter to us, and I am always surprised at how quickly Ruben moves into Real Conversation, that is, about an idea he has been considering, how he feels odd these days, how he worries about Anya, how as a child he fell in love with animals because they seemed to love him back and, as he said, we are fools for those who will have us.

When we meet at the post office or Violet's Grocery, we immediately launch into such a conversation; I ask him, *What did you do today?* and he responds not by telling me what he's done, but rather by what beautiful thing he's witnessed, or what human or animal pain he's encountered, and I listen a great deal.

What these conversations do for me is relieve me of some bitterness, for if one thing has made me angry at this world, it is the silence of others; their decision not to respond, their holding back of themselves. Although in addition, I am sympathetic, since silence is how we defend ourselves, and we defend ourselves because we need to.

Ruben and I rarely speak of my animals or his girlfriend because for these few moments, we allow that they be invisible so as to create space for these other thoughts. Besides, we do not want to give word to what exists, but to that which does not. On the other hand, we don't speak of the invisible thing, either, though we both know it is there. I want to tell him, but do not, about my daily mantra: *He's not interested. He's too young. Not possible. Not reasonable.* I want to tell him, *Ruben, you have taken over my life, have mercy!* I want to tell him, *How can I live, never having this love?* I want to ask him, *Just how much erosion and effort is this going to take?*

In the past weeks, I have also gotten to know his new girlfriend by greeting her at the grocery store. Jess is her name, and she wears a wrist brace, from typing, already injured though so young, and she volunteers at the fire department, mainly by bringing food and cleaning up, and as she told me, she had no particular love of the fire department, it was just that it was the only thing around to volunteer *for.* When I see her, I think: *You never feel as large and important as when you are in love. And you* are, *because you are living in the center of your best and bravest self. You have an appetite for every single second in the day.*

∽

Then came this day, which was yesterday: I was out in the Vreelands' pasture, checking on cows, and I was remembering a different winter, long ago, when Sy had come with me, given that there was an injured cow he needed to check on, and he told me about the angels who visited him—he was not religious and these were not particular angels, such as Catholic angels, although that is the religion he grew up in, but general-all-purpose angels, is what he called them, and how beautiful and kind they were, and that was the first time I realized Sy was ill, or that his version of reality did not match mine, at least, and I was thinking of Sy, remembering him and missing him and aching for the time he did not have anymore on earth, and suddenly someone shot a gun.

The sound ricocheted around the valley, the birds flew into the air squawking, and my dog started to bark, and a horse in a far pasture spooked and started to run.

After some time, I made my way across the ridge and looked down into a draw and saw a man in a jean jacket with wooly stuff underneath. The man was dragging a dead heifer, the cow he had just shot, up a slant, a slant created from a large piece of plywood, from ground to white truck. He had picked the smallest heifer, which was smart, because otherwise the effort of moving her body would have been too great. The dead cow left blood in the snow, and blood up the ramp, and the man was working hard to get her bleeding body into the bed of his truck. He did manage, though, and when he was done, he put a blue tarp on the cow, so as to cover her, and then did something odd, which was to pat the blue mound before swinging himself into the truck and driving away.

It had snowed again, and his truck tires left a pattern across the white pasture as he drove around the occasional tree or irrigation ditch. It reminded me of the patterns my ice skates leave on ice; fluid soft arcs of motion.

It is for these reasons—him patting the cow, his tire marks— that I did not tell the police or the Vreelands what had happened. If someone had asked, about the noise or tracks, for instance, I would have told the full truth, but as is always the case in life, the conveyance of information is often reliant on someone asking, and rarely do they ask, which is not a matter of oversight, as we would like to believe, but rather a conscious decision to stay oblivious and separate. Also, I did not tell anyone because by this time, I felt some sympathy for this man and woman. This couple, the meth lab couple, I now knew to live in the run-down house a few miles away, and in my own quiet anxiety I was feeling a bit of commiseration for the things people do to survive, which is not to say that I approved, but I understood.

I walked over there, though, along the snow-packed county road, to their junky trailer house. The man was out by the garage unloading the dead cow and did not notice me, partly because he was absorbed with the dead animal, and partly because his truck radio was blaring country music. The woman—or girl, rather—was inside, sleeping on the couch. I could see her through the window, thin and tall and mousy-brown haired. I didn't want to bother them anyway. I whispered for Ruby to sit, which she did. From the notebook I carry in my pocket to record births or injuries to cows, I tore a page, and I wrote a note: *DO NOT TAKE ANOTHER COW. COME FOR DINNER, SOMETIME, IF YOU'D LIKE—I'M LILLIE IN THE WHITE TRAILER WITH ALL THE ANIMALS.* I stuck it in their door and as I left, I imagined white crystals inside, scattered across their bodies and house like fairy dust. On the way home, I sat down in the snow and cried, and Ruby sat next to me, panting and occasionally licking the salty wet from my stupid, contorted face. Before I left, I did something I have never done before, which was to get down on my hands and knees and press my face into the new snow beside me, as deep as I could push it, so that for a moment I could not breathe but did not care since the cold crystals melting on my hot skin offered another form of nourishment.

Once upon a time there was a story, and it ends like this: There is a woman, some figure in the far distance, a shape that's hard to make out, and she has a task ahead of her, which is to expel a feeling best she can, or at the very least, maneuver it so that the place it occupies inside her is comfortable, or if not comfortable, then bearable. She laughs at herself about this, for what an odd thing to do to love!

I drove into the village, at last, because I needed help doing this. The roads were black, but the pines in the shade were dripped in white from the blizzard, and so there was a nice contrast to the world. When I walked into the vet clinic, where Ruben was vaguely still practicing, he walked toward me, straight up to me, and took me up in his arms in an embrace. We stayed this way for a full minute, and I pressed my head against his chest and put my hand up to his heart.

From there, I said, "Just tell me. Do you ever wish—?"

He said, "Sure, Lillie. I wish many of us could connect in all sorts of ways." Then he pointed out a window, up into the blue sky, and said, "Lillie, look at the stars."

I smiled into his shirt, for he was telling me that the stars are present, even when they are not visible. This brief moment, this impression, allowed me to catch his eye and nod good-bye.

When I got home, I went straight to the pond. I found I could not ice-skate, for the ice was suddenly slushy, the sun having come out today. I kept hearing noises; I thought an animal was moving about in the dry grasses near the edge. But there were too many sounds, first here and then over there, and it took me some time to realize it was the ice melting at the edges, slipping into the water below.

Ruby ran out on the ice anyway, and the ice supported her, though it cracked in displeasure, and she nudged a chunk of blue ice with her nose and chased after it as it sped far and fast across the pond. I could have called her back, but I did not, because her joy outweighed the danger.

I began to walk alongside the water and noticed that in certain places, the snow had formed tiny ridges of intricate crystals that jutted up at an angle from the ground. I was surprised to discover the degree to which patterns create snow. Then I looked up and saw the degree to which patterns create the world. Then I considered the degree to which colors create the world. Then I considered the degree to which light creates the world. After I came to, I continued walking, and continued to create the collateral damage we all do as we go through life, but then I could no longer crush those snow crystals with my feet in such a clumsy manner, even though I knew they'd melt anyway, and so I retraced my steps carefully as I walked back to the pond. I sat in the grass at the edge and watched the ice slip into the absorbing water, and sometimes I helped it along by brushing and dabbing the slush down with a stick that had been left to rest beside me.

## Chapter Four
# Calypso

It was eight in the morning and still they were in bed. The sun was only now above the mountain—winters were so dark, the shadow of the mountain so long—and Ruben kept his eyes on the strip of weak blue outside the window as he rooted around the back of her neck with his lips. "But really? You don't ever want to get married?"

Jess pushed herself backward, more fully into his chest, her rump against him. "Give me a break. Have you ever seen a good one?"

"There seem to be some solid—"

"Enviable ones, Ruben. Enviable marriages?"

"Well, there's Violet and Ollie. They're enviable. Thayne and Celeste? I think Zach used to really love Dora. At least, he took care of her all those years. And maybe Gretchen and Joe—"

She laughed. "Gretchen and Joe. Boy are they being watched. And you realize we are too? The two new couples of the mountain. They're the mid-life ones, the now-or-nevers. We're the young ones—"

"Speak for yourself, youngster—"

"We're the young ones, full of both more promise and more potential to crash and burn." She picked up his right hand and placed it on her breast, over her heart, and held it there.

He leaned up to look at her face but it was not sex she wanted, only frowsy comfort, so he pushed himself closer against her. They were now skin to skin on every plane, from toe to shoulder, and he touched his forehead to the back of her head so that they would be touching there too. Wasn't there something to be said for *this*? Full-on contact? For better or worse, sickness and health? To the effort of getting inside another person and staying there? In the intentionality and work of commitment? Of leaving the worst selves for the better ones, with someone as a guide and witness? And for putting up with someone even when they *were* taking you for granted?

"I love you, Ruben. And I see what you're really saying here. Something like Sy—well, it makes us all want to look around and take note of the only antidote. But look at the old couples at Moon's. The dining dead, I call them."

"But we won't be like them." Then he stopped. It was akin to asking her to marry him.

He felt a shift in her body, a small hardening, and he was sorry for it. He pushed his lips against her scalp and then stared at the zigzag of the part in her hair and kissed again. She turned around to push her nose into his chest, trying for playful. "That's what everybody thinks. Don't go all conventional on me, Ruben. The zeitgeist has shifted. Commitment is a lovely idea, though, and I'm all for it. I'm here with you. But marriage, no."

He held her against his chest but propped his head on his hand and let his eyes drift across the snowy mountainside. Past the aspen trees was the rise of pines. Many of the lodgepoles there were dead, from the beetlekill epidemic, and someday they would burn; it was a dangerous spot to live, and they'd admitted that perhaps it would be best to consider the cabin a temporary structure.

"I miss the blue." He heard the glum in his voice and squeezed his eyes tight, trying to purge himself of the weight. The churning gray of the clouds was doing something to him. Perhaps he should see a doctor. His throat kept closing, his GI system didn't seem to be working right, his wrists and knuckles hurt more than usual, and it seemed more than age, more than the old injuries from all the animals, more than the shock of Sy, and, in fact, predated Sy's death by several months. It was something deeper, something like a cancer or a gloom that had settled into every single possible nook and cranny of his body. He felt allergic to himself, allergic to this winter. Jess was the only antihistamine.

"It has us all feeling restless and unsure." She was turned around now, looking up at him, her dark eyes rotating color, her dimple deep, her skin clear, looking young, perhaps too young. "Especially you. Come on, now. We agreed to go one day without talking about Sy."

He turned away from her; she was too beautiful and he was too miserable. He looked outside again. The clouds reminded him of a vast sea; if the world were turned upside down, it would be difficult to distinguish if one was looking at sky or water.

"Ruben, I am in love with you," she said, resting her head back on his chest now. "You are Paralos to my Piraeus."

He kissed the lightning bolt on her head. "Tell me again."

"It was a ship," she said. "Paralos was the sacred ship of the Athenian fleet. Piraeus was its home port. They needed each other."

"It's no good, being lost at sea."

"It'll warm up soon, Ruben. Yesterday it was sunny for a little while."

She climbed on her hands and knees over him and kissed him, brought his hand to her breast with a different energy. He felt a something—victory or triumph or the bloom of kismet—spread in his body, even his spine, even his throat, even the base of his neck. He loved all this. It was the opposite of winter. The smell of her morning breath. Her lust. Her direction in the matter. The magic she had—sex had not always been like this for him—of forcing himself outside of his body, his head, giving him a break from his own self. For this reason, he'd never turned her down, never even considered it.

He moved his fingers to her nipple, raised his head to the other, and when her back arched in response, he moved his fingers inside her, and then he was inside her. It was not sleepy morning sex; it was intense and focused, and just once he had an actual line of thought, right before he came, which was: Odysseus shouldn't have left Calypso, what a fucking fool.

⌒

Jess loved this most about their relationship, perhaps: waking up dreamily on the days they allowed themselves just to do that. Or, rather, she allowed it. Allowed herself to escape her ambition, her calling, her art. On those Days of Push, which was most days, she hated the mornings, or rather, hated the annoyance of coupledom: showers, bathroom needs, talk—all the while, she wanting him to leave so that she could write. She sometimes thought that she'd be better as a single person, the main reason being her love of solitary mornings, some absolute nonnegotiable need to leap right into her ideas. Mornings like this, though, they gave her a chance to reconsider. To appreciate a different kind of life.

Steak and eggs is what he was making. If it were up to her, she'd eat a banana and a cracker. Or half an avocado and a handful of almonds. But he believed in food. In the preparation of it, in the romance of it. He also needed the calories: He had several big animals to work on today, it was very cold out, and some of the calls would be difficult to get to with some of the blizzard snow still unmelted.

Lots of calories and sleeping and slow mornings were what they all needed now, since Sy.

She watched him—slippers, sweat pants, shirtless—pad out to the grill to light it, then again to put on the meat. Unbelievable, how handsome he was. Arms and back that always seemed alive with different motion of tendon and muscle and bone, a stance that was comfortable and solid and frankly just sexy and manly. He was thirty-two and in the perfect prime of his life, the most handsome and perhaps the most needed man on the mountain. Everyone had animals, and for a long time, Sy had been the one, but as Sy started to check out, Ruben stepped in, and, in fact, he was brilliant with animals, perhaps even better than Sy, though Sy had the formal veterinarian degree and Ruben's education stopped at vet-tech status, but the way he moved his hands on animals implied a certain grace, as if he understood the problem and could heal—which is what had made her fall in love with him in the first place, ten years ago back when she was a teenager and he was visiting her grandparents' and her parents' ranches at the base of the mountain. She could see this magic in him; everyone could see it in him. He was treated with a certain reverence. Perhaps even worshipped; yes, that was not too strong a word.

He was staring up at the sky, then back at the grill, then at the mountain, as if looking for something he couldn't find. Jess watched his face closely. It was the other most unique thing about him. His mother had been from Mexico, and his father a full-blooded Czech, and something about the high cheekbones, the strong set of the jaw—his bohemian gypsy quality, he called it—combined with dark eyes that seemed to have extra fluid in them—well, it simply made him mesmerizing to watch.

She was sad for his sadness. He was stricken in ways he didn't understand yet, she realized; Sy's death was surprising him in ways he didn't see. Truth be told, he hadn't always enjoyed working for Sy. Like any relationship, it was fraught with personality differences, and Sy was simply frustrating—dreamy and perpetually late, sometimes barely able to sustain a focused operation or exam. Ruben had often said how glad he was that he and Sy rarely ran into each other—one was doing a farm call while the other was at the clinic, or vice versa, and so had joked, even, that it was like a good marriage—avoiding the other most of the time so as to have the reservoir of patience required while in the presence.

But still. He was clearly not himself and the best thing she could do now was simply love him. She rolled out of bed. Her crotch was a bit tender—he'd been oddly rough—and wet streaked across her thighs. She pulled a thick red robe over all of it and pulled on wool socks and went to the kitchen. She hugged him from behind as he stood staring at the melting butter in the pan. "You okay?"

He kissed her ear, but she could feel the sorrow, could tell he wanted to talk about it more, the status of their relationship. But there was simply no more to say. Not until more time had passed. Time would clarify their relationship. Time and all it wrought: Boredom. Annoyance. Restlessness. Or, continued kindness. Care. Deeper knowledge. Somehow she wanted to tell him this, that he needed only to be patient, but she knew that this is what he feared, and he was trying to guard them against the corruption of time. He wanted the lighthouse of marriage to keep the ship safe.

"It's nice of you. To volunteer, to go to the bear den."

"Well, Sergio asked me. He needs someone to administer the tranquilizer. It should be Sy, of course—"

"Well, it's nice of you."

"And the state vet canceled."

"I know. It's nice of you, is all I'm saying."

"It'll be a good adventure."

"Did you know, Ruben, that the word *laconic* comes from Laconia? Spartans were known for being short on words. I'm thinking of using this all somehow in my book."

He let out a genuine bark of laughter. "*Laconic* and authoring don't go very well together in the same sentence, Jess."

She smiled and rubbed his back, down to his butt, and up again to his shoulder. "The history of it. The metaphor of it." She turned to set the table, glanced outside at a dove alighting in a dead pine tree. "They—the Spartans, that is—always gave the briefest answers to complicated questions. For instance, when they were asked by the Macedonians whether they wanted to meet at the border as enemies or as friends, they replied with a one-word answer. 'Neither.'"

"That's not much of an answer."

"And this one: In Thermopali, they were told that the Persians had enough arrows to block out the sun. You know what they replied? They said, 'We will fight in the shade.'"

She went on, delighted now. "Okay. Here's a good one. The Persians sent a long message that basically told them to surrender their weapons. You know what they said? They said: 'Come and get them.'"

"They don't sound laconic so much as just solid in their opinions."

She considered that and then brightened even more. "Well, yes. And here is my favorite. They were threatened by the Macedonians, who sent a message: 'If we conquer you, you will become our slaves.' You know what the Spartans' response was? One word. Ready for it? Their response was: *If.*"

He paused. "So, *if* I asked you to marry me . . ."

᠆

Ruben couldn't believe those words came out of his mouth. "Sorry. Jess, I'm sorry! Forget I said that. I'm getting the steaks." He wanted to punch his fist through the clouds, or crawl out of his body into them.

He kept his eyes down as he came in with the steaks, stood at the stove and nestled the eggs against them, added a wedge of orange and a strawberry, which he'd bought especially for her. He wished for a moment that he could find his old self, the one before he knew her. Or had he always been so fucked up? When had his brain started to be such a heavy weight in his skull?

"Let's eat." He turned around. "Jess, I'm so sorry I said that. I'm a mess. You know I am. Worse than usual today, though. I'll learn to be more laconic. Let's have a nice breakfast. This morning was so nice. Still is nice. The Vreelands' horse is in labor. One of Lillie's cats needs to be put down. Zoë's cockatiel has a tumor on his throat and I'm taking them some pain medication. I hope it doesn't die soon; they need a break from sorrow. My brain feels weird. Just know that it comes out of love. But still, I'm sorry."

She paused, uncertain, her eyes clouded. They sat down and ate silently and near the end of the meal, she caught his eye and said, "Did I ever tell you about Calvin Coolidge?"

He snorted. "No, Jess, you did not."

"So, Warren Harding died in office. Calvin Coolidge took over. Remember that?"

"No."

"Well, Coolidge was not extraordinary. But anyway. He was at a ball one night at the White House, and a young flapper was attempting to engage him in a conversation, and he just wouldn't talk."

"A Spartan reincarnated, perhaps."

She smiled genuinely and he was glad for it. "Yes. Anyway, she goes up to him and says, 'Mr. President, I made a bet with a friend that I could get at least three words out of you.' And you know what he replied? He said, 'You lose.'"

"I guess he wasn't feeling very gracious that day." Then he added, "That's too bad, really. That was a lost opportunity. Perhaps she was a brilliant and beautiful person." He winked at her. He had something poetic to say, but it wouldn't form in his mind. Something about how intimacy and love were the only sanctuaries, safe places for the human soul, like this mountain was a sanctuary in the rest of the crazed world, and the only road to intimacy was communication, and that Sy's death was circling around in him like a cement ghost, and he needed her to witness that.

As if reading his mind, she said, "Ruben, I think being laconic is the greatest danger to a relationship. So I'm glad you're talking. I'll try too."

When he left to do his Saturday-afternoon calls, Jess put on Suzanne Vega's "Calypso," stood with her back to the warm wood-burning fireplace, and stared out the window at the churning sky.

She didn't want to embrace the zeitgeist of her generation, detached and ironic; she wanted to believe in love. This morning, when she'd woken, she'd stared at Ruben, still sleeping, and had been thinking of her grandfather, Ben, who'd killed himself with sodium pentobarbital, which he'd stolen from Ruben when they'd been putting down a dying donkey together, long ago. Ben didn't believe in the zeitgeist of his times either; he believed in an individual's right to decide. Alzheimer's was on the way, and Ben was a rancher and knew about suffering, and Ben was the one who should decide.

It was with the money she'd inherited from him that she built this cabin up on the mountain. A few months ago, she invited Ruben to join her. She'd been in love with Ruben since she was a teenager, a crush, really, surely based on the fact that he was the one who came to the ranch to help animals, help *her* animals, some odd mix of savior/teacher/helper obsession. She knew that. So did he. It was weird; a therapist would have a field day. And yet. It did seem to her that they had been careful, and waited, and their attraction and respect had grown into a real love. He'd been too old for her at first—he newly out of vet-tech school, she just finishing high school—and yes, she'd traveled around, left for a summer here, a winter there—but the place kept calling her back, so finally she took the money she'd inherited from her grandfather and built this place.

Now she was twenty-five. So the relationship seemed less problematic. But still, it was weird, perhaps even fucked up, and needed to be treated carefully, and so why must Ruben complicate it by introducing the future?

As Vega sang *I watched him struggle with the sea*, she knew Ruben was doing exactly that, struggling with his sea. She wanted to help him without endangering their future or herself. What they needed now was someone to cling to. And stop. Right. There.

Surely, Ruben knew that this love, of all loves, should be held lightly.

Now she grew angry. She thought of Del and Carolyn, her parents, or at least, the parents who raised her, and their divorce last year. She'd seen it coming for some time. They were both good people but also caught in that claustrophobic pattern of Days. Without. Love. Years of such days. She was angry at her siblings, who seemed so surprised. Surprised in a way that infuriated her. It was so small-minded, so banal to think that they should just continue on, regardless. It was such an obviously good thing, the parting. Del and Carolyn had made sense together, and then they hadn't. Simple as that. At one time, they were ranchers running a ranch, raising kids, busy with the stuff of life. Then that stage was over. And look how they'd grown and changed, particularly her mother. And wasn't that what life was *for*, to grow and change? She'd said to her siblings: Look at her! She's beautiful! She's come into her own. Has a tattoo, for godssake! She was exploring herself and the world! She was Odysseus, on a journey, literally in Greece, and it was about time *she* got to be the one to launch her ship! It bothered her—panicked her, really—that her siblings seemed so endlessly restless about it, so wedded to their version of the story, so wedded to culture's version of love.

The song ended and she went to her computer to write. She had worked herself into a bad mood, a frantic mood. She had ruined her morning quiet.

She was capable of love, she was in love, she just simply doubted the longevity of love, hated the assumption that it should last, and, at the very least, this was not the time to think about it. Ruben would simply have to embrace what they had, not push for more, not have his eyes so firmly fixed on the future.

She poised her fingers above the keyboard. It took a long time to settle, and she spent that time staring out the window at the pines and sky. She'd hoped the clouds would clear, but they were only becoming denser, and perhaps it was her sorrow and anger that made the words come so well. It happened rarely, but it always felt like a gift from the universe when it did. Her story unfolded and she was surprised at a few turns of events, but she didn't fight them; characters had a mind of their own, made their own decisions, and she just listened.

She believed writing to be an act of listening. It wasn't logical, it was counterintuitive, but there it was. The magic of it. The trick of writing, she once told Ruben, was about shutting the fuck up and extending oneself, listening for something far greater than the sum of one's individual inclinations and desires.

⁓

Ruben attended to his vet calls in the order they arose as he descended the mountain road. First was Lillie's ancient cat, and he was grateful to Lillie's no-nonsense acceptance of the death and yet her desire to have it done well and peacefully, grateful that she shooed him out of the house soon after the tabby was still, leaving him free of the obligation of consolation and friendship, free of the work of mitigating or deferring the odd feelings she seemed to have for him; Anya's house, which he had to brace for and in which he felt like he was holding his breath the whole time, the kids gathered around the cancer-ridden cockatiel, listening to his instructions on how to make the bird comfortable during its dying days; Anya patting him on the back as he left and saying, "We'll talk more later," she not ready for anything more, either; the Vreeland horse was not yet ready to foal but while he was there he doctored a cow with pinkeye. He got a coffee at Moon's, where he visited with Angela when she served it to him, and they also avoided talk of Sy except that she said, "That was a nice ceremony, wasn't it? Gretchen did a nice job. She stepped up to the sudden task of that, and that wasn't easy, I'm sure." He waved to a few people and ducked his head and powered out, feeling both the need to have seen them, and the need to escape them.

On his way home, he drove into the national forest lands that overlooked the meadow, put his hands on the steering wheel, and stared at the clouds.

The one person he should visit, he knew, was Joe. It was Joe's gun that Sy had used, just like it was Ruben's pink juice that Jess's grandfather, Ben, had used. Both he and Joe had inadvertently provided the means to end a life. In Joe's case, it had truly been inadvertent; Sy had gone to the trouble of stealing the key to the lockbox. In his own case, well, that was still something he was struggling with. Jess believed it to have been a gift, when he left the bottle of pink juice next to the donkey he was putting down on the Cross Family Ranch, right after Ben had been diagnosed with Alzheimer's, because he'd want someone to do that for him. Ben had had a full life, and, as the donkey huffed its last, Ben had looked Ruben in the eye and said, "I don't want it, of course, but I'm ready for it, and I'm going to do it regardless. Sure would be nice to have a reasonable way." And Ruben had averted his gaze to the mountain, pretended not to know that

Ben had reached out and taken the bottle and slipped it into his Carhartt jacket.

But Joe would come later. They would share this odd bond later. First, he needed to get his own brain and heart straight.

Jess was too young. Needed more life experience. Should not, under any circumstance, get married. To him or to anyone.

But he loved her. She was perfect. There were so many things he respected: how she had a complete life of her own, that he did not at once become its center. Her preference for action over speech, but when she did talk, it was imbued with culture and oddness. How she pursued her best self. Engaged with the world with confidence and trust. He appreciated her desire in bed. But mostly her desire for life. He felt physically better when Jess was around, both less anxious and in less pain. She was a force to be reckoned with, but she was gentle. She did not seem like a person who would taper off, and therefore, it seemed impossible that they would taper off.

He rested his head on the steering wheel.

He was only seven years older, but it seemed like too much. He knew what he wanted to do—work with animals—and he knew he wanted to stay on the mountain. She was a siren, and he wanted to stay and listen to her music. But when she was ready to leave, he simply *had* to let her go. It was the right thing to do.

When he reached for his keys to return home, he felt a heavy cloud roll across him. He took a breath and was surprised to hear himself choke, and he knew a panic attack was coming. He heard his lungs laboring for breath, heard his mind racing and also tempering it away: *You're thinking too much, too much has happened lately, you're scared, calm the fuck down*, and his lungs listened a little bit and he held the steering wheel and closed his eyes and

breathed, four-count in, four-count out, and when he opened his
eyes, the sky had darkened considerably, but since it was cloudy, it
lacked the blue twilight he loved and was just sinking into a low-
contrast gray. His throat tightened again, and right as it seemed
unbearable, and he promised the universe he'd go to the doctor, he
would, he'd call on Monday, his phone beeped with a text. "You
are Odysseus to my Calypso. The pilot to my Little Prince. The
Athens to my Sparta. May we meet in Corinth."

He started up the truck. Who knows what she meant, exactly,
except the vague message of: Why the fuck can't some stories have
a happy ending?

⌒

When Jess had the log cabin built, she used the same design that
her grandfather had once used for a simple cabin that he built on
the back of his ranch. She'd put her writing desk so that it looked
out a window at the meadow and the rise of the mountain behind
it. From here, she was looking east, and somewhere down there,
far past the rises and dips, beyond her sight but on the same
longitude or latitude, or whatever it was, was the ranchlands of
her youth at the base of the mountain. It felt close enough to offer
some connection; far away enough that she could begin anew.

She would not lose what this cabin offered. Solitude and
independence. The chance to pursue who she was and what she
wanted to do. She would share this space only on her terms. It
was the lighthouse to her past. To her biological mom, who was
murdered by her father when she was a child, and her mother's
dream of someday building a house. To her grandfather and his
poetry and his way of loving the land, which she believed she

inherited from him. It was a place to shine a beam of light so that she might see her future. Perhaps she would get a job, the sort that involved getting up and dressed and to some place each day, or perhaps she would go to New York or Australia, or perhaps she would go to college. But first—just in case she wasn't afforded much time—she would do her Realest Job, which was to write and thereby give her truest hope an honest go. She believed that the most regretful people she knew were those who never gave their main dream a chance. She believed that all people, but especially those in their youth, should do all they could, with all that they had, in all the time that they were allotted, in the place they most loved. She stared at the window, exhausted now, though she hadn't moved in hours, and looked at a thin strip of pastel blue that opened up for just a moment on the eastern horizon, the last bit of glow before the sun set in the opposite direction.

She summoned her energy and stood. She wanted to help Ruben somehow, and the small good thing she could do was to make him some food.

⁂

It was only five but already dark when Ruben arrived home. Or rather, Jess's cabin, which he was just starting to call "home," but only after he'd heard her use the term—our home. Wind—very high winds—had come with night and it struck him as painful that air was literally howling—smashing into the mountain, crashing snow about, twisting into rock and wood and trees. He was going to go crazy, the wind was going to make him crazy. It seemed nearly unbearable; the only way to continue on was the knowledge that it would, at some point, stop. He was glad he couldn't see the sky anymore. He'd had it with this winter, with his brain, but most of all, with the sky.

He kept his eyes trained on the small squares of light as he ducked his head and fought his way across the stretch toward the cabin, toward Corinth.

When he opened the door, she was there, pulling him in, laughing in the face of the wind. Behind her, he saw the rise of steam and he knew she was cooking something, and it smelled of salt, of trout, perhaps one from the meadow stream that they'd caught and frozen, and as he struggled to get the door shut he opened his mouth to ask a question but she was already saying, "There are hopeless romantics, and there are hope*ful* romantics, and you know that Tennyson poem? Better to have loved and lost, than never loved at all? Well. If you wrote that poem, you'd write, 'Better to just have loved and won.'"

He tried to pull away from her arms and say something, but she was still holding on and still talking. "Remember in *The Little Prince*, when the pilot draws the snake that ate the elephant, and the Little Prince instantly recognizes it as something other than a hat? Remember that? Or when the pilot draws the box? With the sheep in it? And the Little Prince says that that drawing is the exact one he's always been looking for?"

He wanted to say *I don't know what you're saying, I don't know what you're talking about,* but he was so grateful for her words, her gusts of air that blocked the wind outside, that he could not. She went on, talking, and he relaxed into it because he did not want to miss a word, could not, at this moment, afford to miss a word. Neither could she, it seemed. So they stood like that for a long time, heads bowed into each other, sharing.

## Chapter Five

# Recipe: Dandelion's Devil

INGREDIENTS:

Ephedrine or *Pseudo*-ephedrine
Iodine
Red Phosphorus
Ether
Hydrochloric Acid
Sodium Hydroxide
Methanol

EQUIPMENT:

Jars with lids, Coffee filters, Eyedropper, Glass dish, Funnel,
Balls—the stupid-brave kind

TO START:

Even at the very beginning I was always on a horse and I was a
barrel rider in the rodeo and it might sound cliché but my horse
and I were *one creature* and we would *explode wonder*. From
Montana originally but I came to Colorado for the Steamboat
Springs Rodeo and met HIM and got a crush on HIM. I did my
first line of meth when I was fifteen after I'd won a race and HE
was a bronc rider and invited me into his truck.

Take Sudafed pills and wash them in the ether. Crush up the pills and put them into one jar. Then put in the methanol and shake for twenty minutes. Let it settle and separate, which means that the pseudoephedrine part floats on the top and the wax and crap from the pills sinks to the bottom. Like how cream rises, or milk sinks, depending on how you look at it. I was going to go to the University of Wyoming and become a lawyer because they have a good law school, and so it was four years ago when that clusterfuck dream evaporated. Sometimes I can still see the mist.

I had nice parents and a nice brother on a nice ranch with nice horses so there is no excuse for this separation. (Who I am now rose to the top. Who I could have been sank to the bottom. Even I can see that. Crank does not make you *stupid*.) So: Separate. Then put one of the coffee filters into a funnel and hold the funnel over the glass dish. Pour the separated mixture into the dish. I used to cook with my mom of course, mainly oatmeal cookies and devil's food cakes and so on. She had a lot of recipe cards. She was a hippie ranchwife and I do believe she was actually happy. I use an oven, not a hair dryer. It blows my mind. Happy.

Obviously the fumes from this are gonna make you sick. So wear a painter's mask and go to the mirror and see how devil-crazy you look because it's fucking hilarious. Remember how you used to look in the mirror and your mom would stand behind you and curl your dirty-blond thin mousy hair and how, with enough work and hairspray and love, could make it full and beautiful.

Me and HIM live in a trailer high up in the mountains which is of course ideal and if we drive twenty minutes down a dirt road there is one small grocery store and one restaurant and one post office and one vet clinic and one volunteer fire department. I have a cousin who lives down in the trailer park by Moon's. But I like it up high on the mountain.

At first I did meth just before races. Because I could do anything and I would win. Then I started cooking with HIM. I am never not high. But I am never high enough. A never in both directions means I am fucked and my life has been a recipe on how to ruin perfectly good ingredients.

At the rodeo I used to fly around the barrels on Alma, my quarter horse. She was beautiful and frankly I was too. I would fly and fly and fly. Now I'm bruised from the needles and not the horse. If I am not cooking on my stove, I am shopping for ingredients. Violet's Grocery which is on this mountain and thus is *not* the place to go unless for the occasional Sudafed or coffee filters. We get iodine from the vet. But we have to go all the way off the mountain and into town for the rest, and the law is in town. I hate that. Because while this mountain is safe, the rest of the world is not, a fact that is proved to me each day when I watch the birds—I love bird-watching, my mom knows them all—the crossbill and black-capped chickadees, the broad-tailed hummingbird, the yellow warbler, the yellow-rumped warbler, and the slate-colored junco, and the saw-whet owl, and the wild turkey, and the goshawk, and the nighthawk. If birds like that can fly (like I used to fly on Alma) and choose to live here, well, then I believe that this is a safe place to be.

HE shake shake shakes me sometimes and I hate the way he treats his dog, our dog, though he always says to me, Dandelion, get the fuck away, it's *my* fucking dog, *my dog not your dog*, I can do what I want. I'm in charge here!

I told him: Please take a look at your ego and your humanity. One is too big and one is too small.

Once you have the pseudoephedrine all by itself, add it to another jar with iodine and red phosphorous and hydrochloric acid. Screw the lid on and shake the hell out of it. This is how you get your exercise, har har har.

HE sometimes leaves me for days with no food, car, phone. Just me and the dog. Still I'm never high enough. Once I was scared. I thought I had overdosed because I began bleeding out of my vagina everywhere. It would not stop. I ran past him and I drove myself to the doctor. It took forty-five minutes to drive down there, into town. I thought maybe I should call my mom and at least tell her I was in Colorado. I also thought about stopping at the veterinary guy's clinic; after all, that guy, Sy, he knew more about being kind to people than most people doctors. But something about it made me ashamed. I'd seen him, once, out in the meadow beneath Blue Moon Mountain, and he was making cairns, all sorts of little cairns on the streambank, putting the darker rocks and the whiter rocks together just so, so that it was pure art, and I thought maybe he was calling to me: Be beautiful. So I couldn't stop by the clinic, since clearly, in my state of blood and mess and general life, I was not.

It turns out, the miscarriage I didn't even know about, which was months before, was not fully finished. I didn't die so I didn't call my mom. I miss Alma more than I miss my mom and there is no reason for that whatsoever other than I am a fuck. I did ask for birth control, so you can see that perhaps there is a tinge of goodness not separated from me yet.

I didn't die, but Sy did, which makes his call somehow stronger. It echoes in my ears. I swear to god, he's talking to me: Dandelion, be beautiful.

I do keep lists of the birds. Crack. Explosion. Ka-POW.

So let it sit for half an hour. Then open it back up, try not to breathe the fumes. Add in the sodium hydroxide. Now gently swirl it until it gets cloudy. This means the chemicals are reacting off each other. Then screw the lid back on, shake it for another ten minutes. Look for a middle layer in the jar.

Normal people do not look out the window to see deer and elk and think they might be spies. I saw a fucking bear once, no joke, but she is no spy. Too wild and beautiful. That was right before the blizzard hit. I hope she found a den in time.

You may think I am the devil, but I'm not. The devil has power, and I have none. Well. Consider this: I am giving you the power to fuck up your life by giving you this recipe. And like the devil, I am my own antagonist. And like the devil, I still have a soul.

Go in with the eyedropper. Be gentle, as if with a baby. Start taking the middle layer. Don't get the bottom layer. Fill up the third jar with water and drop in ten drops of hydrochloric acid. The bottom layer is what you want to keep. Evaporate it by heating, which leaves behind crystals. Some people call this the cold cook method and I call it "how to make a devil method."

Remember that all the stuff can't be left where the sheriff or one of the neighbors can find it. You can go to jail just for having the ingredients. You would think I might care about explosions. You might think, *Oh, this stuff might blow up, in a minute I'll be dead, and I should have called my mom and asked about my horse.* But oh well.

I am going to live on this mountain forever (which probably won't be that long, even I can see that) because it is fucking beautiful and even though I don't know anybody I still know them the way we know people in our periphery. All kinds of crazies up here. The bald conspiracy theorist; he owns this trailer. His neighbor, a lady ranch hand who seems agoraphobic like me, but who is sweet on that horse of hers when she's out checking cattle. Violet at the grocery with the big smile. Joe and Gretchen, the lovers. The handsome vet-tech dude who doesn't like selling me iodine. My cousin whom I don't know, a woman named Flannery who moved into the trailer park because it's cheap and who emailed me about getting together—weren't we relatives after all?—but I never responded because I want to be left alone, I want her to live some good healthy life, and I want to waste away by myself just watching the people who live up here, because they mostly do have good souls. Souls that have not evaporated.

Evaporated souls sometimes get caught in purgatory, but sometimes they get caught in the first circle of hell. Which is where I am. You can't break past the barrier and move up once you're caught.

My name is Dandelion, because my parents made love in a field of them. They'd been hiking, individually, in Montana, and both had stopped for lunch and to make cairns on a large boulder field, stacking rocks to show themselves and others the way. They saw each other doing that, and spoke of cairns and directions, and then fell in love. I was conceived the next morning in a meadow. I too was supposed to show them the way, which, they said, I did.

*Chapter Six*

# Storytime

PART I.

We're standing at the threshold of his door when he clears his throat and says, "The truth of it is that you're gonna have to fake it, Joe. Half of parenting is faking it." Tate glances at my pickup, parked outside this suburban hellhole, and keeps his eyes trained on his daughter, who is duly buckled up inside. "*Fake* being interested in her paintings, in her chitter-chatter, in her dancing. At night, when you're tired, you're going to fake your desire for story time. It's tiring. Do it anyway. Some of parenting is faking it. The love part is real."

*If it comes.* I think it but don't say it, although I do find myself snorting and hawking snot into a rosebush with a few dying flowers hanging on. No doubt my sister planted the bush before she died. She loved roses whereas my life always lacked dignity. "You'll get better."

"Joe." He says it like he's disappointed and then he waves his arms toward his own body. There are tears blurring in his eyes. My own eyes stay on him and it's true he looks like hell. He's had his head shaved and his teeth pulled after the chemo made half of them fall out anyway. He's lost maybe fifty pounds, and he's not the strapping Nebraska boy my sister married. Still, he is more human than me because he says, "I don't have long now. Blood, it's in my blood." His eyes shift to me. Green and steady. "I wish there was someone else too, you know. You are not ideal. And I wish you were married, or had a girlfriend or something, because it would make it easier. For you. So I'm sorry, man. I'm sorry. But here it is. We're down to this."

"I do, Tate. I do have a girlfriend. Finally."

"Well, good. Maybe she'll like kids."

I keep my mouth shut on that one. No, she doesn't. Never wanted any. Said it sounds exhausting, and that her own childhood was shit, and the idea of kids puts her in that same mode she's spent a lifetime escaping. Asked me four times if my vasectomy was tested and secure. And here's the problem: Her presence in my life has caused some strange joy to be flip-flopping around in my body and that is a by-god miracle. The whole fall has been a miracle. "Her name is Gretchen."

"That's great. I'm happy for you," he says. "Joe, this is just a test-run weekend, but I want you to do certain things eventually. I want you to get Honey a rock tumbler, she's always wanted one. She's a tyrant. She will strut around the house and howl for what she wants. Sometimes she can be a snot. All seven-year-olds are snots sometimes, because *all* people are snots sometimes. She has opinions about everything, and they will rarely coincide with yours. I want you to be patient about all this. She hates shoes and socks and clothes that touch her too much. She's not being picky, it's how she experiences the world. In certain ways, she's precocious. In others, she's way behind. Probably because of me. Having to live through this. She still wears Pull-Ups at night, for example. Read her *Goodnight Moon*. She still likes it and it's a tradition. She'll expect a bedtime story. Stories help. With teaching us all how to be human. Take her to the ocean someday."

Yesterday Gretchen was naked on her back below a spruce tree on the mountainside, the sleeping bag below her and the bursts of pine needles above us and her beautiful body lifted to mine, and it keeps on surprising me, this ferocious fight for the full experience before we suffer our own version of what Tate is facing. I should have told her about Honey but I could not form the words, and now I cannot get rid of the image of naked Gretchen and form the right words for this situation. My brain is so often one situation behind.

Tate is shifting his weight and wiping his eyes. My whole life, I have been too distracted. I find myself saying, "Shit, Tate. Well, I guess it's only for the weekend, right? This time, I mean. I can't fuck up too bad. I'll quit cussing, too, you know, I can do that. I'm pretty sure I can. I realize that's the least of it. It's just a little weird for me. I realize it's weirder for you. You know?"

He does know. On top of that, he knows I'm a coward. Which is worse: having to adopt your niece, or die of cancer? He'd trade places with me anytime. But some things, you try not to say.

We just stand there, staring at each other, and I know for damn sure we're both thinking of my sister, Cara, who is still supposed to be alive, Cara who wasn't supposed to die in one of the most mundane and stupid ways possible, car crash, and Cara, who is needed here, and most of all, how this sort of thing isn't actually supposed to happen. It's supposed to happen in stories, maybe, but not in reality. I'm a horseshoer in the mountains of Colorado with a new girlfriend and I live in an off-grid house with no flushing toilet and I eat venison and this sort of thing doesn't happen to guys like that. It happens in *stories* but not to me.

And Honey. A mother dead and a father dying and grand-parents who are too old and ailing and who don't want to be dying out from under a kid who has suffered too much. That's supposed to happen in fairy tales but certainly not in real life. No. I'll tell you why. Because fictional people always have crap happen to them, the tumor is always cancer, the crash is always bad, because that's what is most interesting for the story, and furthermore, stupid mistakes are more interesting than wise conduct, and so, it would be stupid, for instance, to have your mother die, your father get cancer, and be forced to have your incompetent Uncle Joe care for you. That is a fiction. That cannot possibly be real life.

Tate puts his hand on my shoulder. It feels like a claw, and I have to work not to flinch. "Whatever you do, Joe, do *not* let Honey feel your resentment. She doesn't deserve that. If you do that, I'll come back from the grave and kill you. You see? That's what parents do. They give their life, their time. And the good ones, they don't make the kid feel the resentment about all they've offered. Can you do that?"

I say, "Probably not."


**PART II.**


Honey wakes before I do and I hear her feet patter from the couch into my bedroom right as I sit up. She climbs on top of my body, stares into my just-opened eyes for a long time, and then says: "Meow." She says it many times, in fact, a long series of meows that seem to be telling an entire drama. She's wearing a diaper pull-up thing I was instructed to put on her at night, and it's puffy and stinks with pee. "I'm a cat," she says, after she's done with the meows, and she climbs on me and plops the squishy diaper on my chest. I have just enough time to get my hand around my privates, in part for protection, and in part because I woke up with a half-hard-on. I was dreaming of Gretchen. "Actually, I'm a kitten," Honey says in a tiny, high voice. "You're my owner. You found me, lost and abandoned. My paw got cut! I need warmed-up milk in a dish." She actually licks my whiskers, then backs up, regards me, moves her freckled nose back and forth. I forgot a million things about being a kid, one of which is that your teeth fall out—how weird is that?—and one of her lower side teeth moves back and forth, getting sucked in and out as she breathes.

I hold her away from me. "Morning, sweetie. Let's take off your diaper."

"It's *not* a diaper, Uncle Joe. It's a Pull-Up. Diapers are for babies."

"Okay."

"I'm not a baby. I just can't hold my pee. I can't *sense* it yet, the doctor says."

"Okay, I know that." I guess I should have taken out her barrettes before she fell asleep. Now they're way down on her hair, barely holding on for dear life, two red patches in a mess of straw.

"I'm a kitten. Kittens don't wear diapers, either."

She pulls the not-diaper off and throws it on my floor. Her vagina, or vulva, or whatever it's officially called—and I suppose I should know, *why don't* I know?—is so hairless. A hairless V. Tate had said to me, "Joe, it might be weird for you to see her naked, but it's just her body, you know, and she's not ashamed of it. And don't you act like she should be, either." I looked him right in the eye and said, "No, Tate, that would never happen, I give you my word." I said that because if I were a father, I guess I'd need to hear that too, which is exactly what he said, "Thanks, man, I needed to hear that. Let her love her body, and don't look away when you see her naked. She's *seven*. She's not going to feel weird about being naked. Don't you ever make her feel bad about her body, do you understand? I'll come back from the grave and kill you. There's enough women in this world feeling bad about their bodies, and my Honey is not going to be one of them. You love her the way she is, man. You got that?"

Honey follows me to the kitchen by walking on her hands and knees, a thin little body with ribs and juts, except a round butt sticking up in the air, like one of Gretchen's yoga moves, and it's just that I never considered what a female looks like without that hair. I pour some milk into a cup.

"Meow?" she says. "Meow?" like a confused, forlorn thing. I pour it into a bowl and put it on the floor. She crinkles her nose at it and I have to rack my sleepy brain to see what requirements I'm missing. Fuck, she wants it warm. I don't have a microwave. It's going to take ten minutes to get out a pan and warm it up. I tell her that, and she gets teary, and laps up the milk, cold. This is why Tate wants me to move to Denver. She'd be in familiar surroundings; she'd have her own room and grandparents nearby and microwaves.

It could be said that I'm hoping Honey warms to this place; that it's a compromise, since living in Denver would kill me. You could say that. But that would be a lie. It's more like I'm buying time, because surely some other option is going to present itself. Because this just cannot happen; I am quite clear on the fact that I do not want to raise Honey. I should have told Gretchen about all this. But that would be like shoeing a horse and then shooting it in the chest.

I go to Honey's suitcase and find some underwear. I find several pairs, rolled up, each one covered in pictures of princesses.

"So you like princesses, huh?"

She says in her high cat-voice, "I used to be a princess's kitty, but she got captured by an evil warlord, and that's how I got abandoned, and you are the human that found me. Some cereal please," she says in a tiny, high voice. "This kitty likes cereal."

"In that bowl? On the floor? Do you want a spoon?"

But she only purrs and mews until I put the Cheerios that Tate had packed for me in the bowl, and then milk, and then she eats it with her face, until it gets down low, and then she sits up and drinks the rest. Then rolls over on her back, her four paws pointed into the air, while I slip on her underwear and, at her command, scratch her tummy.

She demands I tell her a story. She demands I tell her that I am really a knight in disguise and that we'll find her mommy hidden up here in the woods. And she wants a story about my girlfriend, and she wants to know when she gets to meet her.

"Later," I say. "Next time. I'm no good at stories."

She regards me, disappointed, and she starts up a long stream of words, a barrage against the silence. "My mommy died in a car and my daddy is sick and that's why I'm here with you and are you going to teach me to shoot a gun," to which I say, "No, but how about a bow and arrow?" and she says, "Sure, all right, Robin Hood is okay I guess. Do you have that movie? No, you don't, do you, because you don't have a TV, which means you don't have an Xbox or a Wii, and my daddy said you were different, not different bad, but just different, which is okay, because *everybody's* different. But maybe you're more different than most people because you live in the mountains and don't have anything that normal people have." She crinkles her nose at me and regards me without blinking. She says, "Well, but you do have pinecones, and spray paint in the garage, I saw it, and that's what we're going to do. Ready, Uncle Joe? Ready to have some fun? Do you have gold? Do you have sprinkles? Glitter, I mean. My daddy says one of the best things about me is that I remind him how just to be and to have fun. Which is what love is. He told me to tell you the funny names I make up for things. Like you know that part of your bum where the crack starts? I've always called that a butt-sprout. Because it looks like your butt is sprouting." She points to her own, stabbing the concave indention below her underwear elastic, which, as she intended, makes me laugh, but holy shit, I am not the right man for this job.

Outside, the sun is blazing. It's too warm for October and I stand there, in the gravel driveway, annoyed by it. I need to go hunting; to put away some meat for the winter. But a straw-haired child is stabbing my leg with a stick, so, at her direction, we spray-paint pinecones every color I have on the ground outside the garage. She wants glitter, but I don't have any, so we glue on red berries and pine needles, and then tie on orange bailing twine, and we end up with some crazy-looking ornaments. The truth is this, though: I could be at Moon's having pancakes, or I could be horseshoeing Violet and Ollie Vreeland's old mare, or better yet, I could be with Gretchen.

Instead I'm watching Honey write her alphabet in the dirt of the garage with a stick. I guess she's got it down already, though her Ks and Js are backward. ILoV EMyDaD, she writes in the dirt. Then she wants to know how to spell my name. ILoV EJOE.

"Thank you, Honey. I love you too."

"Just because I love you doesn't mean I don't love my Dad, too.

Even when he's dead, I will love him the most." Her look makes me so fucking sad that I want to crush the pinecone in my hands. It seems so easy, for a kid. Love is so interchangeable, so fluid.

"I would like to give one of these pinecones to Lillie. I think she's kinda lonely."

"Who is Lillie?"

"One of my neighbors."

"You don't have any neighbors, Uncle Joe." She looks around the mountain, as if to show me the evidence.

"Well, I do. We're all just farther apart. She lives down the mountain. Everyone lives down from me. We're highest up. Top of a kingdom. There's a couple named Sy and Anya, and they have two kids you could meet sometime. And there's a man named Ruben, who is sort of like a veterinarian, and he has a girlfriend named Jess. And Violet, she runs the grocery store, and her husband's name is Ollie, and a daughter named Korina, who is a teenager and maybe a babysitter for you someday. There's a guy named Sergio who works with wildlife, and he also likes wood. His sister, Gris, lives with him. They're both really nice. We're all like a family."

"And Gretchen, your girlfriend."

"And Gretchen, yes." Last night, I faked being interested in Honey's drawings, I faked my compliments. I made excuses to Gretchen for why I couldn't visit. I was tired. But one thing is serious and genuine and I-want-to-know: When do we get the crazy notion that our life has a predictable trajectory? That it's not just one crazy winding story? I'd like the answer to that one. I'd like to hear a story about how, at some point in our lives, our stories get blended up. Then I'd like to hear how this particular one sifts out.

## PART III.

First it was Tate doing most of the talking, then it was Honey doing most of the talking, and now it's my turn, I suppose, because I guess it's true that eventually we have to clear our throats and string together a long sequence of words, so that we are simply not responding to the others of the world, but articulating our own likes and dislikes, our own wishes and sorrows. If I'm honest I will tell you that I prefer listening and responding, not coming up with the words myself. I am not much of a talker.

"I wish I could have been with you. The day of the bear." I say this to her as I stand on the stoop of her trailer house, not coming in, as she's indicating I do. "I wish I would have experienced that with you. Also, there is something I wanted to tell you that day. But you'd just chased away a bear, and were full of the energy of that."

She steps outside, barefoot into the snow, which although has been shoveled away since the storm, has refused to melt. She kisses me full on the mouth, and she pulls me inside her door and sinks down first, pulling me with her, and then I find myself on the floor, objecting, but she *shhshs* me and somehow my lips end up between the legs, in the V of a woman who was once a girl, a place of the body I have no good word for because they're all wrong and I want to call it *moooon* because it changes like a moon but the only thing I can do is hold her thighs and push my tongue in further and hum.

I can't help myself. I simply can't. But when we are done, I say what I came to say: "Listen. Please listen to me. There was something I wanted to tell you that day, Gretchen. When I came home early from Denver, because of the storm. But you were so full of energy from the bear, it wasn't the right time. And then. Well. Sy. We wake up to Anya's calling, we wake up to a blizzard, we wake up to the mess these last weeks have been. So what I am telling you next, I should have told you weeks ago, and I know it. But I ask that you forgive me, considering the timing of it all."

She stares at me, expectantly. We are still on the floor of her trailer, on a blanket she has put there. "If only Sy could have seen the sun like this. So bright. Maybe if it hadn't snowed early, he wouldn't have taken his life. Maybe he wouldn't have taken my gun from my truck, maybe now I wouldn't be thinking of his frozen body. Maybe this could be a normal winter with a normal trajectory."

"Oh, Joe," she says. "Joe. That's why I brought you in, to love you, to help you through." She is gazing at me with love-drugged eyes, and outside her trailer, I hear the *thw-ump* of snow falling from trees. "We got through the shock of it. We got through the ceremony. We all got shot-through, didn't we? And now we're all starting to catch our breath. I can feel it. Not that we're not still suffering. We are. Anya is a mess. We got gut-punched, and we're just gasping for air. That's good. The snow is starting to melt. It's going to be okay."

I open my mouth to speak. Odd, how long it takes the words to come. Odd, that I find myself saying them at all. "I simply do not know how this story will go," I say. "But I'd like to write a story, about real humans who do indeed exist, and I would probably call it 'On the Mountain' or 'Blue Moon Mountain,' and it would be about the real people up here, and their real hearts, and it would be about how we all have secrets, and how we all have awful decisions to make, and how we hurt others in our love, and mine would start with describing our shadow against the wall—see there?—

and how there we look like we are one big creature, bizarre and beautiful. But first, first, listen now. Listen, Gretchen. There is a story I need to tell you right now, and a question I need to ask."

## Chapter Seven

# Last Bid

"Starting at three dollars a pound. So give me four four four, Okay! Five, then, five and a quarter." The auctioneer barks a slur into the cold, his voice loud and deep enough to carry over the bawling calves and the drone of conversations and the dusty shuffle of boots up concrete steps and, she hopes, the wobbly way air is coming out of her nose and the tap-tap-tapping of her stubby fingernail on her knee, neither of which she can stop.

"Who'll give me five? Beautiful Angus calves here."

A bidder nods, his ball cap dipping down and then up. The auctioneer jumps to five and a half, and then six six six, and the calves churn in the dirt arena, milling together in their nervousness, bawling and nuzzling each other as they pace.

Violet watches another man lift a finger to bid. He wears a sweat-stained ball cap advertising Erase, a chemical that kills corn rootworms. *No, no, no,* she thinks in unison with the auctioneer's six, six, six. *No, he's not the one.* She smooths her bangs down with her palms and presses her lips together to even out the peach lipstick and pulls her jacket closer. It would be so much easier if he would find her, but if he doesn't, she's prepared, this time, to find him.

The room is too big and too cold, and she's tired of feeling that way. This winter has been tough and she would like to go to

Mexico for the whole rest of it, she would like to heal somewhere else, go a little bit nuts. But there is always the ranch, the damn ranch, and even with the help of their ranch hand, it's just too much work to leave. So instead she's going to do this, by god, and at the Last Chance Auction House, no less.

Violet watches as the calves are chased out and a new group is chased in. They cluster, backing into one another. A few brave ones stand on the edges, their front legs braced, staring up into the bleachers that surround them. It's not so crowded today, and the benches are only spotted with bidders. Sunlight slants through a high window and lights up the floating dust and hay bits and cigarette smoke, and for a moment, it's almost quiet. Then the auctioneer's husky voice starts up again. "Got a group of Hereford-cross here," he drawls, then changes to a speedy staccato. "Start with four, four, four, who's gonna give me four?"

She's watching one calf in particular, a soft, ruddy-red bull with a white face. He stands frozen, blinking at the crowd, and then takes a few galloping steps, kicking his hind legs into the air. He mounts another calf, his front legs gripping and slipping on her hindquarters. As she moves away, he follows, stumbling on his two hind legs. He falls off, then jumps on her again. The female bucks away and kicks at him, but he mounts her anyway, clasping her back and lurching after her.

"Got an ornery one here." The auctioneer chuckles and slows his voice and momentarily stops the bidding. "Not quite old enough, but darn ready for when he is. He'll get the job done for you. So someone gimme five, five, five."

A man takes a bite from his doughnut and tips his hat, and another spits tobacco into his cup and gives a nod, and the auctioneer goes back and forth, goading out an extra three cents per pound as the young bull calf gives up and stands panting, flaring his nostrils with his nose pointed up in the air, sniffing.

It's been a long time since she's been here. It's been years, which is why she recognizes no one. And no one, she hopes, knows her, although it would be easy enough to explain why she's way down here, in town, way east of town, in fact, at the only remaining live auction around, the only way to acquire new animals and meet people at the same time, the only way to get the hell away from her ranch and her grocery store and her grief and her life.

For a long time she stares at the ear of a man sitting several seats in front of her and to the right. His blond sideburn comes down to the middle of his ear and then is cleanly shaven off, leaving red, tough skin. She can see he has a mustache, Western-style. She's never kissed a man with a mustache before. She has been faithful for her entire marriage, faithful to their daughter, faithful to her community, faithful to showing up for her job at the grocery, faithful to the belief in the stretch of time before her—and all this has been good. But then a friend of hers died in a horrible way no person ever should, and something about that has scattered her apart. She can't tell what she is doing, but she thinks she should perhaps not miss out on kissing a mustached man.

This particular man runs his hand down his cheek as he watches the calves, then scratches his ear—perhaps because she is looking at it, she thinks. But he does not look in her direction. Instead, he takes a sip out of a cup and spills some coffee on his denim shirt. He ducks his chin to look at the spill and brushes it away with the tips of his fingers, shaking his head slightly, and she thinks, *He's the one.*

She grabs her purse and walks up the bleacher steps. In the bathroom, she tightens her face against the faint smell of urine and menstrual blood, puts a peppermint breath mint in her mouth, and leans forward over the sink to stare at her face in the mirror. She is still pretty. Still has her trademark smile, lovely and genuine, and even though her ponytailed gray hair and eye wrinkles suggest a certain age, it's her smile that has always made people feel good, has softened and encouraged and cheered them. She has been, on the whole, a person who used that smile to good end. Benevolent manipulation, her husband calls it, teasing her for her ability to cheer. She smiles at herself, now, shyly. "I hope this works for you, kid," she says. "Good luck."

She buys a cup of coffee and then returns to the auction pit, this time descending by a different set of stairs. She pretends interest in the cows that have just been chased in, but really she is aiming toward the blond man, who has taken off his cap, revealing a line across his head where the hair is matted, and she stares at that line until she's right beside him. "Excuse me," she says, and shuffles past his knees and down a few paces and then sits. She drops her purse to the cement floor and sets the coffee cup on the aluminum seat beside her. It will be too hard to start a conversation later, so she's got to do it now. *Now, now, now*, she thinks, and then turns to him and smiles and says, "It's cold in here. Looking to buy some calves?"

He turns to her, jolted out of his thoughts, but not angry, not intruded upon. "No," he says. "I'm here for the sheep. Guess I got here early."

"Well, they should be up soon."

He nods and turns his attention back to the calves. He's being friendly, nothing more, and she thinks she should just let it go, and besides, her hands are shaking. But she sits on her hands and promises herself she'll quit after one more try: "I had a sheep when

I was a little girl," she says, "and I remember how we tied a rubber band around its tail so it would fall off. How do you do that, anyway, with a big herd?"

He considers her question for a moment, then scoots over across the smooth seat so that they won't have to strain to hear, and she lets out a long, shaky breath and fills her lungs again before he is beside her.

"Well, sometimes they dock them with bands, or they just cut the tails off when they're castrating."

"I've heard the men castrate, you know . . . with their teeth."

"Well, there's that."

"Some sort of prove-yourself-a-man ritual."

"Not partial to it myself."

"But you've seen it done?"

"Sure. It's very fast."

"I just can't picture it."

"I'm not sure you'd want to."

"You have a herd?"

"I work for a sheep rancher in Wyoming. I had to bring a horse down here for a cousin of his, so he asked me to see if I could bring back a trailer full of good ewes. Plus I'm snowed in, more or less. Lotta snow up north. Although I see you have plenty here too. Not sure what I'm going to do, exactly. How about you?"

She hesitates, because she cannot remember the response she has practiced. Once the words start, they come out all wrong, in a jumble, and she speeds up to find the end of the sentence. "We, my husband Ollie and I, own a small cattle ranch up west of town, Angus and Herefords mostly, up on Blue Moon Mountain. My husband is gone for a few days, he up and took our daughter on a vacation, one last father-daughter trip before she leaves for college, which is fine, they could use that time together, and I stayed behind to manage the store and the ranch and because they need to be alone, and so do I. But I got a little lonely today, really lonely, so I thought I'd head down here to see if any old friends were around, but they're not. Not today, I guess."

She presses her fingertips to her forehead, alarmed that she might have revealed something, but also hoping that she has. After all, she no longer knows how to proceed. How can she convey to him that she has not kissed another man besides her husband in twenty-five years, and that she's kissed only three others in her life, and that she's not even sure how a first kiss is supposed to feel anymore? But now she's got to know; she's got to kiss someone soon, now, now, now, and she needs to feel something new so that she can hold it inside her.

So could he please help her out with this? she wants to ask. If she could, she would tell him, I know I'm not beautiful, I'm not young, and you don't have to adore me the way I imagined a lover would, the way I thought it would be for all these years—you admiring my back while I'm asleep, naked, in your sheets; holding me to you because you don't want to lose me. No, you don't have to do any of that. But if you could just find something I say funny or clever, or see something special in my face and tell me about it and then kiss me, it would be enough, it would be enough.

He surprises her, suddenly, with a torrent of his own words. He lives in a trailer, he says, in the middle of nowhere, with his horse, Blue, and his dog, also named Blue. It's the last place, that dry open prairie, where a man like him can go. In the winter he moves to town, but he doesn't like it. He feels strange now, in this crowded room, in this Colorado town. But it's good for him, he knows. He's got to stay in touch with this other world every once in a while and—he says, looking at her with a tilt of his head—it's nice to be talking to someone other than Blue and Blue.

He is genuine and soft, not flirting or wanting anything, and his kindness drains her. But it also sends her a wave of courage; his honesty has made way for hers, and she will try to get as close as she can to saying what cannot quite be said.

So she says, "I heard once that getting old is the loss of desire. Desire for something in the present, or the future, and not just reliving the desires of the past. So I've been thinking lately, *What is it in the present that I desire?* Because I don't want to be growing old." She laughs, trying to make it light, but he's looking at her with serious gray eyes, so she continues, her voice barely above a whisper. "And I was just wondering if there's anything, up there in that flat, quiet place, that you find yourself, well . . . desiring."

His eyes drift from hers to the center of the arena, where a large bull is pacing around the edge of the pen, waving his head in the air, as if trying to catch something in his horns, snorting at some invisible foe.

"There is plenty I desire," he finally says. "And not all of it I could put into words, even if I were going to tell you." He bats her knee with his palm, a playful, innocent movement. "I didn't realize that folks at auctions talked about more than the weather. It's nice to meet you. I'm Jack."

"Violet," she says, holding out her hand and curling her fingers tightly around his as they shake.

"Violet," he repeats, and she holds the sound of his voice saying her name in her head.

The drive back was startling in its contradiction, how river and road offered two parallel winding black paths free of snow in a world that was otherwise variations of white: trees, mountainsides, fences, fields. She watched him in the rearview mirror as he followed her west, up the mountain, she in her truck and he in his old truck and trailer.

The sheep he bought are now in her corral. Even from inside her house, she can hear them bleating. But they have access to hay and water, so their scared bawling, after Jack *whooped* them out of the trailer, has disappeared. She'll explain their droppings to Ollie and Korina by telling them that a stranger from Wyoming stayed the night so he wouldn't have to make that long drive back so late in the day, with the roads being so iffy up north and all. She was offering kindness to a stranger. It is the truth, so far. But she hopes there will be more, another truth, which she will also tell her husband if he asks her.

She will say to him: I am greedy for something new. And I felt guilty because of that greed, because I love you. But I don't have time for guilt anymore. I'm sorry.

She hopes her husband will forgive her. His kindness has always prevented her from justifying what she is about to do. But after all, it isn't about greed, she tells herself. It is a chance to understand and recognize desire. There is plenty of desire in her, more than can be embraced in whatever time she has left, and the only way to survive this winter is to do this crazy thing.

So much desire. Desire not only for a kiss, or the tingle spreading from her pelvis to her spine, or the feel of a tongue against her lower arm and circling her breast, but also for warm days and the smell of wheat drying in the fields and the chance to be alive in someone else.

Greed and desire. They are, she thinks now, not separate things; they are the same, and they are good. Why couldn't Sy hold on to that?

She pours Jack a cup of coffee and sets out a plate of crackers. She wishes she had put the dishes in the dishwasher and wiped the countertops before she left this morning, but she must not have believed then that a man would be sitting in the kitchen with her now. She did change the sheets, though, and they will smell clean, and maybe that will remind him of his Wyoming nights, and he will be pleased and roll over and touch her shoulder and speak of stars and remember her that way.

He's quirkier than she first thought; she sees that now. "I like to think about beautiful words," he is saying. "What if you could taste *turquoise*?"

She doesn't know what to say to that. Finally, she says, "I thought Wyoming sheep people thought about words like *beer* and *poker* and *sex*."

"Well, that too." His grin reveals a chipped tooth.

"Is it enough?" she blurts.

He leans forward and looks into her eyes. "I don't know. It's enough for the usual day. But the usual days aren't what really make up a life, are they?" He says this as if he's not quite sure himself, and then he stands up and walks to the kitchen sink and looks out the window toward the snowy mountains in all directions.

"Do they make you claustrophobic?" she asks him.

"Yes."

"They make me feel grounded and protected."

"I can see that."

"The mountains hide things. Two months ago, I came across a couple making love in the woods. It was the sweetest thing I ever saw. I want something like that." She looks at him, then, stands, moves toward him, leans in toward him, all the time an auctioneer's voice murmuring in her head—five five five decades and a quarter, who wants to bid?—and without a trace of embarrassment, she tilts her head and touches his lips with hers.

The kiss is clumsy. Her teeth knock against his lips, and the two of them bump foreheads, and he pulls away. But she leans toward him again, before he has time to move very far, and their lips meet in a soft way until he moves his hands across her back and presses her hips to him. Then the kisses are hard and compact, much as she always thought they would be. Only more scary and more grand, because they are real.

She leads him to the bedroom and pulls back the clean sheets. In the instant before flesh touches clean cotton, she knows that this moment was impossible in her life until now, that it might be wrong, might turn out wrong. But still, she sends a thank-you up to all the lonely souls, for giving her the courage, for the flash of something new, for this moment she can hold inside her.

She imagines the end will come someday, as she lies on this bed, loving her husband and her daughter, the mountains hovering above their land, the flat meadows stretching from the foothills to their door. And now she will also have this: a sudden rise in the earth, this small outcropping of rocks that breaks up the landscape.

## Chapter Eight

# This Imaginary Me

Daydreaming is all I can seem to do this winter. My feet are propped up on the dash of the truck, my eyes directed out to snow-draped pines and granite sky, and I'm imagining a man falling for me, so very in love with me, and that's why I barely see Sergio's face, how it contorts and pulls back into a grimace, as he shouts, "Oh, fuck, wait, what?" and while he is gunning his truck to pass a white junker he's been cussing for a mile he is also breaking to slow down to be *next* to the white junker, all this at once, or nearly at once, and it jolts me back to here, though mostly I have been elsewhere, daydreaming of an alternate me in a nonexistent life. I am looking ahead to see what we'll crash into, how our lives are about to end. My eyes search down the mountain—a deer? the snow? what danger?—and my mouth starts up a Hail Mary, an old reflex from my Believing Days. It's only a split second but it is also forever. I see what he does. Which is. In the white car we are passing, a man drives with one hand and punches the woman next to him with his other.

Punching. Full force.

Then the car is not beside us anymore. It is in front of us. Sergio has reentered the space behind it, right as both cars curve around a steep bend. I cock my head in confusion, squint my eyes. My brain offers different sequences of slow-motion words to explain what I saw: How strange! A man is punching a woman, there is blood smeared across the woman's face, there is a man with dark hair, there is a red-faced man driving with one hand, there is a woman cowering, there is a woman with a thin jean jacket ducking down and away, there is a man punching a woman who has pressed herself against the door.

I turn and blink at my brother. Sergio, in turn, lays on the horn, speeds up to tailgate the car, yells out, "I think that's the goddamn meth couple! Is it? Write down the license plate, Gris!"

I grope around for a pen. I knock my head on the glove compartment as my body sways forward and then back as he accelerates. I look up to discover that the white car has sped up and so has Sergio.

"B-Y-2-0-2-something. Write it down. Gris, write it down! Stupid fucking phone, stupid reception!" He throws his cell phone at the dash and it ricochets and hits me in the knee.

I scrawl the marks across the front cover of the book I'm reading. I see myself as I was this morning, tossing the book in the car, hoping to enter its imaginary world.

"Four-door, Honda, eighties," he says, and he says, "Did you see that woman's face? Did you see that woman?"

Only now has my brain registered the image: Through the bits of a mild dusting of snow, I see a woman, a swoosh of straight thin hair and the exact moment her mouth is just starting to open in surprise, or maybe in a cry.

My daydream was about the same man who is always there, the one who has lived in my head for years, the one who falls in love with me again and again for various reasons and in various circumstances. He doesn't have a name, even after all these years, but he touches my jawline, brushes my black hair behind my ear, and looks into my eyes.

I'm no idiot. I see these dreams aren't about him, and they're not even about love. I know this because my brain is interested in imagining the falling-in-love stage, and after that, the relationship blurs out of focus and my heart goes numb, and I start a new fantasy altogether.

What these dreams are about is me, a different, better, fascinating me. I am the star of my own romance novel, a million different copies sold.

I like to know that through the work of my brain, I can still feel my heart swish open with excitement, constrict with pain, that I can bring myself to tears, all with imagination. I like to know I am still alive. That my grief about the losses of the world have not yet numbed me. That the death of faraways, like immigrants, and that the death of nearbys, like Sy, doesn't shut me down entirely.

Daydreaming is my antidote to reality.

Now we are going way too fast around the corners, and the shady parts of the road are still covered in the snow from That Blizzard. Behind us is the post office and grocery where I work. In fact, there is Violet, my boss, heading the opposite way as us, down into town. Here's the sign that advertises YOU MISSED MOON'S RESTAURANT. NIGHT-CRAWLERS, BEER, FOOD, GOOD COMPANY INSIDE—GO BACK IF THAT'S WHAT YOU SEEK! And another hand-painted sign: NEVER TRUST ANYONE UNDER 7,000 FEET. Finally, I speak. "Stop here, up ahead, Gretchen's house!"

Sergio hesitates. We can see from the silhouettes that the man has stopped punching and is instead hunched over the wheel, glancing in the rearview mirror, trying to get away. The woman is slumped against the door. Their car backfires and makes a loud explosion, which makes me yelp and cover my ears. I beg. "Sergio, let's not follow—what would we do?—he probably has a gun— let's call the police. Stop here!"

Gretchen's driveway is coming up fast. I do not know Gretchen very well, as in, I do not know her heart, but I know she buys lots of cleaning supplies and often braids her long graying hair into two thick beautiful pigtails that hang down to her chest and I believe her to be kind, and I know she is dating Joe, who is a farrier, who I do know because I share a horse with a few others on the mountain, and we split the expenses and share the joy of a beautiful quarter horse. He is our horseshoer, he is everyone's horseshoer. Gretchen, though. She chats with me whenever she is buying groceries, and I know that she loves poetry, especially Whitman, and that she cleans houses. But I have never been to her house. I am thrown forward and Sergio decides last-minute to turn and we are flung to the side as he pulls in her driveway, I am struck with the sense of seeing something familiar: Such a little trailer is where I have imagined meeting my falling-in-love lover, a snowed-in quiet place, such a place where we eke out our quiet, simple lives. Such a place transforms me.

Sergio stomps on the breaks, jumps out, yells, "It's an emergency," and pounds on her door, all at once, or almost once, before I even get there. Gretchen opens the door, startled, and I walk in after him and see her handing him the landline phone, which everyone has up here because cells don't always work. She has been crying. "My cell phone isn't working," Sergio says, and then he is turning away, preparing to speak. I glance around her house, which has houseplants everywhere, pots of basil still blooming, even now, in the winter. There is the smell of pot. There are books and torn pages from the *New York Times*, cans of WD-40. Her refrigerator, which is what I'm standing next to, is messiest of all, covered with tacked-up poems and a sticker that says WELL-BEHAVED WOMEN SELDOM MAKE HISTORY and flyers about how many people in the world lack sanitation, or the average household use of toilet paper per capita per country, or the average pesticide load on average fruits and vegetables. Her house is very cold and I wonder if she is very poor. She is staring at me and so I say, "We were going to go cross-country skiing together, up in the meadow, and have a little ceremony for Sy, for our parents, for all the souls. We saw . . . something . . . bad. He needs to call the police." And then, because she looks near tears, I say, "How is Joe?"

"We just broke up," she says. "We haven't told anyone yet."

"I'm sorry," I say. "Why?"

"Things break," she says. She looks at me with a soft, worn-out look and I know exactly what she is saying. Yes, things break, and our imagination is the only tool we have to patch bits together.

I look around some more. This is the house I would like to have, but this woman is not happy. Finally, I find the courage to ask: "How is Anya?"

"She is focused on the kids. Talking and taking them to do fun things. She's a zombie, going through the motions. She'll feel it more later." Then she goes to the kitchen sink and splashes water on her face.

When I turn back around, Sergio is telling the phone what we've seen. I listen, silently urging him to better convey the seriousness of it, the momentum of the man's fist, the woman's bloody face, the way her body ricocheted from the force of his blows.

Sergio tells the sheriff the make of the car and apologizes that he never caught the full license plate, that there was so much mud splattered. But he believes them to be—and here, he hesitates—he's not sure, but they might be the couple that lives above the Vreeland Ranch in an old trailer. He does not say the word *meth*. There are certain things you keep quiet about on this mountain, there are certain troubles you avoid. Especially Sergio. He wants to take care of the mountains, he wants to make things with wood, he wants to someday meet a woman. He doesn't want the sheriff in his life. He answers questions about our location and names, and then there is a pause. He's searching, I know, for a way to end this conversation right, a way to ask for help for this woman. I am searching, too, for something, anything.

"Tell them to hurry," I whisper.

"It looked pretty bad," he says. "You might want to hurry."

Then he hangs up the phone, turns to me, and holds out his hands.

As he takes my elbow and leads me out, and back to the truck, he leans over and whispers in my ear, "We must do what we set out to do," but there is only sadness in his eyes.

⌒

"We couldn't find the car, but we'll check back by the house," the sheriff tells me that evening, right as the sky is turning deep cornflower blue. He assures me that they did send up a patrol car but no one was home, the place was locked up, and they could not enter lacking a search warrant and all.

*Oh, Jesus, Mary*, I think. *We should have followed. Why did I tell him to stop? Why did I not help that woman?* By now, of course, the image has taken hold in my mind—a frozen moment that I cannot shake away and that I cannot help but examine for details. I can see the man, the black stubble on his pockmarked red cheek, the dark blue of a T-shirt, I can see the hair of a woman, the bloody face, her denim jacket.

I write a letter to the Colorado State Patrol in big, loopy handwriting and bad grammar. I don't know why I want to disguise this, to make it different than our own report. I write, *Dear who-ever, I saw a man beating up on some body in his car and it looked real bad so I'm writing to tell you his license plate number. I think it was BY2002. Please, I hope you do something about it. I am pretty sure they live on County Road 44 in a house that might be selling meth.*

After that, I sit down and cry. I am tired from our skiing, my eyes stinging from the burning sage, from weeping, my throat tired from the old prayers of our childhood, my body exhausted from the startle of seeing the meadow, the stacks of rocks, like cairns, the footprints and snowshoe tracks of others. I didn't know that so many people came. I didn't know there was so much hurt in this world. I want my parents back. I want someone to love me. I want to close the woman's eyes, transport her somewhere else, take her away from the real. But her eyes are locked open, so instead I close mine. I try to conjure up my imaginary romantic man, the one who isn't concerned about the terrors of the world, because he is too intent on me. Or he *is* concerned with the terrors of the world, and holds me to him, and we push our foreheads against each other's shoulder for comfort. He is not there, though. For the first time, I cannot find him.

I stare into the dark and listen to the conversation I realize I am now having in my daydream. I am speaking with the woman who was in the car. We talk about her leaving this man, I assure her of her worth, we work out the details on how she can live alone. I offer advice on safe and welcoming places to go, including moving in with me.

She reaches out to hold me. I concentrate on how my heart feels, the way it swells with the joy and approval of this imaginary me.

*Chapter Nine*
# You Win

The fact that it was a Ducati motorcycle seemed to be significant, which left Flannery feeling shamed. She didn't know anything about motorcycles, including the brand Ducati, or their Ducatisti, or what made them special. Di was solicitous, though, first by accelerating before Flannery had time to develop any serious anxiety, and then by reaching back to pat Flannery's leg on straight stretches. But best of all was that Di pulled over twice on paved areas next to the river, turned around, asked if Flannery was doing okay, and her voice and look indicated that she really meant it, that she'd stop if Flannery needed her to.

Each time, Flannery nodded her big helmeted head and yelled *I'm loving it*, not entirely true. Then she closed her eyes in wince as Di pulled out and zoomed on. Flannery tried to breathe in and send the air specifically to her right leg, which was vibrating uncontrollably. It was just insane, leaning toward the pavement like that, right into the thing that would kill you.

Ten minutes into it, though, she'd relaxed enough to move her helmeted head to a more comfortable position that involved sitting back, away from Di, just enough to straighten her neck instead of having it so painfully tilted backward. This allowed her to look around. Now she could see the dark wave of the river, the glow of the yellow aspens, the rocky granite slabs and the slopes of pines that rose up alongside the road. Since they were going up the canyon, she could also see who was going down. Gretchen, the house cleaner; Sergio, the wildlife guy; Violet, the ranch woman who ran the grocery. She wanted them to see her, the world to see her, but they'd never recognize her.

When they found a pullout to turn around, they had to come to a full stop. That was when Flannery got to implement what she'd learned from Di on how to execute a full stop—keep one hand around Di's waist, but use the other to brace herself on the Ducati, so the driver wasn't pulled too hard back and forth. A little dance of hands. The irony of this did not escape Flannery. That's exactly what she and Di had been doing in the last weeks, and it had come time—surely it had finally come time, because it was crazy-producing not to know—to pick one path or stop for good.

Much of this was a first. First motorcycle ride ever. First time hearing the word *Ducati*. First real emotion since her first boyfriend, seven years ago, with that long long long spread of lonely in between. First potential for sex in over three years. Not her first female lover, but her first female love.

Perhaps Di felt her relax into it, because she waved the Ducati back and forth on a straight patch, and it made Flannery yelp and squeeze. Her leg started shaking and she let it, believing it was best to allow the body to let go of all the shit it was carrying around.

∽

Flannery jumped up and down like a kid when they got off. She laughed with genuine delight now; she was delighted to have survived, to be off the thing, to have gone in the first place. The air was cold and bright but the sun was shining and Di watched her with a tender look as she helped get the helmet off and pulled Flannery in for a kiss, put her hands in Flannery's wild blond curls and said *you're so hot*. Unzipped the leather jacket and kissed her and said *Today is the day, I want you so bad*. Held Flannery's hand out so they could both see how it was shaking, and pulled her in for another kiss, tongue and teeth, moved her hand up to her breast, cupped her crotch and pulled her toward her and said *now now now I want you now.*

The lust roared and Flannery kept holding on tight, even when Di released her, so that she could get one last smell of Di's dark hair, one last hold of Di's solid body, one moment of muscle and tendon and skin, one more moment of the furious burn and wet—one last moment before Di would leave her. As they walked toward Flannery's trailer, which was in a small cluster of them next to Moon's Restaurant and Bar, a bear darted away from the dumpster in the back, a bag of candies or something hanging from her mouth.

⁀

Flannery had herpes, the genital sort, contracted when she was eighteen from the second guy she'd slept with; a one-night stand that changed her life forever. She told this to Di when they were on the couch, about to kiss, and as she said this, she pushed herself up to look in Di's eyes and she spoke very quickly: "I love you. You don't need to say it back. But I need to tell you. There's no mistaking it. You could not believe how badly I want you right now. Want you, and *want* you. As in, for a relationship, for the real thing. Many women have herpes and don't know it. About a fifth of the population. I could not tell you, I suppose. I'm making the choice to tell you, because what I want is love, and by telling you, I start the relationship off on the right foot. But it does kill me, I want you to know it *kills* me, that some small fuck of a virus could get in the way of the largest possible thing, love."

Di made a small, beautiful, confused noise. Her long dark hair swirled around her face and she pushed herself up, away from Flannery, and Flannery accommodated her but kept her hands firmly holding Di's hands in order to keep her grounded, keep her attention. She'd rehearsed it in her mind since she was young, but it never got voiced as hoped. Little fragments came out: It's not usually a problem, I don't often have an actual outbreak. Yes, it's painful. I won't lie. I can sometimes feel it coming, a little buzzing on the skin, I take the medicine and catch it in time. I'd want you to have some time with this before we continued. Especially if you ever want kids. There are other things we can do until you're sure. We can use that female condom. Doesn't guarantee. But before we make love, I think you should do some research. Maybe even talk to your doctor, so that you feel more at ease. I've only had two lovers since, one woman, one man, and the woman had it already and didn't care, and the man took his chances. Neither were love. This is, though. I really, really want you.

Several looks crossed Di's face—her freckled, high-cheekboned, slightly pudgy gorgeous face—and they all broke Flannery's heart. There was openness, confusion, absorption, hurt. There was the scanning of the brain that meant Di was trying to recall what she knew about the virus—was that the one that was incurable but medicine was available? Or the curable one? And shouldn't she know, shouldn't by now she have kept them all straight?—and how should she respond politely?—and Flannery watched it all register. Noted the embarrassed shrug, the big exhale of breath.

Flannery closed her eyes and focused on her own body, how it moved from electrical lust to cold numbness—that old and familiar shift. She sat back on the couch and waited.

～

In Flannery's daydreams, Di responded this way:

* Oh, I know that I already have it, and I was about to tell you. We're compatible.
* It's not true, what they say about "No good deed should go unpunished." You did a good deed by telling me, and I won't punish you for it.
* The universe is always throwing up various sorts of walls. All kinds of walls! This is your particular wall, and we'll climb over this one together. Don't worry.
* Something so tiny should not hurt something so grand. It's too unjust.
* I don't care. I love you so much that I don't care. I want more moments with you. I'm nearly thirty and I know what I want now and I want to spend a good stretch of the rest of my life with you.

～

What happened was that Di flopped to the side, and her body said *I give up* and her voice said, "Oh, that's why you kept your panties on all the time," and Flannery said, "Yes, I'm asymptomatic, but the virus is shed even when there's no symptoms," and Di said, "Thank you for telling me, but maybe you should have told me sooner?" and Flannery said, "It's tricky, you know? To know when. There are three rules, they say. Never tell a person right away, if, for example, you can't trust them to keep your secret or respond with care; never tell them after sex, too late; and never tell them in a moment of passion, since, you know, attraction might cloud clear thinking." Di was still, said she was absorbing it all. After a while, she said, "No wonder. I always felt you pulling back," and Flannery said, "I am really attracted to you. But yeah, maybe it changes the way I approach all of it," and all of it sounded so technical and un-lovely and un-loving that Flannery went flat with the simple sorrow of love never progressing in a graceful mindless passionate way.

Di stood, closed her eyes, took a huge breath, and let it out long and slow. She opened her eyes, looked at Flannery, mumbled a few words of departure. She said she wanted to leave before dark—adrenaline-junkie that she was, she didn't want to be on the roads at dusk, when the deer would be out. There were limitations to what dangers one wanted to embrace, after all.

⁓

Flannery waited a few days for the call in which Di said, "I just can't live without you, I need you, we'll work it out, we'll find a way," or anything resembling that, and when it didn't come, Flannery looked up at her spinning ceiling, uncomfortably drunk, as she'd been every night since the motorcycle day, and discovered her mantra: Okay, universe, you win.

Then she got up. She was never one for lying in bed, even in the most depressed times of her various depressions; her body just couldn't stay still for long. Even when moving about, though, she felt heavy. Her chest, without a doubt, weighed thousands of pounds. This fact had to do with a loneliness caused by a tiny weightless virus.

She continued to get up and go to work, she continued to brush her teeth, she continued to take out the trash from her crappy little trailer and throw it into the bin behind Moon's Restaurant. She continued to lock the bear-safety lock, even though it seemed like no one else did.

No one in the little mountain town noticed a difference in her mood. How could they? She was new, after all, had worked only as a very-part-time helper at the vet clinic for a month now, in order to get to know some folks, and otherwise did some web design on the side. But her world was foggy, as if inside many panes of glass. She watched her hands answer the phone, hold a dog on the weight scale, write an appointment. She heard her voice respond to her boss, Ruben, telling him where she'd put the new shipment of antibiotics. She cleaned up dog shit after an old German shepherd lost control. She sold iodine to the meth couple, a huge amount of birdseed to the old man who'd just lost his wife, expensive cat food to the beekeeper woman who looked like she couldn't afford to eat herself. She stroked kitten ears and purred at them for their human owners, so that they all could feel warm emotion, feel special. She watched as occasional snowflakes sporadically spit themselves around and wondered what it looked like up close, the virus, and if it resembled crystals of snow.

She saw them on the roads now, the Ducatisti, as they called themselves, the little groups on their motorcycles. Funny how that happened, how once you were infected with knowledge, you saw it everywhere. She knew cyclists of all kinds from down in town loved this mountain road, scenic and deserted as it was, but she'd never paid attention. Now she found herself looking at the bundled-up riders leaning into the curves, how the passenger, if there was one, had a hand bracing for a stop.

From her car or from the vet clinic, she watched them go by, and her mind would narrate the same narrative it had for years, a little singsongy list that had become an addiction, one that she tapped a finger to note each point:

It was hard, so-o-o-o hard, to find someone who was

* queer,
* your approximate age,
* interesting and compatible and worth loving,
* at the right place for a relationship—timing was perhaps a stronger force even than love—and finally,
* would not grow cold when you told them about something beyond your control, not like a personality quirk, which could be changed, but something sturdy and huge, something that had enough power to assure its victory.

⟂

It started getting cold and she was not doing okay. This was her first fall in Colorado, and she'd figured it would be much like Seattle, but it was not. She was surprised by the sheer cold of the nights, how short the days were becoming, the strength of the wind. She found herself muttering *you win, you win* at random times, in a bitter way that surprised even herself, even once said it to Ruben, who said, "What? I win? What do I win?" to which she laughed and made some joke and told herself to stop saying it, both aloud and in her mind. She tried Tinder and Match and PinkSofa again, and expanded the mileage range. "Looking for woman within 2,000 miles," she typed in once, drunk, laughing with the saddest noise she'd ever heard herself make. She kept going to the grocery store and cooking, although she spent more time looking at the night sky than she'd ever done before.

Then suddenly there was a blizzard and there was a suicide on the mountain. A nice man, a gentle man, a man who was technically the owner of the vet clinic but whom she'd rarely met because he'd taken time off, leaving Ruben in charge, which is why Ruben had hired her, he not being able to do it all. This man, Sy, was known to have schizophrenia, also something out of his control, and she'd heard he often spoke about the stars whispering to him.

His death hurt like a motherfucker. She didn't know the guy, after all. But she cried and cried for him. Perhaps because they were both at the mercy of some little off-kilter thing in the body, perhaps because she'd started considering it herself.

Now she was saying it all the time: "Okay, universe, you win. You win." During random times throughout the day, in her sleep, to cans at the grocery store. "Okay, virus. You win. I kept trying. I kept looking. I kept hoping. Now I'm done. Truly done. I give up. Look what you do to everyone. You win. You win."

She was sure that Sy had killed himself out of loneliness; most of humanity was suffering an epidemic of loneliness, and clearly, he had finally said to the universe: *You win.*

❧

She went to the ceremony, held a week after his death, and wrote it in the snow outside the grange with an ungloved finger before she walked in. YOU WIN. The others on the mountain had spent the week digging themselves out and various cars and trucks were pulling into the parking lot of an old brick building, or over at the parking area for the post office nearby, and people were trudging through the snow, and so in one small sense, the universe had not won, here was evidence of the fight against it. In the larger sense it had, and always would, and worst of all, was indifferent to its success.

Flannery stood, gazing at her writing in the snow as people started to filter by. A few stopped to say hello or ask if she wanted to join them inside, but she said she'd come in a moment. She waited until they'd all gone inside. Hard new flakes settled over her letters and she decided she'd move off the mountain in the spring. Moving was not the solution to everything, perhaps nothing, but as she saw how fast her marks would be impermanent, she was clear that she had to do something tangible. Her move here hadn't changed anything, after all, hadn't led her closer to family or community or love, and so she'd simply move on, to keep from doing what Sy had just done. She couldn't be rid of this virus. She couldn't make someone love her. She couldn't make the universe cause her path to career into someone else's.

What could she do? The roar of defeat was so great that she couldn't move for a long time. An idea came to her, then. An idea that even made her smile. She glanced at the grange. No one could see her out here; she was facing a bricked wall; the windows and door were on the other side. So she pulled down her tights, held up her black skirt, squatted, and peed. She melted the letters herself before the universe had its chance to cover them up. She smiled the whole time that the urine hissed, and then she stood up and pulled up her tights and smoothed her skirt and looked down at the melting letters. "You win, but fuck you," she said. Then she went inside, to be among others and to grieve it all. Come spring, she'd pack her bags, load up her car, and drive off the mountain. Perhaps she'd get a Ducati. Although, no, she didn't want a motorcycle herself. Just something similar, something so sturdy that she could lean toward a danger and be held.

## Chapter Ten

# Boxed Up

No way around it. *Un*-hinged. That's what she is. I'm always having to move, there's some fuck thing wrong with everyplace, and now she's ruined the mountain for me. I wanted to maybe even settle here for good and now look. I thought maybe I'd found a relationship and a place that would work. She said she didn't like the way I treated my dog, but what she doesn't understand, that unhinged bitch, is that it's a *pit* bull. *Any* way it gets treated is better than its other fate, which would be to be put down. In fact, that's why I had to leave the *last* town, now that I think about it. Pit bull ordinance. But also, and most importantly, I treat this dog really well. It sleeps with me at night, cuddled in my arms. We have an understanding, me and this dog; we both love love.

How I got messed up with this girl, I don't know. I must not have been thinking correctly and I should learn from that in the future. She seemed nice at first. We had some good times and she was a good cook. Fantastic sex, including third input, which is my fav.

She said that anytime a dog shits in a house, it means it hasn't been out enough, that I need to let this dog out, but I'm sorry, Dandelion, in the meadow are things like mountain lions and bears, not to mention an expanse of about a zillion miles in which a dog could, and would, get lost and die of starvation. Talk about suffering then. What she fails to understand, and maybe I should feel sorry for her, maybe I should try to be more compassionate, because she's so mentally ill—bipolar I would guess, if I had to—is that the dog is just being passive-aggressive. He's shitting inside on purpose just to show me he's pissed. Because it gets a rise out of me, sure. I lose my temper. And so BW does it when he wants to make me mad. Can she not see that?

I'm not kidding. Anyone who has had a pit bull knows how smart they are. The dog gets out plenty. The dog doesn't particularly *like* the outside. The dog is an inside dog and is, frankly, just happy to be alive.

For instance, BW, at this very moment, is looking at me looking at him. Puts his big boxy head right on my lap. What a doofus. I love this dog.

Before I leave the mountain, I want to get her back. She's suddenly moved in with her cousin Flannery, one of those gorgeous women who thinks she's gay but is just a man-hating bitch. They met at the funeral of the dude who offed himself. What I want is for everyone to see who this bitch really is. She's got them thinking that she's this sweet, horseback-riding country girl who got mixed up with bad company, and probably *every*one thinks she's lovely, and I don't blame them. That's the thing about mental illness. She can be charming, but underneath she's just a psychopath or something. Sociopath, that's the word.

Because she has no emotion. Like, told me she was going to call the police on me if I texted, called, or emailed her one more time and that would be the last thing I wanted, given my business and all. What I was trying to do was work it out. Apologize for some stuff, get her to apologize. Communication is the key to relationships, I told her. And she said to me, stone-faced, totally without emotion, Not when it's with you, Luce, there's something really wrong with you.

This sort of behavior is called gaslighting. Ingrid Bergman and all that. If you don't know what I'm talking about, then fuck you. There should be justice. Some fairness. I just got to figure out what to do.

I think she is unstable. Maybe even delusional. She can say things that cut right to the bone. Like, criticizing my dog, when she knows full well that he's the one thing I love the most. That he's all I got. Now I realize she was gaslighting me all along.

Everyone knows I love this dog. That I would never hurt this dog. He's still on the couch with me, with his tummy up in the air. He loves tummy rubs, man. L-u-u-ves them. So exposed and vulnerable like that, his dick exposed like that. I thought about killing the dog and then making it clear she did it. But that's an outright lie and I want people to know the truth. The truth is bad enough. I'll just expose her for the unhinged bitch she is. I got to be very careful here. Because I can do stupid shit, and I don't want to get arrested.

What she does is try to dehumanize people. She comes across as being oh-so-human, celebrating humanity, but all she really does is stab people. But not in the back. No. Right in the front, right in the heart. She said we weren't "a good fit" and she "needed to move on, into something where a future looked not only better, but like it might actually happen." But she never would explain what that meant. What if I needed more clarity? Well, fuck Luce for wanting more clarity. She's a narcissist, that's what she is. Couldn't even reach out to me for a moment, to just help me *understand*. To give me some good reasons other than "we weren't a good fit" and "I don't like the way you treat your dog, leaving him in that kennel so much, who wants to be in a box?" I think she has borderline personality disorder. I should have written her a note and told her to look it up.

What I did do was write to her mother. I told her that her daughter was unhinged. I said it all professional, though, emailed and formal. That I had concerns about her mental health and wanted her to be aware of it. That Dandelion had seemed charming and gracious, which is why it was such a surprise to discover she had severe bipolar tendencies.

I told Dandelion specifically: I am having a breakdown. Like serious. Like I need your help. I'm sorry I was an asshole. I'm not trying to manipulate you. Please look past my recent behavior. If you can find some empathy, please call me. Please.

But no. Dandelion knows how to stab straight in and then twist the knife. Because she knew she could, and she was good at it. Do I sometimes say the wrong things? Yes. Do I sometimes act rashly? Yes. I am a messy human. But instead of loving that about me, or accepting it, she just pushed me away.

Well, I boxed up my stuff. Everything's boxed up and will fit in the car.

Except the dog.

I just called my sister, because I got a landline here and I didn't pay my cell phone bill and I might as well make a long-distance call before I bolt. My sister's the only one in my goddamn family who is sane, although that is most certainly a relative term, and she said, "Oh, Michael Bradley, moving again? Do you not see a pattern here? Do you not see it could be *you*?" Then she lost her temper. "You don't cook. You rely on Dad for money. You don't *do* anything for anyone. You don't go to church—" at which point I lost it and said, "Shut up, you fucking bitch, my name is Luce, and you sound like Ma, and I don't believe in a god, that's why I don't go to church, why do I have to be related to a bunch of wacko religious fuckheads?" and she said, "Maybe it would help you because I don't know what else will, but my point is, when you think everything is someone else's fault, that they're all crazy, maybe you should look in. Look at *yourself*," at which point, I hung up.

What a bitch. I should do something about her as well.

But I feel sorry for her, and I will find compassion, because we did not, shall I say, have an easy childhood. When our ma died a few years back, I went through her last diary. It said and I quote, I never turned any of my children over to child pornography. Nor medical experimentation. Nor did I abandon them. And I said, Awww, thanks, Ma. What a stellar set of decisions. When I was young, I told her about the priest and why I didn't want to go to church, and she said it would keep me from Latching Up, or whatever the expression was, and when I stammered that was the exact thing the priest was doing, she said, "Oh, that's all malarkey. Boys make stuff up. I know it's in the news, how priests fiddle around, but we know that those boys are either liars or they had it coming to them anyway." That is how her logic worked. As fucked up as fucked can get. So when my ma died, right before she died, while she was on her deathbed, you can better believe that I said, "Ma, I hope your god forgives you. 'Cause I sure the hell won't. You were a disgusting mother and a disgusting human being. Good-fucking-bye."

But first, Her.

What I want to do is wreck up her life for a bit. Not break her leg or something, although that would be satisfying. It would be nice for her to feel some pain. What a sociopath. The thing I could do that would most hurt her is to leave her with a sense of unease. Like, there's someone out there, watching her forever. Like a god. I'll post some things on the Internet and Facebook friend her— under a pseudonym, of course—but something else, something a lot more painful that will keep her guessing for her entire life.

One great movie is *Dr. Strangelove* and if you don't know what I'm talking about, then fuck you. There's that line, We would suffer modest but acceptable casualties. Great line, great line. Plus the precious body fluids thing. That's my goal here. Modest but acceptable casualties, having to do with body fluids that will leave her uneasy forever.

Yes. Now I know.

I just think it's so unfair. I was born into the wrong family and thus feel like an outcast. I have the wrong kind of dog, and the world makes me feel like an outcast. She says I have an affect, tics, and that makes me feel like an outcast. I move to a little mountain town and my woman breaks up with me and again I feel like an outcast.

The dog thinks I'm just a charming oddball, in a world full of boring Normies. When you get tricked, I tell the dog, it gets painful.

She made me think she loved me and then she does something like telling me to either walk my dog three times a day or build it a fence, and then makes me think *I'm* way off base. This dog doesn't even like going outside! The dog *likes* the kennel; it makes him feel safe and secure. Plus, it's his punishment for shitting in the house. He likes sitting on the couch next to me. He's basically a baby. A wuss. Look at his fuzzy little dick. Look how trusting he is. Like me. Suddenly this sweet dog turned me and Dandelion into a we're-over. A bait-and-switch. Because she is unhinged.

I'm going to go back to Santa Fe. I'll leave today. It's warm there. I'll feel better there. I like it there better anyway. I even asked her to dig deep and find some empathy. This piece of shit trailer smells bad and I'm glad to be leaving it. I got rid of all my drug equipment, threw it into the woods, where I dumped most everything else too. Surprising how little you need. Rent is paid for the next month. By the time the landlord comes. Yes, by the time he comes.

There's fewer crazy people in Santa Fe. BW wouldn't fit in the car anyway. All my stuff is boxed and bagged up. Got BW in his crate. Lots of fluids will leak. Goodbye, BW. It is, in a way, BW's fault that I no longer have a girlfriend. So lovable, him staring out of his crate at me like that as I shut the door, giving me a good-bye friendly bark.

## Chapter Eleven

# County Road

"Tate, life is unfair but not unworkable. I am ready to commit. I *want* your daughter." This from my brother-in-law, Joe, the lucky bastard who has it all, including, and most importantly, time. He's yakking, like he always does, into my old answering machine. For a guy who doesn't talk much past a fragment, he leaves the longest damn messages; it's almost like he's relieved no real person is on the receiving end, which gives him permission to go on and on. "I want Honey. I want to adopt her. I will raise her, and I will do a good job. I'm sitting home alone, because I feel lousy, although I'm sure you feel worse.

"Listen, man, I'm sorry I didn't get this straight before. Let me pick up Honey. I'm sorry about the fight. I'm sorry I'm talking fast but I just realized your machine is going to hang up on me. Listen. Sorry about all that last week. Gretchen. When I told her, she ended things. And I wasn't thinking right. But listen. I won't be able to live with myself if I don't. And do it right. Which maybe sounds like a half-ass reason to you, but for now, it's the reason I've got.

"She can move up here with me permanently when you both are ready. Or I can move there. But here is good, because here I can make a living. There are other kids on this mountain, she won't be alone. I hope you're feeling good, feeling better, that the new chemo drug is working. But if it's not, I am ready. I am ready when you are ready. I am. I want to sign those papers. I want—"

*Beep.*

I should try to get up and answer the phone when he calls back, but I can't, or, I won't. I can only finger the strings on my Martin D-45. I may well die with my finger muscles being the strongest thing about me. I need to change the strings, but of course it's not worth it. I've been writing one last song for Honey, which is how I've always talked with her, through song. Stroke victims; they can't talk but sometimes they can sing, because both sides of the brain are used for music. My love for Honey crosses every part of my brain and heart. 'Course, she's a pain in the ass to raise. All kids are. But I tell you one thing: This dying business would be a lot harder to take if I didn't have her to look at. Perhaps it's uncool to say such a thing, but it's easier going when a little piece of your DNA is left behind in a beautiful young creature singing over there in her bedroom. It's easier to die knowing you loved like you did. That you gave it all for someone else.

Honey is a little tired of my singing and playing already. I play too often and every musician should know how to limit the playtime so that the other person can really hear. Limits, edges. That's what death is good for, I suppose.

I wrote one song on the day she was born. Another for the day she turned two. I didn't write or play for a year after her mother died, but then I wrote one about that, too, and I sang as a way of getting Honey to talk about her and remember.

This last one, which she hasn't heard yet, is a simple tune. About me simply hoping she leads a good life. Not a happy life, because that's a dumb wish that's bound to become untrue. But a good life. A life full of family, even though she's technically about out. There are different sorts of family, though, such as Joe's community on the mountain. There's also an admission that her childhood was rough—both her parents dying—but a hope that better times are on the way and that she shouldn't go feeling too sorry for herself, because being too sorry wastes valuable time. In the song, she's a grown girl, a teenager, and she's walking down a county road, County Road 46, which is the road Joe lives on, on top of a mountain called Blue Moon. The song is a bit of a tearjerker, a sad bastard song if ever there was one. I won't play it for her in person, but I recorded it, burned it onto a CD with a photo of us together on the cover.

I called it "County Road."

I knew Joe would call. I knew he'd adopt her. I knew she'd grow up there, on County Road 46.

Today is not a good day. Today the steroid has worn off. Constipation, bloating, ache, weariness, I could go on and on. Hair gone. Teeth gone. Life-force gone. By the next full moon, I'll be full gone.

The phone rings again. Joe, Joe, Joe. Selfish coward. Brave fragile man. I wouldn't want to be him. On the other hand, I wouldn't want to be me, either.

Message machine picks up, and I swear I can almost hear Joe's initial silence and how it is brewed and thickened and seasoned with guilt and shame. "I mean it, I really do," he says. "I want to adopt Honey." Then, "Gretchen and I broke up. That's okay. She wasn't up for kids. Or a kid. Which means, you know, she wasn't the right person for me. I was hoping it was a temporary thing, a fight of sorts, that she would come around, but kids scare her.

"Our town vet committed suicide. One month ago. With *my* gun. Which he stole from my truck.

"I never told you that because you had your own problems. But I need to talk more, now, don't I? That is the lesson I have learned.

"He killed himself while I was over at Gretchen's. He had stolen my key in advance. I keep the gun locked up, I'm smart about that. Thanksgiving has come and gone and I'm glad you were here for one more. That Honey got to spend it with you. I thought maybe Gretchen was the one. I'm going to keep talking, Tate—"

*Beep.*

"—Did you know, when the sun drops, the world turns blue. The snow is blue, the air itself is blue, and above it all are the blue stones of Blue Moon Mountain. I can't wait to show that to Honey.

"I'll admit that Sy's death is doing a real number on me. So is yours. You mind me saying such a thing? I had my first panic attack the day after he died. And another at his ceremony. And another just now. I wouldn't have known what it was, even, except that my friend Ruben told me about them. Apparently, it's something he's been dealing with most of his life. Since teenage years. I had no idea. He's a tough vet tech that carries himself like he knows himself and you wouldn't think he was capable of having a weak moment.

"Anyway, I would have assumed I was dying right then. In fact, it worried me. What if *I* die? Then where will Honey go? This is ridiculous.

"When it happened, my lungs cascaded down into my feet, I literally had no lungs in my chest. I know that sounds impossible, and of course it is, but if you would have asked me to point to my lungs, right then, I would have been clawing at my kneecaps or thereabouts. Plus I couldn't breathe. And not being able to breathe made my heart beat like it was in its last sprint. What I should have done is call Gretchen, of course. That is what relationship is *for*. Or Ruben. I could have called Lillie, because I know she struggles with anxiety too.

"But frankly, I don't know how to do that. I don't know how to ask. I have never had an honest, long-term, real relationship, Tate. I never saw them modeled to me, nor have I figured out how to do it on my own. I mean this literally. Honey will be my first. That scares the crap out of me.

"It's not something they teach in school. How to build community. Foster friendships. Care and be cared about. Perhaps there are books about it? The one called *How to have Unfucked-Up Relationships*. I just like to shoe horses, man. I'm known as the quiet one on the mountain.

"Anyway, I just had another one. Panic attack. I stayed on the floor, counting. One. Two. Three. I felt like I could sense a piece of good in me, but just then it was not available to me. I think it's in there, though. I do—"

*Beep*

"—See, I didn't realize that a kid might *add* to my life. In beautiful and unpredictable ways. She'll detract, too, but she'll also add. I'm capable of love. I know that I am. I'm going to grow up now. I just haven't . . . needed to until now. I could float around, doing my own thing. That time is over. I get that now. I'm coming now, to get her. I'm leaving the mountain now. See you in a few hours."

⤸

Two days later, the phone rings. "Tate," says Joe. "I don't know what hay bales are. Why does she want hay bales for breakfast? She's crying. Please call."

I call him back. "Shredded frosted mini-wheats," I say. "We call them snowed-on-hay-bales."

"Motherfucker," he whispers. "Why didn't someone tell me?"

⏝

"Tate," says Joe. "Honey is in time-out right now. She threw her orange juice across the room because I made pancakes the wrong way, and she wanted to go home, and she said I was an evil warlock holding her captive in the mountain, and she was a princess, and she was going to fight me, and that I better watch out because she was going to make her gecko grow big and huge and it would bite my head off, which is what I deserve. She's got a terrible throw, man. Good stories, terrible throw. You haven't taught her to get her arm back. I'll fix that. Or you will, when you're better. Although I realize I need to quit staying stuff like that. You're in hospice care, for godssakes. It's just hard to accept, that you're dying. I'm sure it's hard for you too.

"Anyway, what I want to know is: Would you put her in time-out? You want to talk to her, or would that make things worse? What constitutes a good pancake?"

I don't pick up on that one, but that's one I'd answer if I could. Couldn't get out of bed anyway. Hospice nurse due in ten minutes. Lawyer preparing papers. Don't have the energy to talk, even to Honey. I saved what I could for her, as long as I could, I hope she knows that.

⏝

"Tate," says Joe. "When Gretchen said good-bye like that, it took the air out of me like a horse kick, exactly the same. She said: 'We'd pretended more than we felt.' Do you think humans do that? Pretend to feel more than we feel?

"I don't even remember what we talked about, all those times we curled together. Gretchen and I. Isn't that odd? It seemed like so much. It seemed big, bigger than anything. I hope it doesn't take long to forget her. Not that you forget people, I guess. As in, Honey won't forget you. Sorry if that came out wrong. I'm always saying the stupidest shit. Also, I'm cutting down on the cussing.

"I read the articles you gave me. Taking care of a traumatized child. That book. *Adopting the Hurt Child.* Who writes these titles? *Post-Traumatic Stress Disorder: Clinical Child Psychology and the Adopted Child. The Emotional Tasks of Adoption: Transition, Attachment, Separation.* Okay, holy cow, they've been helpful. I got her some frosted mini-wheats. Honey is outside now. She wants to talk to you. When you're up for it. That cereal is lousy. Too sweet. I just didn't know what she wanted, before. I just don't know what Gretchen wanted. I wish you weren't dying. There should be better words."

~

"So, Tate," says Joe. "Honey says to me this morning: 'Uncle Joe, you're fussing me.' She was curled in her pink blanket on my couch, which has turned into her permanent bed. She likes it better than the other options. It's near my room, near the fire, near the window, she loves staring at the Big Dipper. Next to the couch is now a pink dresser, and lined up in front of her dresser are her pairs of pink shoes. To the side of the couch is a line of stuffed animals, largest to smallest. She lines things up. I guess you know that. Okay, I just wanted to describe it. I sent pictures, did you get them?

"So, anyway, I said, 'I'm fussing you? What does that mean?'

"And she says, 'You're fussing *over* me.'

"I said, 'I just asked if you wanted hot cocoa. If you wanted me to add some snow to it.'

"She says, 'That's fussing and that means you love me. My dad loves me.'

"I said, 'I know, I know, he's always loved you like crazy, and always will.' I thought that was, you know, something you should hear, Tate. She misses you, but I try not to talk about it too much. To you, I mean. I let her talk and talk, because that's all she does. What a talker. I never get a word in edgewise.

"Her eyes remind me of Cara's. We were talking about her, and Honey said, 'She died in a car, and that's no fair, and life is no fair. My dad says it's the worst lesson of all to learn.'

"Then she told me she loved me. I hope it doesn't hurt, hearing all this. I just mean to convey that things are going . . . well. Better than expected. Not always great, you know, because this is reality. It's been a week now. The community always has a solstice party. It's coming up. She'll get to know everyone then. I wanted to give her a quiet week first, but that will be the perfect time to introduce her around."

꒰

I call Joe. "Bring her back. For a visit. Doc says a few days now, but I feel like it might even be less. It'll be the last time."

꒰

Honey hugs me hard and the pain feels like heaven. She hands me a pinecone that's been spray-painted orange. In her face, I see the fear. See the tears well. Spill. I don't look like her daddy at all. This is all going so fast. Much faster than I would have thought.

I hand her a picture, one of the two of us when I looked normal and she looked untroubled, just to remind her it once was true, then I give her a stack of CDs. Listen to the songs someday, I tell her, especially "County Road 46," about that family you now have. Soon you'll have your first Christmas with your new family. Santa finds people up on that mountain, don't worry. I'm so sorry this happened to you. It's not fair. It's just not fair and you should allow yourself to be sad. And angry. But don't feel guilty if you feel happy too. In the end, I want you to be happy. Not all the time, but lots of the time. Okay? I gotta go now, honeybird.

She's crying hard now and so my mother leads her out.

You, I say to Joe, You stay, you hold my hand.

He sits down next to the bed, takes my hands in his. I would like to thank him for all his damn calls, for yakking nonstop, for trying to tell a story that made some sense. For trying to break that boundary that separates us all. Despite the beeps. But when I say thank you, he thinks I'm saying thanks for holding my hand, so I add, For the story, for the slightly happier ending. I breathe out, a little hum.

## Chapter Twelve

# Water out of Sunlight

But I forgot to tell you of this meadow. Why Sy picked it, what his death did to it.

There are large-scale reasons we all love this meadow. The fact it's framed on all sides by mountains, butted against national forest lands on the west and north, state lands on the east, the county road on the south. There are shady parts to offer relief from the heat of summer, protected parts to offset the wind of spring. Ideal for cross-country skiing, snowshoeing, hunting, fishing, making love.

Then there are the particulars.

How, for example, in the mornings, sun takes up mist, light sucks up vapor, and how that process reminds you that there is great power in one particular moment, which an age of prudence can never retract. One such moment changes everything. But to refrain from waxing poetic, and to stick with the facts: the coyote, the bald eagles, the owls, the willow, which turn redder as winter goes on. There are plentiful wildflowers most springs—first the pasqueflowers up in the pines, then Indian paintbrush and blue flax and meadow rue splattered, and the meadow is also threaded by a fantastic trout stream, better than anything I have on the ranch, so that my grandfather and father brought me here from earliest memory.

So you can now picture this meadow and realize it holds the memories of our community; more memories than many houses do. I am an old man and my relationship with the meadow has been a long one. Certain memories stand out: The time Sy and I came upon a nest of swirling baby rattlers—a hibernaculum, he taught me that word then—and we wondered what to do, being that many of the other townsfolk went fishing there as well, including children, but neither of us being likely to kill a wild animal in its own habitat. The fishing trips I took with my own daughter, and how we would meet Sy, with his two, Zoë and Michael, and we'd spend all day getting their lines untangled. Sometimes Anya and Violet came along, spreading out blankets and fishing themselves. Gretchen joined us once, bringing her sketchbook and showing everyone how to make marks from the special pencils that turn into watercolors. Ruben would wander in too, his big boxy ruined fingers unable to tie on a fly, and so we'd do it for him. He'd keep most of the fish, freezing them for winter, he said, so that he could remember the sunlight in the meadow when the snow came.

Suffice it to say that everyone on the mountain comes here for something. Most of us have made love somewhere on the edges of this meadow. It has that kind of pull. More people have sex outside than city people think, I suppose, and I've come across— or heard—more couples than ever I would have guessed. And if you don't think two old codgers don't sometimes get carried away while resting on a picnic blanket, well, I suggest you rethink what you'll be doing in your old age.

So what Sy did was astounding.

What he did to our meadow.

Which is why I'm here, standing at the edge of it, staring at the expanse of blue and white ice. Backpack on, duffel bag in one hand, sandwich and a whiskey tucked in my Carhartt jacket, corncob pipe in my mouth.

You don't just go barging into such a meadow. You stand at the edge and ask permission. Remind the meadow how you know her. I say to her: It's a true honor, to have lived here my whole life, to bear witness to all your secrets. Or some of them. How, for example, that the bear holed up in the rocky outcrop on the north edge has two cubs, yearlings this winter, and therefore the last winter they'll spend with her, and it's this bear who wanders into town, that she's a cinnamon, and I do believe she's the daughter of the larger bear, the one that had taken herself higher up the mountain years ago, after I shot above her head, since she was always trying for my chickens. I know your mountain mahogany and I know your aspens. I know you have frozen the blood of my friend Sy. Then I nod and give myself allowance to take a step forward, into the crunching snow.

⁓

I've come nearly every day since his body was found—about a month now—which is when Ruben and I found him, all of us agreeing to pair up to search together, the blizzard still full force, the night at its apex, the snow deep somehow immediately, the temperature and wind being dangerous. We were still hoping his absence and the gun's absence was soon to be explained in a happier way, but if not, Ruben and I were hoping to get to him before the sheriff's folks did, if only to offer our friendship before all the chaos of law and death set in.

I didn't know for certain, but I suspected where he'd be, and so did Ruben, and so we clamped on our snowshoes and headed out into the meadow in the dark, in a blizzard, which is something crazy to do, is something you would only do for a person you truly love. We'd just gotten a frantic call from Anya, who said, I know it's bad, but if only he can be talked down before it's too late . . . and so I picked Ruben up in my truck and we drove to the meadow and hunkered down, bundled up, and started out and crisscrossed the meadow in a pattern, a rope tied between our two hands, as difficult a physical endeavor I have ever borne, and on we went until right as daybreak was launching, which is when we saw a glitter of something purple, which turned into the blue of a glove and the metal clasp upon it, reflecting in the first ray of light. We stood, together, silent, until our eyes had scanned and found the rise of snow, the white lump that did not belong.

Everyone else was looking for his truck. We didn't see the truck parked, but still we went to the meadow, guided by the same pull that brings us here for other happier things. The truck was found later, up the mountain a bit, pulled over and hidden in the trees, covered in snow, politely waiting.

That daybreak, when the snow was just starting to let up, Ruben and I huffed and gasped our way through the snow, our feet sinking despite the snowshoes, our lungs burning from cold and exhaustion, and knelt above the mound and scooped the snow off with gloved hands to reveal a face blown to smithereens, more blood than you'd imagine and frozen like a kicked-over paint can, an indelible pattern . . . well, I suppose I don't need to tell you those details. Only that ever since that day, I've visited. Despite the shattering cold. Except for the two days I was out of town, which is when Violet had a brief and tender affair, one which she needed but now will never need again, which she told me about yesterday—it was something about Sy's death, she said, how that made us all double-check that we were okay, that our lives were more or less full, and that was my last chance, I'm getting old!—can you understand?—and somehow I did, I truly did, and I didn't hold it against her and I told her so.

And this morning I told her, I can see I need to reckon with him myself, in my own way. I'll be back tonight. I loaded up bundles of firewood and my snowshoes and a lunch.

Most days, I come midmorning after the ranch chores are done. I tell Violet I'm going to Moon's for coffee with the group that call themselves The Never Sweats because they are tired and worn-out from a lifetime of sweat and work and wish to do so no more. But instead I come here and walk. I kept it a secret from her. But not today.

Here I am, snowshoeing to my friend.

⏤

And here is Sy. Not his body, of course; that was cremated and a ceremony has been had. But his blood, still here. Can you imagine such a thing? The snow from the first storm has turned to ice and this ice melted some, but not all, which means that Sy's blood is frozen within layers of cold clearness, like oil soaked in ground underneath a tractor, or like spilled iodine.

I take off my snowshoes and kick away the light dusting of white from the night's winds and then get on my hands and knees and wipe the rest off with my glove. You son of a bitch, I say to the swipe of dark. You go to hell.

He would have laughed at that. He would have said something like, What will suffice becomes less and less as we age.

He would have said, If we could internalize the flowers of the earth, we could deal with life better.

He would have said, I've been to hell, Ollie. God took me there and showed me. It was completely empty. Big empty caverns. Stalagmites and stalactites and fires and dripping water and the whole bit, and completely deserted. Hell was empty.

You son of a bitch, I tell him. Who the fuck am I going to go fishing with come spring? Did you think about that? Did you think about Zoë and Michael? Did you think about Anya? Or Ruben? Or this meadow?

His blood stands, frozen, silent, whereas everything in me is clacking against each other; my heart into my collarbones, my collarbones into my brain, my brain into my ribcage.

Well, damn you to hell, Sy. I am angry as hell, and I came here to tell you I think you're a true son of a bitch. You go straight to hell, whether it's empty or not. What a thing. What a thing you did to us.

I pound my fists into the ice until the pain shoots fierce. I don't even make much of a dent; the snow is packed here from all my previous visits. But I want to. I want to fall into the center of a sea, a frozen sheet of ice-sea. I want to get to the wildflower roots and seeds that are resting in wait. Find him, somehow.

I sit back to rest; the sweat is running down my face and then it will freeze. I shrug off my backpack and dump out the tinder, all the small sticks of apple and pine from the wood stack.

Well, here we go, I tell him. Were you in pain?

Of course I was in pain.

Well, damnit to hell.

It was real bad, he tells me. You know it was. Only you know. There was nothing that could be done about it.

I know it, I know it. I'm sorry. Who am I supposed to be mad at, then? Your brain? The universe? Goddamn it to hell. I've got fury in me, and it's got no place to go.

I dump handfuls of dried hay—I brought plenty, there being no shortage in the corrals—to make a large flat circle. The fire flickers, reluctant in the cold. But it will go.

Damn you, Sy. Don't you see what you've done to us? I howl. I clap my hands. I stomp. I howl again.

⮑

Nothing could be done about it, his pain. It was for that reason that he'd quit mentioning it years ago. People, on the whole, aren't great at describing physical pain, and if they do, they seem guilty about it, as if a body wasn't supposed to ache, and also, if there's nothing to be done about it, why give it voice?

But I knew he was hurting. All the time. Every moment of every day. Never have a moment's break, not even a second, he would tell me. Imagine, he'd say, just an hour, or even ten minutes, of being in a body without pain. Boy, I'd love a moment or two of that. Just to remember what it feels like. Boy, would I soak that in.

I often wondered what the pain did to his sanity. Violet and I spoke of it. We agreed that perhaps it was the pain that first sent him talking to god. After all, the schizophrenia, or the delusions, or whatever you want to call it, didn't hit when he was a twenty-year-old boy, like it is apt to do. No, it came in his thirties, after he first screamed like a horse and went buckling down to his knees, grabbing his head like he was trying to crush it. I wasn't there for that, but I heard about it from Ruben, who was the one who hauled him to the doctor.

Oh, how he hoped.

He'd gone to the bone doctors at first; that would have been best, some spur easy to identify and relatively easy to fix. Some nerve being crushed by a cervical bone. But no: That was not it. So next he had scans. MRIs and CATs. Some dye injected into the blood vessels of his brain. It was that neurologist in town, that woman doctor, who finally came up with the only reasonable explanation, and it was one that had no cure.

The fire is hissing now, eating up the hay. I put on the dry sticks, small and well chosen. This is no big sloppy bonfire. This is ceremony.

In return, the fire eats. That's what fire does: It chews and swallows, always hungry, always willing to consume more.

 

I came back by myself, that summer day we found the rattlers. I didn't want to upset Sy, but I didn't want my daughter or Antoinette's grandkids getting bit, either. Or Celeste's horse. Or Jess's horse. Both women had taken to riding up in the meadow, and my own greatest physical injury came from a horse that threw me sideways, smack into a cottonwood, after a rattler spooked her. The mass of movement turned my stomach a little. It seemed there were dozens of them, writhing and twisting. They'd dispersed, but I got plenty of them, halving them with a shovel. Chop, chop, chop, fast as I could, standing back and with my thickest leather boots on. I hated to do it, but I did it. Simple as that. I never did tell Sy.

Earlier this fall, we were hunting near that same spot, and I noted that Sy's attitude wasn't what it used to be; it was as if he was just out walking and happened to be carrying a gun. He wasn't trying to hunt anything. Anya had requested his guns be taken away a long time ago, a few years ago, when he first started talking about talking to god and angels and such. So I kept them.

He didn't seem to mind nor hold it against me, just accepted it
with a gentle shrug when I asked if that was okay, that I'd return
them each day we went hunting, or that he could borrow one of
mine, depending on his mood. But that particular day, he had no
intention whatsoever of getting a deer. I could just tell by the way
he walked, by what he was choosing to notice and choosing to
ignore. He rarely spoke of his pain, but that day, he said it was
worse than usual. Mostly, he said, it was a low-grade ache behind
his left eyeball and above his teeth. Trigeminal neuralgia of the
second branch, left side. Sometimes it would flare up, enormously,
like a fire. That's what it felt like. A fire eating his brain, he said.

Sometimes it happened when the wind touched his face.
Sometimes it was the way the light glared. It was a cruel universe;
anything might set it off, but that same thing wouldn't set it off
the next day. It was unpredictable and there was nothing he could
do to avoid it or prepare for it, and perhaps that was worst of all.

Then suddenly, as if talking about it made it manifest, he
dropped his gun and fell to his knees and then fell to his side and
moaned. Just like that. Dropped straight down. There was nothing
for me to do except say, *What the hell?* and kneel down and hold
his hand, bring some water to his lips. It only lasted a bit—maybe
two minutes—but it was a long two minutes, and in those two
minutes, I understood, from the way his eyes flashed with fight
and then went dull, what kind of pain this man was dealing with.
He lay there, breathing, for some time. Long after it had passed.
Then he got to his knees, vomited, got back up and sat on a rock.
But we were both shaken.

I asked him if he had any drugs—from the doctor, or even from
his supply of veterinary meds, or anything illegal? Because, by god,
any kind of drug would be worth avoiding that.

Tried about everything, he said. Both legal and not. Drugs made for human and for animal. He looked at me, his eyes still clouded. They call it the suicide disease.

You talk to Anya about it?

Anya, he said. Anya.

Yeah, I said. Your wife.

He looked at me and shook his head, no. Not much. She never once asked me what it felt like. She is worn out. And I can understand. Her hands full with kids, and she's stuck it out with me already. Brain chemistry.

By which he meant, everyone considered him crazy, although he did not, which was one way we all knew he was crazy, but either way, he'd suffered through the last few years of trying antipsychotics and stopping them, gaining weight and sleeping all the time, then becoming manic. The disease was a son of a bitch. Both diseases. Trigeminal neuralgia and psychosis. Can you imagine? Being forced to bear both? Maybe one was the result of the other; maybe they were unrelated. I can't remember the specifics, but I feel like a drug called prednisone also played a part in it all, the psychosis also coming after a bout of that drug. It's hard for me to remember the medical sequence of events, but I remember that day perfectly.

I told Sy that day: The more you talk to god, the more I lose faith in one. Because no kind and just force would put people through such things. I can't fathom it. I can't abide it.

He'd said, Well, it's all in god's hands now.

And I lost my temper and shot into the sky and said, Well, he's got some lousy hands. Any one of us regular humans could do a much better job.

That made him laugh, and we both ended up sitting under the

trees and enjoying the fall air and napping, each of us recovering, in our own way, from his two minutes of hell.

Now I pull out the larger pieces of wood from the old duffel bag. I picked them carefully, mostly from the old cherry tree I had to chop down a few years ago, but a bit of pine, too, since it will go easier. I put them on and the fire responds with a lot of pops—the occasional sparks—and the ice below it is starting to transform.

And now the sun is coming out full force. It was just above zero when I warmed up the truck this morning, but now it must be nearly forty. Ice is melting. By fire and by sun. Although it's not visible to my eye, surely the steam is rising, evaporating, and water is becoming sunlight, a phrase I remember from school, a T. S. Eliot, and I'm setting my friend free.

⌒

I myself have had plenty of injury. What rancher doesn't? Cracked ribs and dislocated shoulders and cut-up hands. Sy's even given me drugs for it from time to time, in fact, when we were working an animal together, and there was no point in driving to town to see a doctor when Sy could palpate my ribs, declare them bruised but not broken, and offer up something stronger than the ibuprofen I had, swipe his hands together and call it good.

Folks knew about Sy's psychotic problems; that was easier to identify and was well known. Sometimes, upon examining a dog filled with cancer, he'd say, "I'll have a check-in with my advisors about it." This would come up at Moon's, and a few people would laugh at Sy, a few would roll their eyes or make a joke, but most were kind about it. It was explained—many of us were always defending Sy—that Sy only meant he needed to think about the options. Sy was contemplating the success rate of the surgery. And the family's finances. And the dog's quality of life. It was not an easy equation; various factors that all had to be weighed differently. More often than not, and unlike most vets, he decided against an expensive surgery. Even if the dog could have gotten another year. Sy leaned heavily toward the let-dying-creatures-die side of the spectrum; he was opposed to prolonging life if it only meant delaying a death. It gave him a certain sense of ease with dying; he had a friendlier relationship with it than most of us do. Plus, Sy actually cared for people, which, in my observation of it all, seems rare; many go into veterinary school because they get along with animals better than people. But not Sy. He hated to see folks go into debt over a horse or a cat with a fatal disease. He was practical that way; as practical as he was insane. Somehow the two went together.

I notice a similar tendency in my daughter. Perhaps the world is turning that way. Korina just seems to assume that people will die, willy-nilly. The part that grieves me is that she seems to assume that the world is full of crazies, and that at some point, you're likely to be shot. In a movie theatre or at college or if you're a police officer or if you're a black man. It hurts me to think she's growing up in a world that has so many shootings. Bombings. Planes disappearing in the air. The constant knowledge of it. Without retreating to the mountains, hunkering in to help a cow give birth, fishing in a stream, how can one remain sane? But now Sy. Even this place has been taken away from her.

Still, I hope we've given her enough of that, Violet and I. So that she always has the natural world to return to, which, after all, is the most obvious god around. I don't care what others believe, but I will tell you that a blooming flower or the spiral of a hawk is about as in-your-face godly as a human could possibly want.

⤳

It was that day, of not-hunting, as we rested, that Sy told me what he might do. But that he would wait as long as possible. He said it in a quiet voice, his energy still depleted from the pain that had just rocked through his body.

I'd said, But your kids.

Don't I know it, he'd said. Don't you go lecturing me. That's what I've been holding on for. But believe me, even my love for them can't make this pain bearable.

That's crazy talk, I told him. Love for kids can make anything bearable. I wish you'd take it back, Sy. Promise me.

You can't stop a man. And you damn well know it. I don't want to kill myself, mind you. Depends how bad the pain gets. I've helped animals, always trusted my instinct on when the time is right. Never have regretted a single decision. I talk to the gods and angels, all of them, and I weigh it all, and I come up with an answer. After careful deliberation, you see. Sometimes I save them. Sometimes I let them go. So I'll know when the time is right. Don't you worry. We all die. But I appreciate you letting me tell you. I needed someone to tell.

I wish you wouldn't. You don't know what the future holds. You'll miss out on the future.

And sometimes, that's appropriate.

No, it's not. Time is a gift. I guess I can't agree with you. It's a hard thing you're telling me, Sy.

I know it. You're the only one I'll mention it to.

Perhaps I could take you to that place. The Mayo Clinic. Just check you in and not let them get rid of you till they help. You don't look so good.

I feel old. I feel about a hundred years older than I am. A lifelong bout with insomnia and pain will do that to a man.

But it seems they can fix most everything else.

There's not much to be done. There's a surgery on the brain. But it often doesn't work, and besides, the gods advised me against it. I'm tired. Somehow this life wore me out. But you know what? All the hours we leave behind are so ordinary. You ever consider that? All those dishes washed, all those miles driven, all the cattle fed, all the cats saved. Ordinary but not unloved. I have loved my life so much. He looked at me and his eyes flickered, from dull to just-barely-coming-alive again. You know that, right? I love life so much.

I'm not ashamed to tell you that now that the fire is going, I am weeping. Openly, and not quietly. Thinking of him saying that. And for all kinds of other reasons. Although I consider myself a good man, I often feel I've made a mess of it. I feel like I've made a mess of it when Violet cries or when my daughter sasses me in her teenage way, or, even worse, ignores me altogether, as if we haven't gone through life together in the most intimate of ways, me changing her diaper and putting food in her mouth and teaching her to fish and to cook that fish, as if we were now only strangers. I feel I've made a mess of it when I lose my temper, which happens from time to time. I feel a mess when my friend kills himself, when I see my neighbors suffering in their own various ways, when I see a deer hit on the side of the road. I feel like I've made a mess of it and all I want, with this fire, is maybe the seed of an idea that maybe I'll get a chance to do it right. Or do it better. Because it seems that life is like this: This will happen and then this will happen and then I become an old man and this will happen and then this and then poof. It's over. And did I do it right enough?

Did I?

Did I?

Fire eats even ice. The flames are licking it now. Once in a while
the whole fire tilts, or sinks, as it falls into a new layer. It tries to
go out on the edges, but I add the hay, the dried tinder, and it
reluctantly flares up again.

I can't see it, but underneath the fire, Sy's blood must be
melting. Turning to liquid. Evaporating or sinking into the earth,
I don't know. No longer frozen tight, tense and bound up, just like
the look I saw on his face that day of hunting, the day he collapsed.
I want him to be free. I want my own heart to forgive him. For
doing this to us and our meadow. I want to forgive myself, too.
What a gift that would be.

Let it go, let it go. I hear him saying it to me now. Tell everyone
to let it go.

The ache of my sorrow. I can hear it pounding hard inside my
ears. I imagine Sy alone out here on that last moment, gun held
to head, the snow coming down fierce, the dark of night. The fire
pops one very loud shot, taking a big bite out of dry wood.

So let me tell you about this meadow. I see two figures in it now,
walking toward me, bundled up and without snowshoes, which
means occasionally one of them sinks to the knee when the layer
of ice at the top doesn't hold.

Violet, hair pulled back in a gray ponytail, Korina, hair pulled
back in a shiny brown ponytail, both without hats, for heaven's
sake, and I watch them like they are a mirage, not real, and I
assume that is the case, in fact, until Violet walks up and hugs me,
her body solid and human. She says, Ollie. How are you?

Better. Some better, not much better.

She looks at the fire. We thought we'd come see if you wanted company.

Korina is staring at her feet. Or the fire. But she looks up, meets my eyes. Hey, Dad.

I gently put on the last log and stand up. I appreciate it.

Korina clears her throat. I love you, Dad.

I look at her: long hair with just a touch of curl to it, both in her bangs and the ponytail hanging over her shoulder, and her youth and beauty, her freckled nose, and best of all, her face isn't closed up, like it sometimes is. It's open and young and true. She walks over and takes my hand and holds it, just natural, like she did when she was eight, and I close my eyes and let the tears drip and tell myself not to forget this, my daughter holding my hand, her skin on mine, to remember the sheer joy of this moment when I myself am dying, whenever that might be, I want this memory.

I feel like I'm standing at the edge of a precipice, the kind I've not known in years, and I have perhaps forgotten what it is like to have so much at stake. Oh, Korina. Oh, Violet. Oh, Blue Moon. Oh, meadow.

I reach out my other hand, so that Violet takes it, and I turn us all around. The fire cracks even as we turn away from it and start walking the other way. It will burn itself out, now, just like he did.

We walk and stumble and walk and stumble, and I wonder how we must look from above, a group of us, parting a snowy sea. In front of us, the crystals sparkle from whiteness of snow, crackles of small bits of color, which is how, I'm supposing, our lives must appear to god.

## Chapter Thirteen

# Smoke's Way

The snow was rotten. Much of the time, Wyn's feet sunk, snowshoe and all, especially her left one since that was on the downward-facing-slope side most of the time. Though there were switchbacks, the bear den was far to the south, and so the climb was not only three thousand feet but to the south by several miles. Her left hip was roaring. It was just dawning on her that this wasn't the sort of injury that would require a few days of soreness, but the other kind, the kind that would require a broad expanse of time to heal, perhaps more than a lifetime.

The mood was rotten too. It had started out sweet, with early-morning bursts of banter when the group had left the parking lot in the dark, right before sunrise, but the situation was fucked. Snowshoes were not supposed to sink, that was the point of snowshoes, and the world was too warm, snow this time of year should be frozen, and it was only noon and they had at least another hour to go, and so on, and all Wyn could think was, *This is not Paris.*

Someone up ahead stopped to adjust straps, so Sergio turned around. "It's not Par-*is*. Just *Ursus american*-us. I've been making a little ditty out of it in my head. Rhymes, you see." He swiped the snot off his face with his arm. There was already a layer of salt right at his hairline, something she knew would expand as the day went on. She'd never known anyone who sweated so much; he drank electrolyte powder all day to keep himself going. She first noticed it during the one August month years ago when they'd been lovers, and seeing it on his jawline always reminded her of the way he looked when he orgasmed, his lips pulled back, like a bear. She'd never told him that, that he looked so oddly animal, so salty.

She swooped her arm out at the treed mountainside, as if to say, *I have this view, don't I?*

He looked at her, unconvinced. Perhaps aware how close she was to tears, he said, "I'm really sorry. It's not December in Paris. But at least it's out here, in the wild."

She tried to smile. It was the least one human could do for another.

"The bear will be great. We know she's up there. Been quiet and sleeping for a few weeks now. The two yearlings, not so sure, they were never collared."

She nodded and tried out her voice: "An adventure is an adventure."

"Cutting off the GPS collar will be the boring part. But—oh, just seeing her, Wyn—that's the part you came for. Hang in there."

"And I can climb in? Thanks for letting me come, Sergio. Really, I mean that."

The others were starting up again and so he turned back around and said over his shoulder, "Just don't tell anyone. Or sue. Especially CPW." He turned around briefly, caught her eye, started to say something, then stopped, then started again. "We didn't expect this, for the snow to be rotten. It was already a push.

Let me know if you're not okay. You can turn back." He looked close to tears himself; she supposed that they were all close to their physical limit. The men were breaking trail, after all, and each of them had heavy equipment in their packs. Her pack was light, and she had the benefit of going last, but she was the oldest, and although she was in good shape, she was not in big-hefty-guy huge-thighs shape.

"Sorry, I should be more encouraging." Sergio said this to the air in front of him, starting to move ahead now. "The bear will be great. Keep thinking of the bear. Touching the pads on her feet."

Then they were off, the four of them in a single line, ducking their heads against the snow that whipped off the mountainside during the gusts. She raised her eyes, sometimes, to watch the men. She wondered if they too were focused on each footfall, if each of their steps was imbued with the expansive hope that the snow would hold their weight for this one, this one, this one.

It was so steep. Even the aspen trees looked as if they had a hard time hanging on, their trunks emerging from the snow and curving ninety degrees, upward to sunlight, and the four humans were not so different from those trees, Wyn thought, all leaning hard toward the mountain, trying to root there as well.

After a while, Sergio took front position, and Ruben took second, and then it was Kevin, the guy from Colorado Public Radio, the stranger, who was directly ahead of her. He looked like an insect, all that padded radio equipment poking out of his pack like antennae, jammed in alongside the avalanche shovel and beacon. It gave her something new to look at, but it didn't distract her from the pain. Tears leaked down her face, and once in a while, she gathered the snot in the back of her throat and quietly hawked it to the side.

"I'm not sure we properly met." Kevin addressed this to the

air in front of him, but said it loud enough that she could hear. His voice broke the silence of the mountain, the swishing of their fabrics, the crunching of their snowshoes. "At least, it was hard to see you in the dark this morning."

"Wyn," she said to his back.

"What brings you out here?"

She didn't want to answer, to add noise to the mountain, and she wasn't sure she could keep her voice steady anyway. "Hemingway," she finally said, and when he turned his head with a quizzical eyebrow that raised his woolen hat as well, she added, "As ridiculous as that sounds. It's a long story." They went on like that, long after even Ruben, the strongest of them, had started to slow significantly, had even dropped to his knees a time or two, and, once, had bowed his head in what looked like prayer, or perhaps a plea.

⤳

This difficulty, she told herself, was nothing compared to the evenings, the fight against another glass of whiskey or gin, which had everything to do with the fight against the old stupid belief of her life, which was that, in every life, some true and good and declarative romance would descend upon each person. This pain was not as bad as being alone, night after night, realizing the depth of untruthfulness of that mistaken belief, and that she'd let too much time slip by, been too picky, too selfish, too lazy, too indecisive, had let herself go smoke's way, drifting along. It seemed unbelievable. It had simply taken her too long to realize that the door of love and family wouldn't just open, that she was supposed to bang on that particular door more loudly. She hadn't, and now it was too late.

⁓

"The reason I wanted to go to Paris was because of Ernest. And Zelda and F. Scott," she huffed when they cut to the right and stopped for a breather. "And Hadley Richardson, Hemingway's first wife. And Pound and Gertrude."

Kevin kept his eyes on Sergio and Ruben, who were farther up ahead, discussing something, but said to her, "To see their old haunts? Find remnants of the lost generation?"

"No. Because we are cowards now. Because they said things to one another. Real things that I don't think we say to each other anymore."

"Wouldn't it be pretty to think so?"

She looked up at him, smiled.

He patted her on the coat. "Well, it might not be pretty. You're romanticizing them, perhaps. Ruben is the vet, right? And Sergio is Parks and Wildlife."

"Right."

"And you?"

"Interested observer. And it's my birthday."

"You live down in town?"

She nodded. "In that little trailer park by the restaurant." She wanted him to know that particular sorrow; that her poverty extended in all possible directions. Literal. Heart. Life. That besides this day, this hope of crawling into the den of the animal she believed to be most holy, that she had nothing of note to offer, share, or receive. She had missed her mark.

She took off her light blue cap and jammed it in her pocket. It was hot, now, the sun shining clear. "Grizzlies were gone in this part of the state by the thirties, you know. My great-granduncle was involved in the effort to save them." She paused to catch her breath. "To convince people that they were not the bloodthirsty devils people thought they were. He was friends with Enos Mills, the Quaker who helped preserve Rocky Mountain National Park. They say he died of a broken heart, after the last grizzly was killed. My great-granduncle, that is. At least he had done something grand with his life."

He clapped his hands to warm them. "Well, drinks on me, when we get back to town. For the bear, for the birthday, for him."

A drink sounded like such a good idea. Drunk was what she wanted, how it would settle over her like a perfect glove of fog, how the pain in her hip would float away from her body like silk.

⁓

It was soon after that Sergio put his palm out to indicate that they stop, a finger to the lips, and then pointed them to a good place to take off their packs and hunker in against a small ledge. Wyn studied the topography, unconvinced. The mountain was the same as it had been for the last few hours. Then her eyes discerned it amid the trees and snow, a slant of outcropping of a rocky ledge that increased in size as it traveled across the mountain, and that somewhere, in there, was an enclave big enough to be a den.

She and Kevin snowshoed the last distance and removed their packs. In silence, they watched Ruben and Sergio, who had taken off their snowshoes and were shuffling sideways, hugging the ledge. They moved across it until they reached an area that was wider and flatter, and here they stopped, conferred, peered around a corner, squatted down, and started to remove equipment from their packs. It was hard to see what they were doing, hunched over and with all the coats and gear in the way, but she did see Ruben use his teeth to hold a syringe, use his armpit to warm a small bottle of what must be the tranquilizer, put together a pole, which she knew would be his way of reaching in the den to stab the bear. He'd told her bears could come at you, straight out of hibernation, at thirty miles per hour.

"This isn't what I expected," Kevin whispered. "I thought it would be a cave or something." They were both sitting on a rock. Kevin had cleared of most of the snow, using his snowshoe as a shovel. He'd gotten his off easily, but she was fumbling with her straps, which were clotted with snow and thick with cold.

"It's not like the cartoons. With the big roomy cave." She kept her voice low. She had her snowshoes off now and was digging in her pack for the ibuprofen, trying to be quiet in her rustling around. "It's generally a small snug place. There must be an indentation, a cubby of sorts over there." But she had to agree— this rocky ridge was so insignificant looking that it simply didn't seem grand enough for a bear.

"I'm exhausted. Look at this view." He was standing, moving about for this view and that, and while she watched him, she stilled herself and felt something was tearing on the inside thigh of her left leg, that's what it felt like, and it took her a moment to realize it was the cut. Perhaps it was peeling open. She peered down at her inner thigh, but no blood showed; but after all, there were lots of layers, the silk underwear, leggings, wind pants. What kind of adult still cut herself? She did. *What a sad, sorry loser I am*, and she closed her eyes against the view of her crotch, and the image of last week floated into her mind, home from the bar, having never bought the ticket to Paris that she'd told everyone she was going to buy, and drunk, and angry she was drunk, angry she was alone, and she hated herself, hated herself, and yelling *You are an alcoholic* at the mirror, forcing herself to say it aloud for the first time, *you fucking alcoholic bitch, you went smoke's way, you drifted around, you're just doing to yourself what Sy did, but slower, I hate him, I hate you, I hate hate hate* and found the old cuts, both the very old, from when she was fourteen, and then those of ten years later, and added a new one to the last year, which is when she'd taken it up full-force again, a small punishment for a grand mistake. The grand mistake of not knocking on the door hard enough.

Kevin was still whispering. "That was an elevation gain of three thousand one hundred feet, putting us at eleven thousand five hundred feet above sea level. Right? I usually get headaches at about ten. I'm a Colorado native, too, but city boy. Which direction is town? I'm all turned around."

She pointed north, to the highest white peak beside them, but he was already speaking into a small device, quietly. His voice was fluid and confident; it was a voice that had things to say and could be trusted. She heard the fragments of it . . . *where several bears have been collared for a study . . . a study is being concluded . . . . I'm here with—*. He paused and looked at her, clicked off his recording device. "Can I interview you?"

She was chewing almonds and had to swallow before she could answer. "No. I'm a nobody. I'm not really supposed to be here. I'm not official. Liability issues and all. Sergio just let me come because . . . I'm an old friend, and I'm not in Paris, and I'll never go, and we all feel like breaking a few more rules these days, and he felt sorry for me." She tilted her head at the men. "And it's my birthday. Interview them. They're the official ones."

She had to pee—what a drag, so much trouble, with all the

layers—and she was too tired to go far. She only walked so that she was behind him—and she could still hear fragments of his voice. *A study conducted . . . state agencies . . . The results indicate that bears will return to their natural food sources when they are available. . . . Drought adversely affects bear habitat . . . climate change . . . that saying of "a fed bear is a dead bear" is not necessarily true . . .*

She purposefully didn't look down to examine the cut when she was peeing. What was done was done and she wanted this day to feel healthy and real. She finished and pulled and zippered and snapped various layers, and then stood apart from him, staring at the mountain, until Ruben came walking up to them. "Yup, she's in there. Beautiful. Never would've found this place had it not been for the GPS. You know, I think Ollie's theory is right, that this is the mother to the bear that hangs around town, the one that Gretchen had to chase away from Anya's kids. Ollie told me to look for a missing claw on the back paw. It was always leaving tracks like that around his chicken yard. Sure enough, she's missing one. And not from a trap, either. Just born that way, looks like to me. Like a human missing a finger. Anyway, she's a beauty. Tiny, tiny cozy place, not visible at all. The tranquilizer dart is in." He took a handful from the baggie of almonds she held out. "Now we need to wait a bit. Sergio and I will pull her out from the den. Then we'll see who she's got back there—if her two yearlings made it through the year, and we'll give them a tranquilizer too—then you two can come up closer. I'll give you a wave. Keep moving, meanwhile. All that sweat is going to freeze."

"And so, Hemingway? You were going to explain?" Kevin prompted when Sergio left.

She kept her eyes on the mountain. "I've hibernated." He didn't respond, so she added, "I suppose I planned on falling in love, having children, the whole catastrophe. The last grizzly in Colorado was killed in the late seventies. That was in the southern part of the state. They lasted longer down there. Things used to be wilder. I thought I'd have more time."

"You think you're out? Of time, that is?"

"For certain things, yes. So I decided to go to Paris, and then I broke my wrist. I was helping a friend move flagstones for her patio. Simple and stupid as that." She held out her left arm now, as if for inspection. "Anyway, the medical bills." She didn't say how surprising this was. She'd been careful with money all her life, socking it away and living humbly in an inherited trailer right near the restaurant, and always assumed it would be there. To have the money so suddenly gone; the surprise of it still made her queasy.

"So you wanted to go to Paris to feel the vibe of the old gang, but a broken wrist sent you to a bear den instead." His voice was kind. Now that he was less bundled, and she was less desperate, she could see him. He was young, in his twenties, probably of Irish descent, freckled and a tinge of red in his hair.

"Isn't love a beautiful goddamn liar?" she said. "But you know what I respect about them? All that group? At least they gave it a shot. I wonder if we've lost it, somehow. This safe and rational approach to love. All this caution. I'll speak for myself. I was always talking myself out of love, listing reasons why some particular man wasn't right for me. And maybe they weren't. Now I find myself alone. I'm nearly fifty and have never been in love."

He looked at her, rotated his jaw as he worked some almonds out of his teeth. "Well, it's true. My dad used to say, 'Son, wasted time and unrealized human potential are perhaps the most unfortunate occurrences in the universe. Never settle for a life of mediocrity.' He said it in a low full voice, and then went back to his natural pitch. "And when he died last year, he looked up at me and said, 'The more you participate in life, the less you will regret death. I don't regret death.' So I hear you. But also, of course, if I remember right, Pound was screwing everyone, and he abandoned his baby in a hospital. So don't be going too far with that line of thought. There are different ways of realizing a life."

"I know. I'm not romanticizing."

"Hemingway was an ass. And I'm sure they all did their own tallies and pro-con lists of their various lovers. How many of them ended up alone?"

"I know, I know." She chewed her almonds and looked toward the town of Blue Moon. "But really, there was some brilliance, some attempt at something grand. No denying that. I am simply wishing, on my birthday, that I had made a little better attempt to be brilliant and to be grand."

The bear den was a simple indentation, filled with the decay of dried aspen leaves and pine needles. When she approached the bear, she could see that they'd covered the bear's head in a ski mask, so as not to scratch up her face as they gently pulled her from the den, onto a blue tarp, which helped them pull her out a little farther. They'd covered part of her with a space blanket, and that fact surprised tears into Wyn's eyes. She loved these men in that instant: That they would care this much for a bear.

She got on her hands and knees, as Ruben was indicating she do, and inched forward, toward the bear. The sow's front end was pulled out, her hind legs still in the den, and when Wyn leaned forward, she could see another figure, the one yearling that had survived. It was bigger than she thought it would be, nearly full-grown, it seemed, and much darker than its mama. Nearly black. But the best was the noise, the huffing of the two bears, the steady breath of sleep. She had not considered what bears would sound like.

"I want you two to have these avalanche shovels in your hands at all times," Sergio murmured. "This is no joke. Bears respond to tranquilizer differently. They can become alert quickly."

He nodded to her, giving her the go-ahead, and she moved closer, leaning to one side so as to alleviate the pain in her hip. She paused, on all fours, looking at the bear, then putting her nose into her fur. Behind her, Kevin was busy with various recording gear. How odd, she suddenly realized, to have a radio guy come—wasn't it the visuals of aspen and blue sky and sparkling snow and the bear that were so effective? Why not a TV guy? But now he had his mike in front of the bear's nose and was recording the huffing, as well as the banter between Ruben and Sergio as they murmured about ccs and hair samples, and she could see why. This was a story told well in sound.

She raised her head and looked at Sergio, his eyes closed in concentration as he felt for a vein. Ruben was helping him, and they drew vials of blood, administered eye drops and ointments, took measurements. Kevin recorded it all, the little bits of conversation that floated around the bear's head—*considering the girth, I'm guessing one hundred seventy-seven pounds*, and *seven years old*, and *two cubs last year*, and *dart in at one fifteen*—and then looked over at her and said, "Hemingway would not have been so gentle."

Wyn wanted to say something to these young men, something about how they should knock, knock loud, for what they wanted. But they were busy and it was not her place.

She leaned forward to better see the bear. She was starting to shake. Her socks were wet, even though she'd been so careful picking out the best wool, and now that they weren't moving, and in the shade, she could feel the bite of cold. Of a body that could not warm. A fear rose up. She didn't care, she deserved to die, she was killing herself anyway, and she kept her eye on the bear, the wild creature; the feet pads looked surprisingly soft. She touched one gently, then pushed harder, her finger between the pads. Sergio lifted the skin of the bear's mouth to show her the yellow teeth; the claws were the same color. Then he handed her the GPS collar, and it was heavier and larger than she would have thought; she was delighted that it was off the bear; how annoying it must have been for her.

"Crawl on in," Sergio said, taking it from her. "If that's what you still want. We did what we came to do, now go enjoy your Paris." He went to the effort of getting down on his hands and knees, difficult because he was a bit tired and because of all the outerwear. Clearly, he wanted to be eye level to her, tell her something. When he put his face near hers, she could see his lips were blueish, his skin oddly lacking in color, and he looked not only cold but exhausted, the way an animal can.

She nodded. "I do. Still want to go in."

She really looked at him, then. Two wild animals, taking stock. They held each other's eyes, and she understood, suddenly, why he had invited her on this trip. A simple shared fear, but surely a great binding one. An understanding of what the other was suffering because of smoke's way. She knew he slept around—had slept around with her, in fact—and so had she—but now understood that he was looking for something great and grand, something different, and he saw it in her too. He was in his early forties and was just realizing he needed to knock, and Sy's death had clarified that for him, and he saw the same impulse in her. They recognized in each other the journey.

The others were busy, so he leaned forward and whispered to her. "I was thinking about this on the snowshoe up here. Even married people, even married people in Paris of all places—well, you better believe they doubt and suffer. That they don't know what it is they want, and how best to get there. Whether they've given their life enough thought, which requires time, or if they've made the right decisions, which requires courage. They know as well as we do, Wyn, that life keeps an account of both the decisions we don't make and those we do. Don't beat yourself up about it anymore. Look forward. Be here. Be with the bear."

She nodded, to him and herself—*you can do this, you will do this*—and broke his gaze and looked in at the den. She patted his gloved hand with her own, and then inched toward the bear, then past the mama bear, first on hands and knees, made difficult because of her avalanche shovel in one hand, and then on stomach as the cavern got even smaller. It was hard to make out how the body of the yearling was positioned, given the lack of light and the amount of fur, but she felt around until she knew she was touching his head. She couldn't raise her head to get a full view; she was smashed on her stomach, but she let go of the shovel—caution be damned—and put her other arm out. In this way, she was touching the mama bear's hind leg with her right hand, the yearling's shoulder with her left, and she lay, gently digging her fingers into fur. They did not smell as bad as she thought they would—not the rank odor she'd smelled when they were near dumpsters, of wild and urine and rot. This smelled of pine needles and cold and something pure. She closed her eyes so she could breathe it in, feel the oily coarse fur, and rested her face down, right on the duff, the pine needles jabbing at her cheekbone.

She heard Sergio saying something to her, probably beckoning her out, but she ignored him. *This is the best moment you are ever going to have*, she told herself. *Please remember it so you can use it. Please find a way to hang on.* Behind her, the sky was starting its turn toward the evening hour, and surrounding her was rock. In the past were the times she'd forgotten to knock louder, and in front of her was the descent down the mountain, in which they'd have to ride their avalanche shovels like sleds in an effort to make it to the trucks before dark. Below her ran the waters of the world, above her was the arc of sky, and she stayed this way, although she knew she wouldn't have much longer now, that sedation was never a full guarantee, and almost all creatures would eventually resist the pull of sleep and awaken.

## Chapter Fourteen

# Painting the Constellations

Anya had been faking orgasms for the last ten years with her husband, and then she'd decided to take a lover, basically to eradicate the heart-sick that came with pretend moans and clenching of vaginal walls. Not to mention pretend love. Or at least, dissipated bored love. But she had kids—what was she supposed to do?—and so she'd launched forth bravely, to still feel like the woman, the sexy and sex-loving woman that she had always been. But now, at this odd but critical moment, she found herself suddenly shy, incapable of doing what she'd set out to do. Perhaps this was a horrible idea. Sick, even. Her husband dead just a little more than a month. And yet, she was so off-kilter she had no other idea of how to spend her evening without literally going mad. She had said this to her lover, Sergio, who had said: "I hear you. We are all just trying to survive right now, darling."

They were in the hot tub together, she and Sergio, and Thayne and Celeste. Naked and high. Anya hadn't been naked in a hot tub, ever, and the high was new too, and legal, she joyful, and was not sad her husband was gone—maybe that would come later?— and she was glad for the buzz of red wine, glad for the float of pot, glad that Sergio's foot was touching her own.

The mountains settled her, too. She was the lucky one who had the direct view of twilight sky and the dark waves of the Rocky Mountains, the Never-Summer Range, with Blue Moon towering above the rest. Sergio, on the other hand, was facing Thayne and Celeste and their small log house behind them, and if he turned toward her, he got the twinkling skyline of the Front Range. It was only if he looked west, away from her, that he could see the deep blue of sundown and shadowed mountains—which was, of course, where he was looking.

She ran her foot along Sergio's leg. Why, she wondered, was it always up to the woman? It was Anya's theory that men had, in the generation preceding hers, lost their ability to move sexual matters forward—one aggressive act and they could be sued or accused or slapped. And so women were in charge of any overt first moves. It was she who had, for instance, invited Sergio into her bedroom two years ago (he had been over, building her a bookcase out of beetlekill, her kids at preschool), after clarifying with herself that she was sure that her love for her husband was over, and that while she still needed to care for him in his illness, she also deserved love. Or at least, some touch.

At that time, she hadn't orgasmed in so long she forgot how good they were, but after taking Sergio as her lover she was sparked alive. But then her husband died, and the guilt and relief did not send her crying, as one might expect, but rather outward. She was only trying to continue on, wasn't she? It was so fucked up, she realized. And yet. And here were three people who didn't judge her for it. Amen to that.

So, it was up to her. It was true that men were capable of mild, first hints, though, and that's exactly how this had all started: Months ago, at the beginning of the school year, at a parent-teacher conference for her child, Thayne had purposefully held her gaze as he spoke about her oldest child, Zoë, a girl in his first-grade class, and it was his kindness, his obvious affection for her daughter that had made Anya, oddly enough, become aroused. Plus she'd heard, through the grapevine, that he'd given up a high-paying job at some tech company to become a teacher and move up to this mountain and buy a horse, and she was a sucker for people who bucked the system. So she stared back, despite the fact she was already married, and despite the fact she was already having an affair. As she sat at her daughter's tiny desk, it was Thayne who then suggested that she should come over to sit in their new hot tub—and then, he added, more haltingly, she and Sergio, or she and Sy, could come over for dinner and then go outside for some hot-tubbing. At that time, he threw out his arms with a warm confused smile, which said everything. It said, *I know we accidentally came upon you and Sergio kissing, I know that your husband is our vet, I know that given the state of your life and the world in general I am in no position to judge you, and that you are welcome to come to my house regardless of who you would like to bring, lover or husband.* Which she had not been able to respond to, not till now, when she called and asked, haltingly, if she and Sergio could come over, that Sy's actions had made her want to connect with others on the mountain, if, strange though the timing was, if *now* she could come? If they could have one evening together, without mention of Sy—a pretend story, a pause of sorts, in the painful universe of this winter?

Thayne was looking at her now, in the hot tub, with that same intense, interested expression he had on his face when he first suggested this scenario. He had curly dark hair and a nose that was a bit too big and a skinny lankiness. He smiled at her, warmly, and said, "I suppose you hear a lot about sex. I know there's client privacy issues, but can you give me generals? Like, what percentage of adults need to talk about it, in one form or another?"

"A hundred percent," she said. "Eventually."

"This is a nice hot tub," Sergio said. "Perfect for a winter night."

"God and love," Thayne persisted, running his hand through his damp hair, then touching his jawline to wipe off the excess water. "Probably the only two things worth obsessing over. I bet you hear a lot about those two."

"Well, honey, but love and sex aren't the same thing, and first you asked her about sex," said Celeste, who had been sipping her wine from a plastic wineglass. She was a blond, too, and the tips of her wet hair reminded Anya of fall grasslands. "Of course you can have sex without love, without messing things up."

Anya breathed out loudly, which was her way of saying she wondered. It was, perhaps, possible to become sexually engaged without any residual waves. But who'd want it? The erotic was a life force, pushed people to live deeply and truly.

She wondered, briefly, if her husband had known about her affair with Sergio. Or, for that matter, if her best girlfriend, Gretchen, had ever found out. She doubted it. She had decided long ago not to feel guilty for loving, but to also try to contain the gossip and pain. It was a small town, after all. It worried her sometimes, though, what ripples might be caused if the truth were known.

She tapped her foot against Sergio's, to send him a signal. On the way to dinner tonight, as they drove down the mountain, she'd told him, "I wonder about this, you know, not everyone invites you over to their hot tub, and then mentions they sit in it naked. I wonder if they're, you know—"

"Swingers?"

"Yes, swingers."

"I don't know," he'd said.

"But what should we do if they are?"

He'd taken a curve fast enough to cause a squeal, which caused him to slow down. "This situation is already so weird, I think we should just let it get weirder. Play it by ear, I guess."

Now, in the water, Sergio tapped her foot back, moved closer and put his arm around her. She was struck, suddenly, with her great feeling for him.

Everyone was looking at her, waiting for the therapist's response to this question of sex and love and messy things. "You know what I think humans want?" she offered. "They want someone else to see the hurt done to them by this world, and they want that someone to care. They also want someone to have their back when the hurt comes again. That's what Sergio has been for me. And I love him for it."

⁀

Sergio scratched the line of sweat trickling down by his ear, then examined his hand, rough from working with wood. There was a long scrape on his knuckles from pulling the bear from her den, his hand colliding with rock. He was trying to keep the hand out of the water; the wound was still new and needed more time to heal.

He put his arm around Anya, and pulled her toward him, and wondered when it would snow again, and how, exactly, he had ended up here with this mother, this woman who had wanted sex but not a relationship, this woman who had, for the last year, encouraged him to date and to find someone to build a life with, all that and now naked in a hot tub with another couple.

He felt obliged to step in and say something. "Occasionally," he said, "Anya tells me what she tells her clients—or no, not what she tells her clients, but what she *wishes* she could tell her clients. What's that favorite line of yours? 'Close your eyes, breathe out, and embrace the puzzle of the human heart.' I really like that line." Celeste and Thayne were nodding their heads, but still silent, so he added, "I like how the air is so cold, the water so warm." This he said to no one in particular, facing the sky. "I love the winter." He meant, he supposed, that lately he'd been feeling his heart's own tributaries and rivers, the odd but predictable flow.

The others had taken his comment about the cool air and turned it into a discussion about Colorado's warming weather, which led to a discussion of kayaking, which led to a discussion of Kierkegaard. Typical. Humans had a hard time being brave enough to stay on fragile topics for long, himself included. That's exactly why he liked working with wood and wildlife. From childhood, he'd been awkward with people, and Anya understood that in him, and, yes, she had cared about the hurt done to him and why he sought refuge in working alone. Of course he was confused. Perhaps beyond repair. He was a man looking for relationship, who wanted real love, but he also wanted to get through the nights, who had started a relationship with a lonely married woman, never guessing that her husband would die—not just die but kill himself—who now felt an obligation not to leave her, and yet somehow it felt more wrong than ever before, and now he was sitting naked in a hot tub.

He was sorry for the grief of the world, sorry for all this mess, but overall, somehow it still all made sense deep down, and he had to admit that at the moment he was content, which, as he had once heard, meant that he was full of *con*tent. You had to have enough content to be con*tent*.

And yet. Perhaps he was not. He'd whispered enough fantasies into Anya's ear to have covered all the bases: images of threesomes or foursomes conjured up for arousal purposes. In fact, sex with multiple partners was, as Anya had clinically put it, his core erotic theme, his particular constellation of fantasies that would repeat themselves with only slight variations. And there was nothing wrong with that, she would add, kissing him full on the mouth. More than anything about her, he loved that he could talk to her about this, and that she could respond in a way that was kind.

He looked at the others, who were now talking about Joe, the horseshoer on the mountain, who'd been over to shoe Celeste's horse. Apparently, he had a child living with him—temporarily or permanently, no one was sure, because Joe wasn't much of a talker. But the child had joined him and sat at the edge of the barn chatting with Celeste while he shoed, asking questions about horses.

There was a gunshot, suddenly, or perhaps a car backfiring, from somewhere up the mountain, and it surprised them all into silence. He was feeling the pot full force now, the blinking odd spaces forming black holes in his head. He said, "Michelangelo once said, 'One paints with the brain, not the hands.'"

That comment, which he knew was out of nowhere, made Celeste laugh deeply and fully, which surprised everyone even more. She was sitting across from him, and he leaned forward to better listen to her, or not to listen, but to encourage her to speak. Her breasts—smaller and pink—were just at the line of bubbling water. She was beautiful, this Celeste, with her long blond hair and deep blue eyes that reflected some certain form of sorrow. As he hoped, she began talking. She spoke about her job as a kindergarten teacher, not at the school where Thayne taught, but one down the mountain in town, meaning she had nearly an hour-long commute, and how she was in charge of children with alarmingly beautiful imaginations, which then floated into a story of how she'd first met Thayne, which floated into a story of how they'd come to buy this house on Blue Moon and put in this flagstone patio and hot tub, which floated into a story of an injury to her spine and the resultant pain and why she needed a hot tub in the first place. He noticed through the surface of the bubbly water that Celeste, like Anya, had shaved, or waxed, the edges of her pubic hair. His groin tickled. He looked at Anya, then back at Celeste, then back at Anya. The timing of this all was strange, but both were smiling, and both were beautiful.

⌒

Celeste took her husband's foot in her hands, after he'd placed it in her lap, and rubbed the arch, which is what she knew he wanted. Silence had, at last, taken over, and all four sat with their heads tilted back, considering the stars.

She was depressed, no doubt about it, had been for some time. She was on an antidepressant, but still, what medicine could take her beyond *So this is it, huh?* Part of this melancholy was due, she knew, to her spine, how it ached, but it was also simply because her life felt surprisingly empty. Which is why, she supposed, Thayne had gotten her a horse, which was nice, but would never be enough.

All this had her thinking of *her* favorite philosopher, which she was too embarrassed to admit was the Little Prince. Call her childish, but it was that book that had, in her youth, caught her brain on fire. There were better ways to live than others, better ways to be more human—which primarily consisted of avoiding conventional and boring people, as well as living full force in the moment. When in junior high, and required to learn a language, she picked French for the sole reason that she could then read the book in its original. Perhaps that is why she had become a teacher, too: to capture young minds while these little humans still had imagination and heart.

But she herself was failing at the job. She imagined that the Little Prince himself was in those stars, begging her to be brave. So she pointed her finger up, as if pointing to his planet, and said, "What did the Little Prince say? 'It is the time that you have lost for your rose that makes the rose so important.'"

"Oh, I remember that line," Anya said, dreamily. "I used to think of that when Sy first got sick."

They lapsed into silence. Celeste had picked that line on purpose; it also was her way of reminding Thayne that she was grateful for his attentions to her body and its needs, because it was in fact time lost. Time lost to pain and words about pain and doctors for pain and medicines for pain. A simple injury to her lower back and it was the reason she didn't want children. Her job as a teacher was enough, was at the very cusp of her ability.

Celeste regarded Anya and Sergio. She liked that they were lovers. She liked that now they all had that particular secret. An image floated into her mind of the four of them curled like grapevines or perhaps playing like puppies, kissing breasts and running hands over hips. Sad people still liked sex, after all. Perhaps needed more loving than others, in fact; needed the small moments of release, of feeling good.

"I need something," she said abruptly, tapping her chest, which caused everyone to look from the darkened sky to her. "What I mean to say is, we're not swingers. But we've thought about it. We've played around with one other couple, long ago, but we are without disease and we are without the desire to mess up any relationships, including yours or ours, or any friendships, including this one. However, we *are* with desire. Is that so awful?"

There was a reverberation of silence. She noticed that Anya was stabbing her feet into Sergio's leg, and Sergio reached over to hold Anya's hand. But it was Thayne's reaction she was waiting for, and he reached over and touched her throat, which is where, she'd told him once, her sadness had taken up residence.

⌒

Where would this lead? Thayne bit his lip and ran his finger down his wife's décolletage, a word he loved, on a body he loved, that housed a woman he loved. He had known Celeste to be brave on many occasions, but not this forward. He was delighted. Perhaps this would actually happen. How rare to bump into another couple who might be willing to experiment. He supposed he'd been hoping for something, back when he'd suggested this evening to Anya, long ago, but so many things had happened since, the timing was awkward, and really, it was going to take one of the women to get this thing going, and he was enormously grateful for Celeste's direct words.

"I need to use the restroom," said Sergio suddenly, slipping out over the tub, wrapping a towel around his waist. As he stepped over the edge, Thayne saw a long scar running down the length of his leg. It reminded him of something Anya had said earlier, how she and Sergio had met because of their love of wood, and beauty, and because he had brought her a breadboard he'd made while building her some shelves, because he knew she loved baking, but that, once they knew each other better, they were attracted by one sad commonality: their exceedingly lonely childhoods, their exceedingly lonely current state, and their not-quite-accomplished recovery from the consequent pain.

Come to think of it, Thayne thought, this foursome seemed like a group of survivors in their own right. Wasn't everyone? Perhaps they weren't homeless or hospitalized, but they were accomplished in weathering life's difficulty as any. Three of them had fathers dead, one a sibling, one a mother who'd had a stroke. Anya, of course, had just lost her husband, although it was also true that she'd lost him long ago in some sense, and had perhaps suspected this would happen for a long time, which is why her grief was calm and regulated. He and Celeste had lost their only child at birth—a heart defect—which is when he decided to become a teacher, moving into this new career by instinct and survival mechanisms only. She'd never wanted to try again, which, frankly, was a bit of a relief. Life was hard enough. Their bodies were painted through and through with physical and emotional and psychological pain, and now all that was blurred together in this bubbling hot tub: depression, anxiety, sorrow, boredom, fear, and the random pangs in the heart that signaled that this was not enough; that there was more to be grasped, and loved, before this short life was over. And now, unbelievably, here they were, curious and hopeful for—what?—for a little simple and messy joy. It seemed, almost, like a bit of a miracle.

Sergio returned, unwrapped his towel, and slipped in next to Anya. Anya reached out for his hand, but looked at Thayne. Thayne withdrew his foot from Celeste and looked up at the stars.

There were constellations everywhere, ones of his own making, ones that told stories only he believed in. He wondered how many of this foursome housed secrets, and what those secrets contained.

"I don't have, well, any experience with this sort of thing," said Anya, after clearing her throat. "I don't think Sergio does either, but I do know we are both disease-free." She glanced at Sergio. "We are healthy," she repeated. Then she laughed and said, "Really, this is so strange. It's hard to be this brave."

Thayne held her gaze but also perceived that she was squeezing Sergio's hand, the motion visible under the foam and bubbles. Then he felt that Celeste was smiling, in her sad way, and she moved forward, against the water, toward Sergio. He set down his plastic wineglass on the side of the tub while keeping his eyes on Anya, who was moving toward him. A lock of her blond hair made a perfect loose spiral down to her shoulder.

They were all thinking of Sy, he knew. Offering him a tribute, thanking him for granting them the insanity of what they were about to do. He wished they all had more time underneath this darkening sky. He wished the heartache of death and the limits of life didn't gnaw so tightly in his chest at times. He wished he knew how to keep love deep and passion wild.

Anya suddenly glided through the water to his side of the hot tub, placed herself on his lap, facing him, her knees on the seat. For the first time in his life, a naked woman was sitting on his lap in a hot tub with others around. She nudged close enough that his cock touched her body. She looked at him, expectantly. Tilted her head. Touched his jaw with her finger. She smelled of wine and her eyes were quite clear and honest and alive. She was waiting. What happened next was up to him.

He moved his head slowly forward, found her lips, and touched them softly. It was all he could think of to do.

## Chapter Fifteen

# Plan B

The blond was leaning over the counter at the pharmacy for privacy but I heard her anyway: "If I understand this correctly, I don't need a prescription for the Plan B thing, right?"

The pharmacy guy's eyes flickered, but he did a good job of hiding whatever judgment. "No, you don't," he said, "but it's expensive."

"Not as expensive as having a baby," she murmured.

I was standing behind her, next up in line, but when she left, I left, so that I could follow her. That's a creeper thing to do, but sometimes your regular boring Plan A, such as picking up your mom's prescription, doesn't seem like the best way to spend your time. I wanted to see what the future me would look like.

〜

I followed her out to the parking lot. She got in her car, which happened to be parked near my junker Chevy, so I went ahead and got in mine to avoid the spitting snow and pretended to be busy with my phone. I watched her unwrap the package and take the pink pill (I couldn't really see that far, but I've taken Plan B

and I know the pills are pink) and while she did that, I patted my
bloated belly, pushed my thumb into the roar there. Shark week.
Because a uterus looks just like the brain of a shark, and because it
feels like *Jaws* is being re-filmed in my stomach.

Then she looked at herself in the mirror (I think she's pretty,
blond and perky, the way kindergarten teachers are, and I like her
name, Celeste). She put on lipstick, got back out, and walked *back*
into the store. She had the light brown plastic bag in her hand,
and she threw that package in the trash can that sits outside. All
evidence gone.

I wandered around the store, tailing her in a pattern that
mirrored her own, and watched her pick up a few items—a
pineapple, a gallon of milk. All the Thanksgiving stuff was on
clearance in the back bin, and I noticed that she paused in front of
it, and I'm guessing it wasn't because she wanted to get a good deal
on pumpkin-colored placemats. It was because if there's any holiday
that represents family, this is the one, and she just got rid of whatever
might someday have created that. Also, I bet we were both thinking
of Sy. How no one celebrated that holiday on the mountain at all
because of him; I doubt a single person even cooked a turkey. My
parents opted to take us all out to Moon's instead, where we ordered
grilled cheeses and chili. His death was like a really loud noise that
keeps reverberating around the whole mountain.

I should have gone home to study. Mom would be preparing
dinner and Dad would be breaking the ice in the water tank, and
my mom will want her prescription (which I picked up when the
woman was checking out with her pineapple and doughnuts and
milk. I also bought some red hair dye, which is the other reason I
came down the mountain to the big store).

I don't think I intended to follow her home, but we got to

our cars at the same time, and like, why not? She glanced in my direction, but I looked the way a bitchy teenager is supposed to look, and so she loaded up her one bag of groceries and drove off. It's a long drive up the mountain, so I got to follow her headlights. Now it was dark, and I appreciated that she was going first and leading the way. She lived in a new log home near Moon's Restaurant, not too far off the road. I didn't pull in the drive, though. But I did pull over and squint through the trees and I thought I could see her walking through the door, with her pineapple, for which her husband would probably be glad because it was going to taste sweet-spicy on such a cold winter day.

☙

After dinner, I helped with the dishes and then I sat at the dining room table and stared at *Mrs. Dalloway*. Here's what I'm guessing: Tonight the woman will feel a little crampy, because that's what Plan B does to you. So she'll take a bath too. While she's in the bath, she'll be pissed off with herself for sleeping with the guy she just slept with, and she'll be worried that he had an STD, although he insisted that he didn't, but she exposed herself and now has to spend moments of the rest of her life worrying. She'll check for symptoms from time to time, but she'll also know that sometimes there aren't any. Then she'll also think of how nice it was to be fucked and touched in a new way; he was really a nice man and in fact very good in bed. She hadn't felt that way in years, or maybe ever, because every lover is different.

My period started later than most girls. Fifteen. Started having sex the next year. Thought: Fuck, if my body is going to do this to me, then I'm going to counteract with some pleasure. Someday

I'm going to be in a bathtub, also having just taken Plan B, which maybe by that time will be available on the shelf, no whispering required, and I'll be thinking these same thoughts.

∽

A bath is the only way to get truly warm in the winter, plus I like looking at myself, I like coming in the bathtub. The hollowness of my stomach, my hipbones, my clit, which, if I flick it with my fingers, hard, pinch my nipples, hard, close my eyes and picture a man spanking my ass, hard, I can make myself come, there in the warm water, in forty-five seconds flat.

So far, my memories with men have been good. I'm lucky in that way. I've been smart about who I've picked. They all appreciated it, and I appreciated how much they appreciated it. We were good and warm to each other. I try to insist on condoms, but no one is a fan, and hence the taking of birth control, which I sometimes forget to take, hence the purchasing of Plan B, which you have to be over seventeen to get, and so until my birthday, I went with my cool neighbor Gretchen who bought them for me. That's how I know they're expensive: I had to come up with the money myself, although she'd always offered to pay. After she bought the package and handed it over, she always said, Kid, I have one request, you know I have one request, which is don't get pregnant, you don't want a baby, you don't want to lose your whole self to becoming a parent, and you don't want to have to decide about an abortion, nobody does.

To which I could only agree.

That woman who walked in her door with a pineapple didn't want a kid or an abortion either. All she wanted was to be half-

loved on a nice night, to have the man say she had nice hair and a
nice heart. It's not such a terrible thing to want. I'll be wanting it
my whole life.


                                    ⤴


I left way early on the way to school this morning, in the dark,
and I let myself into my mom's store, which, although not having
a pharmacy, does have prepackaged bundles of flowers. I got
the roses, not the stupid carnations. Then I drove back up the
mountain and dropped them off at the woman's door. I wrapped
them in a plastic bag, and an old towel I always have in the back
of my car, and I hoped they wouldn't get too cold by the time she
found them.

There were lights on, voices inside; they were getting ready
for work. I suspected she wouldn't be there much longer, so the
flowers would be safe. I won't have kids either, is maybe why I did
that. Maybe if I'd been born at another time, I would have. But the
world is too fucked up and there's no way I'd bring an innocent
creature into such a confused place, where men shoot themselves
in fields, and other men shoot police officers, and whole countries
stone women and gays and where the human heart clearly doesn't
have much inherent kindness.

The man she slept with, whether husband or a lover, wouldn't
be sending roses. People, in the end, are mostly takers. Not givers.
Including me. He probably didn't even know she had to suffer
through the Plan B. And even if he did, he'd never understand the
trouble of it, the cramps of it, the particular lonely of it. Oblivious
to everything.

After I left the roses, I got in my car, drove down the mountain to my school, turned in my paper, went to classes, changed my tampon, took my ibuprofen, complained to the galfriends. Later I went to lunch where I bought a small carton of milk. It went down my throat. I'll keep moving on, for the sake of my parents, I guess—just like Sy should have kept carrying on, just for the sake of his kids—we owe each other some shit. We owe each other some occasional flowers.

*Chapter Sixteen*
# Pinball

Sergio took first dates to the pinball place, all the way in town. In the winter, especially. All those bright lights, chatter of machines, more color than any other place short of Mexico. He also liked getting off the mountain, to remember there were such things as college students and the homeless and the professionals. It was good for dates too, a comfortable family place with lots of middle-agers, and most women were reminded of their pasts, of their first video games, and at least they could talk about that.

One-and-done. That's what most of his dates in the last years had been, not that there were many of them. But he'd just re-upped his Match.com profile, deciding the other day to put himself out there more, ever since his friend Wyn had talked about knocking on the right doors, and knocking hard.

So here he was. And even if it didn't work, at least he got the pleasure of this place even if the date was a bust. He wasn't sure why he had trouble finding the right person—if it was him, a failure of will, his feelings still confused because of his affair with Anya, or a confusion about life and love in general since Sy's death, or if it was just a matter of statistics, how it did in fact take dozens of people to find a good spark.

This date, for example: She was too small for his too big, too athletic to his round. Her name was Flora, even, and she would forever make him feel ungainly and inadequate, and if there was one thing he wasn't interested in, it was feeling not-good-enough. He wanted to be comfortable. He liked himself; he was never going to lose the extra twenty pounds, he didn't want to. She looked far smaller than her profile pictures, which amused him; normally it was the opposite.

They were seated across from each other over *Ms. Pac-Man* now, the console down low and between them. The sticks were old and mushy, but it was the original game, not the new version with the lasers and everyone competing. In this game, it was just two players amicably taking turns, eating fruit and avoiding ghosts—which had struck him, on one date long ago, as a nice metaphor for a relationship. Didn't one want a partner to witness the fruit-joys of life and help one avoid the ghost-death dangers? *Get the cherry! Watch out for the ghost, he's turning the corner on you!* That was what he wanted in a real partner: someone to say those things to him, to let him do the same.

The other great thing about this game—the reason he liked to do it first, if it was open—was that he could sit across from his date and simply watch her play. Even if it was a no-go, he got a certain enjoyment out of watching a woman, her eyebrows shoot up, her face registering concentration. The simple joy of eating Pac-dots and the sorrow of withering once touched by a ghost—seeing all this cross a face was better than the game itself. It didn't feel creepy. In fact, it felt the opposite. Sort of a melancholic appreciation of the beauty of changing human emotion.

Flora looked up and caught him staring. "I just got killed." She crinkled her nose. "Inky did me in. Or was that Sue? Game over, I guess."

"Should we move on to something else? Try a game of pinball? We could get another beer if you want." He made a move to rise from his chair, but she put her elbows on the console and her face in her hands, so he sat back down.

"I have a proposal for you," she said. She took the rubber band off her ponytail, let her hair loose, then ponytailed it up again. It looked the same as it just had, except slightly messier. "We just met," she said. "I realize that."

"True." If he thought this would go anywhere, now would be the time to flirt. He'd say how he liked her eyes, that she was prettier than her profile pictures, which was true. But something about it wasn't right—it wouldn't work, and putting effort into something that would fail would make him feel tired and suspended. He wanted to get married. He wanted a real future with a real someone. He wanted to *build* something of quality, something that lasted. Basically, he'd been fucking around for a while now—had not made the wisest decisions, regretted it, and it had all become so absurd, so ugly, so not-what-he-wanted that he had finally and fully clarified that what he wanted was a real life and a real family.

She blew up at her bangs and sent them floating up for a moment. "Do you drive all the way back home, back up to the mountain, when you come to town?"

"No. I stay at a friend's house, a friend from high school. Run some errands in town the next morning."

"So you're staying in town anyway?"

He nodded, finished his beer, set the empty glass on top of the blue ghosts sliding across the screen.

"Nights are lonely. Nights are the worst."

His eyes watered; the flashes of light stung them all of a sudden. It was still early, and he briefly wondered if he'd slept badly last night, and then remembered that he had, that he had been awakened several times by a rat clawing around behind the wall, not only the noise of it, but the worry about how he'd get rid of it.

Flora blew her bangs up again. "It's hot in here. Feels good, though, because I've been cold all week. What a winter. Anyway, I know a little about you because I know a few people living up in that little town. I called around. I know, for example, that you're not a creeper or a murderer. You're a nice guy, you hold the door for Violet at the post office, you help shovel roads in the winter. You are a biologist. You work for Parks and Wildlife. You also work with wood. You build furniture. And breadboards. Your sister moved in with you, you got her a job at Violet's."

He was surprised. "You've done a bit of reconnaissance, I guess."

She gave a quick shrug. "I heard the story about you, how once you sat down in someone's beanbag, and the pepper spray you'd been carrying around in your front pocket for an aggressive bear, and, well, it went off and it—well."

He laughed and blushed a little, surprised again. "That pain was amazing. Worst ever."

"You jumped in the shower and it only made it worse. You were hollering in there."

"Yes."

"What did you end up doing?"

"I drove home, cussing all the way, and drank a whiskey and paced around my house for a few hours yelping like a madman. I joke that *that* was what scared the bear away. Never saw her after that night."

"I'm sorry." But she looked amused. "Anyway, I know you're not a mean person."

"No, I'm not." Something about that stung. He was tired of a world in which you had to prove yourself a decent human being.

"Well, Sergio, I'm wondering if you want to come home with me and sleep next to me. Not sex. I don't mean that. I mean, just lying there, companionably. Just to, you know, have company during the night."

He scratched his eyebrows by running his fingers toward each other, then pinching the bridge of his nose. Then he remembered that doing so often made his eyebrows big and bushy—a resemblance to Oscar the Grouch eyebrows, he thought—and so he smoothed the hairs back the other way.

"I don't know if that would be hard for you, or weird for you. Or even possible. At the moment, I just want someone to hold me and to talk to me. If you could do that—if you wanted to do that—awesome. If not—awesome. Either way. Just putting it out there." She shrugged her shoulders. "Sorry if that's super weird."

"You know, you're really pretty. I'm just saying so. I'm guessing you don't have that much trouble finding men to sleep next to you."

A sadness crossed her face, and he was surprised at how closely it resembled his own feeling at the moment. "I do, actually," she said. "Especially someone who could just be there and not want to . . ."

"I get it. I'm sorry." He looked around the room. All those flashes of color. *The Lord of the Rings* pinball machine was the closest to them and it roared *Get a hold of yourself!* Someone across the room cussed and hit the side of the game, a gaggle of young kids stood around the change machine, the air-hockey puck glowed in the dark as it pinged across the table.

"What are you thinking?" She asked it genuinely, her eyes also roaming around the room.

"I'm thinking about a rat that's moved in behind my wall. They do that, in the winter. One of the hassles of living in the country. It's really hard to get them out, once they've gotten snuggly in there."

"Don't worry. I'm no rat. This would be an occasional thing."

He chuckled because he wasn't sure he'd even meant that. He looked at her, at the bit of light from the *Pac-Man* caught right above her pupils, at the richness there. "Okay, I'm thinking something else random, which is this: I'm not sure a man could ever ask a woman that question."

"True."

"I don't know if that's our culture or cowardice. It might actually be cowardice."

"I don't know."

"I've often thought that women have a bit more oomph. Willingness to risk."

"Maybe."

"I wish I could ask that kind of question."

"Well, I suppose you could."

"I'm just buying some time here while I think on your proposal."

"I know. I can see it."

"Sometimes I think I missed some kind of call. Because of a lack of courage, and I see that in a lot of early-middle-aged men around me. We find excuses."

"Well," she said, finishing off her beer. "I don't know."

He took a deep sad breath and looked at her. "Yes," he said. "Yes, I'd like to spend the night with you. Without sex. As long as *you* are not an axe-murderer."

"I am not. But you can call Violet. She's the aunt of a friend of mine. Violet doesn't know me well herself, but she can put you in touch with my friend. Then you can call my friend and confirm I'm okay." She used her arms a lot when she talked, weaving them about above the *Ms. Pac-Man* game, her hands signaling the connection between Violet, and her friend, and her friend's phone.

"I'll trust my gut. Can we do one thing before we go, though? Can we play one game on the Big Bowler? It was built in 1959, out of oak, and when it breaks, it's hard to fix. There aren't any parts anymore. They asked me to make a lever in the back, which I did." They were walking now, toward the back of the pinball place. "It's like bowling, except smaller. See? I like this part, this little sign: FOR AMUSEMENT ONLY."

She reached down and touched the oak panel that returned the ball. "Wow. How beautiful it is. All this wood."

He liked that she said that, and they bowled a game, cheering the small bowling ball down the wood paneling. She clapped and he turned his head away from her; he didn't want to think about sex now that it was both more, and less, of a possibility than it had been before. Instead, he thought of all the spheres in this place— the balls of the skee ball game, the bowling ball she now held, the power pellets and Pac-dots, the pinballs.

He won, even though he'd tried to mess up a few, but she was happy about it. "Thanks for showing me this place," she said on their way out. "But we didn't even play a game of pinball. Maybe next time. As, you know, friends. You bring all your dates here?"

"Often."

"I don't blame you. It's a nice first date."

"No one has ever asked me what you just did, though."

"I wonder how many people have secretly wanted to?"

Now they were at their cars, which were iced over with a new brittle snow. It was incredibly cold out, well below zero, and while she was warming her car, he came to help her scrape the windshield, and they complained about how miserable it was, how miserable this whole winter had been. That snow from the first blizzard a month ago still hung around in shadowed places, and the sun had often been covered by roiling gray clouds, unusual for Colorado.

He followed her to her place. He texted his friend, who texted back, "Well, good on ya, ya lucky bastard. See you next time," and then Sergio parked and grabbed his bag and followed her around her house to a back entrance. She was renting the back half of a brick house in the old town area, perfect, she said, for a graduate student like herself. It was quiet and convenient and she helped out the woman above her in exchange for low rent.

When they were inside, he stood in the little living room while she flipped on lights and moved about. It was warm, thank god. There were a lot of houseplants, some with Christmas lights hanging between them, and some good artwork with bright colors and he liked it. It felt comfortable.

"I'm tired," Flora said. "I know it's early, and perhaps you don't want to sleep yet—"

"Actually, I do. The rat kept me up all night—"

"Oh, good. Well, not about the rat. I'm going to go in the bathroom and change into pajamas and climb into bed. Make yourself at home. There's tea and milk and food and all the usual stuff, in all the usual places. You don't seem like a thief, but I'll tell you right now, I don't have anything worth stealing."

When he got to the bed, in his own sweatpants and T-shirt, he said, "Do you do this a lot? Ask people to stay over?"

"You're the fourth person I've asked."

"How did the others go?" He sat on the edge of the bed and looked at her. She was so small and beautiful, the white comforter pulled up to her chin. She didn't look nervous, but he was, and he wondered if he'd sleep at all.

"Three people agreed. One was a one-night deal; a one-night-sexless-stand, I guess you could say." She smiled at her little joke. "Two of them came over periodically, but one of them moved away. The other still comes over every once in a while. We text each other. Something along the lines of 'I'm a little too lonely tonight.' And he shows up at my place, or I go to his."

"And there's never any . . ."

"No. In his case, he's an old teacher of mine. It's off the table. He knows it. What we want is some warmth. I have this theory, which is that people tend to talk about real things, big things, when they're side by side, instead of, say, looking at each other over dinner. Personally, I think more people should be doing this, more of the time. Depression and alcoholism would decrease."

"You have a lot of theories."

"We all do. That's another theory of mine, that we all have lots of theories."

He climbed in beside her, careful to stay on his side of the bed. "Well, it's just brave. There's some assholes out there. But I think you're right about depression decreasing. It's just that people aren't used to such an idea, and once you touch another person, it changes things."

"Yes, true. But I think there are sins of omission. A failure of character. People so often don't get what they want because they don't even bother to formulate the thought and ask. It's almost as if they force themselves to *not* think outside the box. Cognitive dissonance and all that." She turned her head to him. "With that in mind, what I'd like to do is shimmy up next to you, put my head on your chest, and have you wrap your arms around me. If that's okay with you. And no sex. Really, I am so not kidding about that."

He lifted up his arm to create a space for her, and she snuggled into it. He was getting hard, but it would fade. He felt a bit offended that she was so opposed to sex, had so clearly put them into the friend-zone, but somehow it was also comforting to have this clarity.

"Are you afraid of death?" She said this abruptly, in a happy-teasing way, proving her point about conversation getting more real when two people were lying down.

"Sure."

"Do you believe in some afterlife?"

"I'm in a process of investigation."

"I don't. Believe in an afterlife. For one reason, and it's not the usual reason about whether there's a god or not. I just think that when people invent some other world that's brighter and shinier than this one, what happens is that they're not paying attention to this world. And they mess it up. I don't believe in an afterlife because it would take my attention off of this life. *This* . . . sphere."

He felt a pang, then. A flitter of emotion for this woman. Perhaps she felt it register in his body because she said, "Good night, Sergio. I usually wake up at around two and wander around for a bit. Old habit. Feels like an ancient habit, in fact. Checking on things." Her voice was very matter-of-fact, her body a bit more tense. "Then I come back to bed. If you're here in the morning, cool. We can have a short breakfast together before you go. Then I need to study. If you get up and go, though, that's totally fine. Just turn the latch on the doorknob so it locks. There's a bunch of fruit in the bowl by the fridge. Help yourself. It's weird, I know." She gave him a small squeeze and relaxed again.

He took a deep breath. He thought of Sy and where he might be right now. Perhaps Sy's DNA was floating around, perhaps it was in some lovely place with clouds. It made him sad that he didn't know and wouldn't ever know. So much of life seemed to be about pinging around, totally unsettled, and trying to make peace with being unsettled. He wanted to feel comfortable, just for this night, at least, and he'd have to work a bit to get there. He wanted this to work. He wanted to prove her right; that such a thing was possible. He didn't want this night, or his life, to careen about swiftly and in an uncontrolled way anymore, pinging here and there. Now that he closed his eyes, they weren't stinging, and better yet, he could focus on the weight of her head, the smell of her hair, the presence of her form, all bits of consoling evidence that this night had gone in a different direction than all the others that had come before.

## Chapter Seventeen
## *Debitum Naturae*

Zach bent in front of the woodstove, feeding it dry branches, and considered how, throughout the course of this one day, he would come into a new and final phase of his life by gazing in three directions. Up, to the sky. Straight ahead, at a woman's eyes. Down, at a box containing a brain. This was the day that would shape the rest of his days. The day to launch a new era. It sounded grandiose but there it was. A simple, quiet fact. He could feel the sensation cawing in his throat.

It was so very cold out—really very cold—and he straightened his knees with effort and stood in front of the warmth. The dark outside was astounding. Antoinette would be over by six so that they could drive down to the mouth of the canyon before the sun came up, and together, they'd be looking back up, counting the species as they moved down the mountain.

First, though, Dora's brain.

He peeked in on the two pots of chili he'd had simmering all night—one vegetarian, one meat, he wanted everyone to be happy—and then he stood above the white cardboard box on the kitchen table. He'd retrieved it yesterday from the mortician down in town, but yesterday was dreary and ruined. Today was the day. So dark out, still, and full of promise.

He cut open the box with his pocketknife and pulled out another box. He stopped to add a log, now that the sticks were burning, and poured himself a cup of tea, now that the water was hot. He cut open the second box. Inside was a white block of Styrofoam, and it took some time to work the tight-fitted, squeaking mass out. At one point, he had to resort to stabbing parts of it away so that he could work his fingers into it enough to get a grip. It were as if Dora was tormenting him with one last difficulty, refusing even now to show herself.

Finally, he cut the tape holding the two blocks of white and they fell apart to reveal a plastic bucket. That surprised him. It looked like something cookie dough would come in, the kind kids at the school sold for fundraisers. He'd expected a glass jar, or something classier, and smaller. He didn't like it, this white plastic. Cheap and thin, not worthy of a brain.

He looked out the window at the single strand of white lights spiraled up the bird feeder, each covered with a glob of new snow, and which he'd left burning all night to mark the occasion, the start of this Bird Count, undoubtedly the best week of the year, full as it was with camaraderie and binoculars and plumage and ears tuned for vocalizations. And surprises. This week was always filled with surprises. Perhaps it was wrong to think so, but it was lovely that Dora wasn't around to complain about it all.

Peeling the lid off the plastic bucket also proved difficult. When he dug his fingernails under the plastic and pulled, the plastic pulled back and re-hinged itself to the bucket; when he re-pulled that part up, another part re-hinged itself. He had to use both hands, holding the bucket down with his elbows until the plastic gave way. This growing old stuff was for the birds, he was fond of saying, but the younger version of him couldn't have managed this plastic any better.

The brain was stacked in slices. It was the entire brain, for sure, and vaguely held the expected shape of a human brain, only stacked a little incorrectly, like a Jenga game that was starting to tilt.

"What the hell," he said. "I thought you'd be floating in formaldehyde. I thought you'd be *in* something."

There was the smell of chemicals, to be sure, but the brain was just sitting there, cold and alone. He pulled at the skin on his throat, and then noticed he was doing it and let it go. It was something Dora had once noticed about him, that he did that when stressed, when he needed more air. It's true she'd known him in ways like that, better than any human ever would.

It's just not what he'd expected, this brain. It felt disgraceful, and that was not his intent at all. Somehow, it was an act of love. He wanted to pick up a piece, but thought that perhaps he should be wearing gloves. He closed his eyes to consider what he had on hand, and all he could think of were the yellow ones he wore when he cleaned the toilet, and that didn't seem right. He could stab the first slice with a fork, but that didn't seem right, either. Finally, he scowled at himself—to conjure courage—and reached out and picked up the top slice of his wife's brain with his fingertips.

It was cold. And spongy and wet and heavy, much heavier than he would have thought. He held it out in front of him. Breathed out slowly. It looked like a thick slice of a mushroom, he decided, a very meaty gray mushroom. With spaces and grooves, as one would expect, like the picture of brains in magazines. It was denser than he would have thought.

"Hi, Dora." He cleared his throat. Started again. "This is a little strange, I realize. No disrespect is intended. I just wanted to see you, felt I owed it to you." He couldn't stand holding it any longer and he put the slice back on top of the others and pressed his fingertips into his jeans. Now he leaned over and spoke down to the entire stack of slices. "Your results came back. Was indeed Alzheimer's. The report indicated plaques and tangles consistent with Alzheimer's, that's what it said. Although I guess we knew that. But anyway, it's confirmed. That's what you had."

He imagined he could push his hand right into that brain, smash it all up in his fingers. Knead it like bread dough. Or stab at it with a knife. To get it back for the last decade of hell, pure hell, for the both of them. Ever since that day she'd put a hamburger right on the stove top, with no pan beneath it, and he'd taken her down into the town and the doctor had said, Dementia, probably Alzheimer's, want to try Aricept?

But even before then, too. This brain that had caused her depression. And therefore her meanness, her blankness, her lack of curiosity or wonder or joy, the one that had taken away a substantial portion of both their lives. "There is no shame in chemistry," he used to console her, and that was true, but still, they both hated this brain, and its disruption of chemicals and incomplete firings, which had made a life so difficult, so hard for the both of them.

She used to clutch her head and rock back and forth and moan, "I hate this brain, I hate this brain," and he did too. It was her brain, they used to joke sadly, that had ended their faith in any god, ended any belief that they owed a debt to a force who allowed such suffering.

Headlights galloped across the dark outside. Antoinette was early. "Now what do I do with you, Dora?" He quickly pressed the lid back on the tub, put the tub in the cardboard box, put the box on the floor, and washed his hands, twice, just in time to open the door.

∽

Antoinette barged in, big and radiant, clapping her gloved hands together. Her graying black hair sprung out from a red hat and ran down her back in a river. She was wearing dark red lipstick, which was a bit crooked, but which gave her a certain spark that was matched by the whir in her eyes.

"*Dios mío*, it's cold out there. Roads are a bit slick. But not windy, and that's all we could have hoped for. Give me something warm. If you've got it handy. We've got a few minutes. You're all set, yes?" Her eyes were scanning the table, where he had just set out the Rare Bird Documentation Forms, the General Instructions & Information, and best of all, the Tally Sheets, with their long lists of species. "One hundred species this year. That's what we want. Last year, we had ninety-eight. Isn't that right? I didn't check my email yesterday. You sent the map out to everyone? Everyone's ready?"

"Good morning," he said, handing her a cup of tea. "Yes, usual crowd, mapped out the usual way. I sent out Sibley's website link for guidance on distinguishing the geese this year. That's important." He glanced at the box on the floor. "I've got Dora's brain here. Want to see it?"

For the first time, she settled. "Well, no." She blinked at him, then down at the box. "I'm surprised they let you have it. Aren't tissues regulated? Can everyone just go around getting the brains of their spouses?"

He pulled at the skin on his throat. "Well, maybe it was a bit illegal. I requested it back, after they did the study to confirm Alzheimer's. They could release it to the coroner, who can release it to the mortician. You know, for reburial with the body."

"Sanders? Down in town?"

"Yes."

"What are you going to do with it?"

"Bury it, I suppose. Near where I let her ashes go. I wanted to see it first."

"Zach, some people would find that a bit disturbing. She's been dead, what, eight months?"

He shrugged. "It takes a long time to study a brain, I guess." He liked the way she said his name. With the small undercurrent of an old accent. He liked that she was chubby and brown-eyed and full of life. *Round* with life. He found all of it exotic and new and beautiful, and liked looking at her for a few extra moments when she didn't know she was being observed.

He shrugged. "I know it. But I wanted to see it. The report came back, she did have Alzheimer's."

"I guess we knew that."

"But it's nice to have it confirmed."

"Yes. You like data."

"Brains weigh three pounds. Which is a lot, if you think about it. Red-tailed hawks can weigh about that much."

She put out her hand to touch his shoulder blade, and it lingered there, on his flannel shirt. "It'll be nice to go out this year without her. You know, it was just hard." She rubbed her hand up and down on his spine. "I just mean, it was hard to keep her occupied and quiet, hard to count the birds. She didn't like any of it."

He stared out the kitchen window at the sky. At this new day. It was still black with the smallest blur of light way far south. He cleared his throat. "It was good seeing you at the funeral last month. At Sy's funeral, I mean. It will be strange for everyone this year, being in that same meadow where he died. "

She had taken back her hand quickly, as if she'd suddenly

realized what she'd been doing, and now had it cupped below her teacup. "I know. But we need to include that territory." She paused. "It's people dying that brings the living closer. More room for them to make connections. That Sy. We're all still angry with him, I'm sure. But at least he reminded us to take care." She caught his eyes, then looked at the box, raised an eyebrow, shook her head.

He considered it as well. "I thought it would be floating in formaldehyde. Like that brain in a jar I saw as a kid in that museum in Chicago." He added a heavy log to the fire, with the idea it would burn slowly and still be heating the place when everyone returned for lunch. "But no, it's just sitting in a bucket. I think it is soaked in the stuff. But I should keep it cold, right? The room is getting warmer. I'll take it out and put it on the picnic table. No, maybe in the shed. Nothing will bother it there."

Her smile came back. "No one is going to want to know about a brain and still eat lunch here, I'll tell you that much. As our coordinator for Bird Count, you have an obligation to feed us. We're all freezing our tuchuses off for you, after all."

"It's not for me. It's for the birds, for nature. You all love it as much as I do."

She winked at him, and it seemed to him that she was nonplussed by life's oddnesses, that they only made her softer and more curious, and that such a take on life was her particular grace.

He glanced out the window at the dim glow. It was just so far south. It always surprised him just how far the sun went in winter, so very far away before starting the path back.

The cold was to be expected, but it was still hard to endure. They got out of her car on County Road 27 where the creek bed ran down the foothills. There were clusters of cottonwoods and rabbit brush and wild plums, all in hibernation, waiting. There were a few houses and acreages dotted alongside this road and Vreeland's lower corrals, and from here, if they turned completely around, they could see the cluster of Moon's Restaurant and the enclave of trailer homes around it.

This was the lowest territory of the Blue Moon Mountain, as low on the mountain a person could go and still consider himself a part of the mountain community, and thus the lowest area he was responsible for as the count compiler. Some folks liked living here, at the edge, closest to town. He preferred it farther up, tucked in the woods, like certain birds, the ones that preferred to nest and raise their young up high and only came down to feed. The Steller's jays, the hooded juncos, the Townsend's solitaires.

Antoinette had her clipboard with the species list and was rifling through some papers. Immediately, in the flush of soft light, they spotted two kestrels, three house sparrows, and one tree sparrow, which Antoinette penciled in on the tally sheet. It was quiet, then, except for the occasional ding or creak of a piece of metal fencing or a faraway rooftop. Funny how little sun it took to start the warming. Funny how one never noticed the sounds of warming until one was really listening.

They both stood leaning against the car, looking west, toward the mountains, in silence. There was nothing. Good. It was due diligence to get here before the birds, before the sun was at the angle that would send them into motion down the corridor of creek bed. Once they came, it would be a flurry, a flood of motion.

"Are we counting like we did last year?"

"Why not," he said, stomping his feet, hoping to dissipate the ache. "You do the clicker, I'll estimate in groups of ten. Then we'll compare."

"It'd be nice if they'd fly a little high, so we can see them against the sky. Easier to count that way. My eyesight gets worse each year. That's what this Bird Count reminds me." But she said it in a happy way. He was again struck by her burbly joy, some internal happy setting that she didn't have to work for. He believed he had a bit of that, but he wouldn't mind absorbing extra from her. He felt sorry she was so cold, though; her breath wisped in front of her face and she pulled her scarf tighter.

He heard the caw of a crow and his eyes drifted right, toward it, but he didn't see anything. Far away, someone at the Vreelands' was dropping rotomill for the cows, and the smell of it bloomed slowly. He wondered if it was Ollie or Lillie; perhaps it was even Korina, since both Ollie and Lillie wanted to do Bird Count. He wondered who would be minding the store, if Violet went out. In any case, the rotomill smelled a little like the brain, and he felt sorry for leaving Dora in the dusty shed, cold and alone, and also sorry he had spent his life obligated to someone so opposite of the warm creature standing next to him now.

Down the road, he could see the glow of headlights. Now that it was getting lighter, they were hardly visible, but he could recognize the distant sound and knew it was Wendell's old truck. Wendell and Flannery. An unlikely a pair as ever; a stodgy Libertarian conspiracy theorist and a gorgeous gay blond, and it was exactly that sort of thing that made him love this day so much. After all, it seemed sad to gather the community only for funerals; why not a day of joy and surprise?

Antoinette leaned against him a little, the sleeves of their down coats whispering against each other. "Who'd you put where, on the mountain?"

"Well, that's Wendell and Flannery, and they're on the territory north of us. Thayne and Celeste are to the west. Lillie's doing the Vreeland property, probably with Ollie or Violet, depending on who is doing chores. And I have Ruben and Jess near their home, up the highest. That's some tough hiking, but they're young and strong."

"And in love."

"Yes. That too."

"It doesn't bother me. The age difference."

He looked over at her. "Me either. Besides, Jess is an old soul."

She held his gaze. "Plus, when people find happiness. Well, you know. Let them just feel it for as long as it lasts."

His eyes blurred with tears and he was about to make a joke about that—how he was prone to being a soft crybaby—but she reached out, held his chin in her hand, and without any warning or pause, she tugged his face toward her. Their lips touched, a small gentle tug, and then she pulled back but held her gaze steady. He had hoped for exactly this; still he was startled by this new knowledge about the rest of his life.

⤛

The crows came in waves. Some groups swooped down in the field in front of them, some to the left, some came right over them to go farther east. The black blur of them looped, rose up, cackled and whirred, swooped to the side. Antoinette clicked her counter and he murmured his estimates by tens, though he was having trouble concentrating. Sixty years since the last new kiss; a long time, to be sure, and until a few weeks ago, he'd been operating on the idea that he'd not have another.

When finally there was a lull, they leaned in toward each other, tallying.

"About seventy-five, that's what I got," she said, staring down at the clipboard, perhaps too embarrassed now to look up.

He nodded. "I had ninety, so let's put eighty. My age."

She recorded the number and they stood, facing the mountains, eyes searching for more.

"Are you very cold?"

"I'm okay."

"It aches. This cold."

"We'll warm up soon."

"I wish I had more time. I do like living."

"Do you miss her?"

"No. If you want me to be honest."

"I do. Want you to be honest, that is. We should be honest with each other."

"Yes." He cleared his throat, looked at the sky.

"There's so much to lose, otherwise."

"There always is."

"She wasn't easy, was she?"

"No."

"You're probably glad not to be taking her into town. To the doctors and such."

"Those Alzheimer's Association meetings, they were fine, I miss those a bit. I made a few friends there. Renny Cross, for instance. I miss seeing her."

"But Dora had that ailment. She never felt very good."

"An autoimmune disorder." He stamped his feet again, begging for the flow of blood. "It seemed like the diagnoses and the way it took hold of her body was in continual motion, but one thing that stayed constant was that she was miserable."

"She was depressed a lot."

"Well, chicken and egg. One makes the other worse. I sometimes think this world is making people sick."

"Zach." She looked at him and then went back to looking to the mountains. "You've had a tough row to hoe. Most of us do. Living is just hard. But yours has been particularly difficult."

"I have this mountainside. These birds. This view. Here with you." This last bit, he hoped, would elicit a smile, but it did not. She had a pensive, serious look.

"I don't mean to be disrespectful," she finally said. "But I never liked her much. I feel like I should say that now, I want it to be known, in case it matters to you—"

"Don't worry. Not many people did."

"You didn't think of leaving her?"

He glanced over at her. "'Course I did. Doesn't most everyone?"

"And?"

He let his eyes roam across the mountain again, across all the shades of white, the shadows on the north-facing slopes. "Couldn't do it. She'd tried to be a good mother, gave me my kids. And some of it was brain chemicals, a disease, stuff she didn't ask for or deserve. She could have tried quite a bit harder. On that matter, I am sure. But I'm not a leaving sort of man. You can't just go walking away from some stuff."

Antoinette looked at the sky. "I wish your soul well, Dora. I do. I hope you're warm and safe and comfortable and peaceful. But sometimes I'm angry with you on behalf of my friend, here, Zach, you see, and I feel like I should just admit it aloud." Then she finally looked at him. "So you're eighty?"

"Just turned." He was nervous about that; a good bit older than she was, but she was smiling and nodding at something behind him. "On the wire. Pigeons or doves?" Suddenly, again, there was a flush of counting. One hundred sixty starlings, forty-five more crows, twenty doves, two song sparrows, five chickadees. Then the birds settled and stilled. No new ones came; none of the current ones left.

"Let's sit in the car for a moment to warm up," she said, and when they were there, with the heater running, she said, "Do you ever feel that you gave the world more than it gave you?"

"Well, I'm not sure the world ever owed me anything." He looked over at her, her nose red and her cheeks pale from cold, her lipstick worn off, her lips chapped, a little more worn down than she was this morning. "I've been thinking on something of late, though. About the eras of our lives. Mine have been much like everyone else's, I suppose. Happy childhood years, though growing up can be difficult. Then early twenties, the flush of it all. Then the child-rearing years that came a bit too early and were a bit too hard, but had their moments of good. That blurred into the career years."

"That's when you became serious about this. This birding."

"Yes. Taught the kids as I taught myself."

"And then?"

"Those overlapped with the Taking Care of Dora Years. Then the Alzheimer's Years. Now I'm at the cusp of something new." He wanted to say more but couldn't quite form the words. Something about how they could be called the Alone Years. Or Peaceful Years. Or, Southern Sun Years, because when the sun was this far south, it reminded him a bit of death, of the end of the journey. Or maybe, just maybe, it would be the Years of Spotting Something Rare and Beautiful. But before he could get a word out, she'd climbed back out of the car, and they stood on the road again, counting a complicated mixture of starlings and redwings. It was December 17, Bird Count Day, and this particular day was as rare and special as he'd ever have.

⌐

Waterfowl, particularly the geese, moved around less during the middle of the day. That meant the best counting at the lakes was done between eleven and two. There were two lakes; one down low, and this one, smaller and up in the meadow.

Visiting the meadow would be tough because of Sy, but it couldn't be avoided. There'd be some waterfowl and it would likely be the best place for raptors; the golden and bald eagles were strong, both the adults and the juvies. In the cottonwoods by the south side, if anyone could spot them, would be the great horned owls.

As soon as they stepped from the car, his eye stopped on a strange shape in the frozen expanse of meadow; it was the remnants of a bonfire, it looked like. But then another strange shape caught his eye, on the other side, near the trees. Two bald eagles, enormous.

They stood, staring at one another. They at the bald eagles, the bald eagles at them.

"My god," he breathed.

"Yes," she whispered.

They stayed like that for five heartbeats, six, seven, and then one of the eagles took off and then the other. He felt Antoinette shake herself away from the magic and back into herself. "Oh, Sy," she said. "I miss him. He was such a good veterinarian. This place . . ."

He glanced at her. It was at Sy's funeral where this idea had bloomed in the both of them, and they both knew it, though neither had yet said a word about it. How had it happened? At the reception, she had done something—he wasn't even sure what—a vague warmth, flirtation, hint? A strange silent signal? It was akin, he decided, to the dings of the warming metal things he'd just heard; how his heart suddenly pinged with a small ray of warmth sent toward it. He cleared his throat to say something about that moment, but Antoinette spoke first. "I can't believe how this day started."

"Oh, well. I shouldn't have . . . Dora's brain—"

She laughed. "No, I meant Bird Count Day. How people would go out this time of year and shoot as many birds as they could. And now. It has evolved into the best day. Audubon changed everything. Stop shooting the birds, count them. "

He stamped his feet again; the ache was intense. "For me, it's like hearing the national anthem. Everyone coming together, everyone across the whole nation, counting the birds. Citizen science at its best."

They could see some of the other counters from a distance, across the lake, but he didn't see any birds. If they were out there, they were being still, and without motion, they were invisible among the jumble of tree branches and undergrowth. He turned to her. "How much longer you got those grandkids?"

"Till Diego is back. Another year or so."

"That was a raw deal."

"It was."

"Although he shouldn't have been stealing cars, I suppose."

"There's some. Canada or a cackling?"

He paused and looked at the sky. "Cackling. They have faster wingbeats."

She marked her sheet and said, "No, he shouldn't have. But it was mostly a drunken 'I'm-a-single-dad-cutting-loose-with-my-friends thing,' not a regular habitual activity. And now the kids, without their dad around."

"Did you know," he said, "that there are eighty-six billion neurons in the brain and that there are one hundred trillion synapses between them? And those kids already have them all. How you keeping up with them?"

"They're in school during the days now," she said. "I'm cutting back on my hours at Moon's. It's true, that I come with them. I wouldn't mind dating a man who enjoys kids, wants to teach them a thing or two. Sees them as an asset, rather than a burden. Embraces the full catastrophe of life. What did you say recently about Sy making us all braver? That his death would teach us to reach out more?"

"Did I say that aloud?"

"I thought you did. Maybe I was just thinking it too. Surely we all are. Otherwise, the grief of standing in this meadow is too great to bear."

⌒

The Rare Bird Documentation Form was his favorite of all the forms, and, in particular, he appreciated that there were exactly three ways of being rare. Also, that he got to check a box on the matter: Unusual Species _____, Unusual Date _____, and Unusual Habitat _____.

He sat in the car staring at the form while Antoinette tucked herself in the trees to pee. If he had any power, if he were god, he'd let each person fill out one today; his wish was that everyone would see something unique. Not so much if the rare sighting meant climate change, which was foreboding and gave him a sick feeling in the stomach, but a good kind of rarity. To see something startling—plumage or vocalization or behavior—was what they all needed. That's what brains and hearts needed to grow.

"Name the species you consider ID contenders and explain how you eliminated them," the form said. This gave him pause. It sounded like the diagnosis of Alzheimer's, which could have been a lot of things that slowly got eliminated. Not a brain tumor. Not depression. Not normal cognitive decline. He glanced at the trees but there was no sign of Antoinette, so he picked up a form and filled it out for Dora.

Species: Dora

Age: 78

Sex: F

Date of Observation: The last 7 or so years.

Place: The Village of Blue Moon Mountain.

Distance from species: Close up

Viewing Conditions: Constant and uninterrupted

Photo taken, video, sound recording: All yes.

Optics used: Microscope of brain slice.

Other observers: Everyone on the mountain.

Was this report done from notes made during observation or from memory? Both.

Notes: Not rare. Familiar because of time together, familiar disease, familiar footfall of fate. Uncaring and indifferent universe that owes us nothing.

He did it quickly, without much thought, and there was no sign yet of Antoinette, so he filled out another for her. Antoinette. Dark eyes. Crooked lipstick. Large. Bright red plumage. Rare find. Very beautiful. Indifferent universe that owes us nothing but sometimes treasures are found nonetheless. He thought he might be able to check all three boxes.

> Unusual species: Happy human, yes.
> Unusual date: So late in life, yes.
> Unusual habitat: Falling in fondness at a funeral, yes.

He'd wondered about that, if he cared for her, or if it just so happened to be a matter of convenience and random order. Or just biology and human psychology and oxytocin and endorphins and yet he'd fallen for her, in the same way people all over the world fell for one another, which was simply by thinking and feeling in the other's presence, and thereby seeing better, noticing more, as with the birds.

He hoped she felt the same, and he was getting the idea that perhaps she did. He liked that saying about the brain: "What fires together gets wired together," and thus tender connection would get wired to Bird Count Day, for example, and the two would always be connected in their brains. He so much wanted his brain to change, to be rewired for this final era, to be as bright and alive and smart and curious as possible.

She came to the car and he hid the forms underneath the others on his clipboard. As she started driving, he smiled to himself. Perhaps he'd send them in to Audubon. As the count compiler of this region, he had a bit of influence, after all, and shouldn't everyone see something strange from time to time? Today, for instance, he'd seen and touched his first real human brain, and kissed a new woman for the first time in sixty years, seen two bald eagles in a tree, and it was still early.

⁓

"Welcome to Count Headquarters," he said as each birder arrived at his home. "You're part of a great tradition, going back one hundred seventeen years." They would nod and hug him or shake his hand, or, in the case of Flannery, pat him on the head and say, "You sweet dear." They came in pairs, stomping off snow. Some were laughing, but some were wincing, miserable because of the cold, and he didn't blame them. It was bitter out there, and that was his job, to cheer and to warm and to keep the spirits high.

Wendell was sitting at the table, holding his head in his hands, staring forlornly at a form. He likely didn't want to fill it out, because that would require the spotter's contact info, and he was not interested in sharing the fact of his existence. Flannery, after using the bathroom and pouring herself a cup of tea and adding some whiskey, settled herself next to him and started in on one, conferring with him from time to time. He thought he heard her say something about moving off the mountain come spring, maybe with her cousin Dandelion, and thought to ask her about it, but others were coming in, then—first Ruben and Jess, happy and full of love, and then Violet and Ollie, also full of love. Sergio and some friends from town piled out of the truck with something— what was that?—the skull of an elk they'd found. Angela and Lillie and Wyn came huffing in, complaining of the cold but happy all the same. Then Gris came in; she'd been babysitting Antoinette's three grandkids, and now had to go to work at Moon's. Suddenly there was chatter everywhere, a flock of whirs and cackles, catching up on lives and talking about the birds—the feeder versus field preference, the high number of crows this year. One of the kids tripped and was crying, and Antoinette was tending to her, and Flannery went to help, and Wendell was putting another log in the fire.

He closed his eyes so he could feel it all. All this! He opened his eyes and they settled on Antoinette, who was now getting the kids coloring on the back of his extra forms with a handful of pens she'd scavenged from around the house. One spilled apple cider and the other one wanted to add a log to the fire and he didn't think he would mind the chaos of it much, or, at least, he wanted to give it a try. Nothing in life was easy. Whether opening a plastic bucket or standing in the cold or seeing if a relationship would work; it was all hard work. His eyes caught Antoinette's and they both smiled, full with the knowledge that they had a secret between themselves, that they were going to give this a whirl.

He needed to tell Dora. Just this last thing, to say it aloud to her, out of an old and worn obligation. He'd bury the brain as soon as the ground wasn't so frozen, and with it he would also bury everything ugly, and clear his brain of all the things he could only admit to himself, the bitterness and raw rage and exhaustion, the guilt for the times he had not been kinder, and the resentment that he had felt far too deeply. It was either that or succumb, and he had always hoped he'd enter old age gracefully. That was the real thing here, of course, to fight for gratitude and spunk.

He found her in the shed, still in the bucket, which was in the box. He didn't want to talk to the box, or the bucket, and so he went to the trouble of prying off the lid again—despite the fact that he was very cold, and now each of his bones ached with a particular ping—and stared in at the brain. "I'm sorry it wasn't better for you," he said to the brain. "I said it all the time, and I meant it. I'm going to go on now. Start anew. I wanted to do what was right. Death is our debt to nature, our debt to being born in the first place. We have a debt to life too."

He put her back and started his trek to the house, walking carefully in the rut of packed snow. The sun was above him at its noon-high position and still very far south and was a dull glow behind the clouds. He glanced from it to the bird feeder, where there were sparrows and one mourning dove. They'd likely all be dead by now, had he not been feeding them; the winter had been too cold, too windy.

Something small caught his eye. A flash of blue. He breathed in. Tugged at his throat. It looked like a lazuli bunting, but that would be impossible.

And yet it was. Simple as that. He went in the house. "Everyone, everyone, please!" He did not yell it but said it with such emotion that everyone was at once stilled. He was crying, in fact, and once they recovered from the startle of seeing this old man with a wet face standing there in such an unapologetic and unfettered way, they gathered, some at the kitchen window, others at the sliding glass door, both of which offered a view of his feeder. There it was. All of them documenting it, cameras clicking and gasps and note recordings. The orange-yellow throat. The gray wings, the white belly, and above all else, the bright blue head. "A lazuli bunting," several of them said, which confirmed it. Then there was a long stretch of silence, and then the chatter broke out all at once, in fragments from every direction.

"It's magic."

"It's Sy, visiting us!"

"It's not Sy—"

"—It might be Sy."

"Oh, quiet. None of us believe in that stuff."

"I do. Also, it could be a fairy."

"It's a Christmas present."

"It's climate change."

"Never before seen in a winter in Colorado. Look, I just confirmed it on the Internet—"

"They're neotropical migrants—"

"—Did you know, they get their name from the gemstone?"

"I believe in magic."

"I'll call the paper. This is a first. A real first."

Antoinette sidled up next to him and gently took his hand. They stood, quietly staring at the bird, until he took his gaze off the beautiful bird to look at her. The shooting stars of gray in her black hair sprung from her head in crazy directions from the hat she'd removed; her dark eyes sparked as well, and looked straight into his own. Perhaps there were not three directions, but four: up, down, straight ahead, and inward. The compass of a life, pointing him in this new journey, and it didn't bother him a bit to say so. Soon—not too soon, but soon—he would die, and this genius, this debt to nature, would be guiding him more strongly than ever. In the end, he'd have to pay his debt, and this debt had shaped this world more than any other force. He only wanted to resist it for as long as possible, be a part of it all, to stick around for the experience. To see what became of his life, and this world. There was no wealth but time. Perhaps he and the planet were running out, but he would try to notice and love it all while he still could.

## Chapter Eighteen

# The Bear

The day before Moon's Solstice Party, and three days after Bird Count Day, on December 20, the winter's second blizzard hit. There were two feet of fresh snow and it was coming fast as she'd ever seen it when Gretchen snowshoed over to Anya's at 4 PM, Anya having just called and said, Please come, I can't do tomorrow unless you come get drunk with me tonight.

Gretchen now sits at the kitchen table, facing Anya, and the room is quiet and the blizzard is quiet. Oddly so. There are no howling winds, just a pouring from the sky. Everyone on the mountain is silent and staring out their windows, Gretchen thinks. They are considering the first blizzard, considering Sy, considering the two months that have passed since then. Everyone is worried about the trek down to Moon's tomorrow, and how it will be a pain in the ass, but that they'll give it a go.

As if in response to her thought, Gretchen hears the faraway low hum of a machine. It's Ollie Vreeland, she supposes: Of everyone on the mountain with a pickup and attachable snowplow, he is the most likely to start so early on the side roads, since the official county plows will only do the main road, and will only get this far up the mountain late in the day tomorrow. He did the same thing the whole night before Sy's ceremony. Normally, he and the others with equipment—Joe and Lillie and Wendell—would wait until morning. Or see if the sun would do the job. But tonight, they'll be out.

Something about this brings a blur of tears, which makes Anya catch her eye, raise an eyebrow. They hold a silent gaze. The stillness in the room is still new, still catching up with them. Just a moment earlier, a child had been seated on each of their laps—Zoë on Gretchen's lap, Michael on Anya's—chattering away, excited by the snow, by the school break just started, by the loss of a new tooth by each of them, by the news that tomorrow they would get to meet a new girl named Honey who has just moved to the mountain. They've been ushered out now, tucked into sleeping bags with hot cocoa and popcorn, and are watching *Peter Pan* in the next room, and the women are still absorbing the reverberation of silence, each of them frozen for a moment, each with one hand on the table, holding a whiskey glass.

Snow is still melting into Gretchen's hair, from the outside of the braid to the scalp, but she feels warm and settled enough now to talk. She tilts her head toward the living room. "A little magic will be good for them. I watched this flick with them the night I babysat. You've got the bond between brothers and sisters going on. That's good. And the power of imagination."

Anya nods. "It's been a recent favorite." Then she pushes her chair back and stands. She's wearing red pajamas, soft pants and a button shirt, and something about the red makes her hair particularly blond, especially the strands that rise from the static. She walks to the window. Quickly and with purpose. She seems to be searching for something specific, as if looking for the very source of snow, or to see if perhaps Sy is out there. She manipulates her chapped lips between her fingers as her gaze wanders across the sky and snow. Gretchen can see it in her reflection, and Gretchen bites her own lip in worry.

"And that crocodile. What's his name?" Gretchen asks.

"Tick-Tock."

"Yeah, Tick-Tock. The short days are hard. What we need soon is spring. Things are going to get easier, Anya. Hang in there."

"Incredible. Look how fast it's coming." Anya closes her eyes, then, in the way Gretchen recognizes as the moment when the alcohol of a much-needed drink is first hitting the brain, when you just start to let go. With her eyes still closed, she says, "You know, it keeps surprising me that Sy didn't wait for the mountain bluebirds. He was always on the lookout."

Gretchen searches her brain for the right thing to say, but she is strung out on insomnia and tears and grief, having given herself fully over to the emotion of letting go of Joe. Finally, she says, "Yeah, it was Sy who pointed out the sandhill cranes flying overhead this fall. I wouldn't have noticed them, they were so high. But he heard them. That weird garbled noise. Said to be a good birder, or a good liver, you had to use all your senses. That might have been the last conversation I had with him."

"That sounds like him." Anya opens her eyes and smiles sadly into the window. "He loved inspecting feathers. I was remembering that about him the other day when I saw one stuck in the snow. How he'd stare at feathers as if the coloration or the design might reveal something. But especially, he loved the bluebirds. You'd think those would be worth waiting for."

"Well. We can't—"

"That night, the night he killed himself? He was standing outside in the snowstorm watching me fold laundry through the bedroom window. I saw him out there, and I ignored him. I could have waved or blown him a kiss, but I was annoyed. I just wanted to be left alone, I wanted him to go away."

"Oh, Anya. We can't—"

"I know. I've been thinking on this. I believe I gave him what I could the vast majority of the time, which is the best any of us can do. But that's why he didn't wait for spring."

There's a burst of chatter from the room—the kids have spilled the popcorn, it seems—and there's the sound of Captain Hook bellowing at Peter. Anya leaves the window and looks in the room briefly, tucks her blond hair behind her ear, comes to the kitchen table, and sits, facing Gretchen. "You saved them, the kids. From the bear."

"Good thing, too. That fact is helping you forgive me now. You're mad at me, aren't you?"

Anya tips back her whiskey with a flourish and finishes it. Pours another. "Yes, I am."

"Because I broke up with Joe."

"Yes."

"Because I chose to end a love, and you didn't have that choice?"

"More or less. Although it's true that I think my love for Sy had died. But I was assuming it would come back. I was waiting. I was trying. I was sticking with it." Anya reaches over to pat Gretchen on her wet head. "You're a coward, Gretchen. You're stingy. You call yourself an unapologetic romantic, but it's surely on your own terms."

Gretchen starts to unbraid her hair and finger though the strands. "Good for you, Anya. Call it like you see it. Thank you for speaking up. You're right, I am. This might have been the greatest mistake of my life. And all you can do is forgive me for it. I couldn't picture my life with a kid in it. All that talking and explaining and listening and sitting down to do homework and going, going, going. It's a big thing. As you know. And obviously, I didn't want to decide later, *after* the kid knew me. She's already lost her parents, has to be adopted by her quiet Uncle Joe, move up to this crazy mountain, and then, what, deal with me? No, it's not fair. If I can't constantly be on call to do stuff, and I just can't, then it wasn't fair to stay. Joe will find someone who can." The words pour out in a quiet rush, as if Gretchen has been storing them up for too long. "Anya? I'm sorry. We can't help what we want."

"We can," Anya says. "We can help what we want. Sometimes. But listen. I have something I need to tell you." She paused and took a big huffing breath that reminded Gretchen of the bear. "I've been Sergio's lover for nearly two years."

Gretchen stands, sits, stands. Sits. Her hair, loose now and strewn around, is half wet and half dry. She catches her reflection in the window. She looks crazed. The strands that are wet are plastered to her shoulders and chest and the strands that are dry are floating up because of the static electricity. Her head rears back in surprise and she starts laughing. The image and the news are too bizarre. "What? What did you just say?"

"I didn't tell you because at first it needed to be a secret. Then, right as I was about to tell you—because I trusted you, and you're my best friend, and I believed you'd understand—you took up with Joe." Anya starts smiling now, amused by Gretchen's giggling. "And Joe and Sergio are good friends! And Sergio had decided not to tell Joe, which meant *you* couldn't tell Joe. And how could you start a good relationship with Joe while keeping a secret from him? I didn't want you to have to hide something from Joe. Secrets are no good. This mountain is small. So I'll forgive you and you forgive *me*."

But something has broken in Gretchen, a damn of tense grief is exploding out of her, and Anya is laughing too, if only out of the sheer joy there is in seeing someone laughing beyond their control. It is Gretchen who now goes to the window—she wants to look deep into the eyes of that crazy laughing witch she sees—and inhales deeply to try to settle the laugh. She can barely make out the tracks she made coming over here, the sunken path of snowshoe indentations that are lit by the house lights. Her eyes follow the path toward the apple tree. To the light of her house. Across the beautiful weighted, white world. She breathes in, deeply. "Well, holy shit," she says to the window. "Has it been good?"

"Very good. Although there's a guilt factor to it all, of course. Although I do think Sy did, or would, understand. In the end, it sustained me through a lot."

"Is that where you were, the other night? When I was babysitting?"

"Yes."

"Not at a grief-counseling meeting?"

"He is my grief counseling. Was."

Gretchen turns around and raises an eyebrow.

"We're ending," Anya says. "Like you and Joe. Not because we dislike each other. But because it's the right thing to do, so the other person can move on. I even love him. But I couldn't have a life with him. So, see, that's why I'm telling you. We're in a similar spot. I ended it because it's right. I need time to think. To get straight. And he needs to find some real love. He's a good man, and his life is going by."

"Exactly."

"Yes, exactly."

"Sometimes the right thing to do is to walk away. If it's gonna end in disaster." Anya raises her glass and waits for Gretchen to clink it. "A toast. To being alone. Because it's the right thing to do."

Gretchen toasts the glass and drinks. She feels suddenly warm, flushed, still sparkling inside from the laughter, and she winces with the realization she'll have to muster the courage and energy to go back out in the cold in the middle of the night. Perhaps, she thinks, she could even get lost, the snow is coming down so hard. Maybe she should just spend the night here, on the couch, and wake to the sounds of a family, just to see what that was like.

"This way we can all be friends," Anya is saying. "We can make this mountain work. You'll be able to be a nice neighbor to Honey. I'll be able to see Sergio fall in love and start a family."

Gretchen notices that Anya's eye crinkles have deepened. In the last two months, she has fully fallen into middle age, and Gretchen feels it too. "Anya, did you know that Joe told only one person about his niece, Honey? That Tate was likely dying and that Joe had been asked to consider adopting her? Did you know he told Sy, back in October?" Gretchen watches Anya's eyes rise in genuine surprise and so knows the answer even before Anya shakes her head, no. "Sy told him to do it. To adopt Honey. That he wouldn't want to live the rest of his life knowing he hadn't stepped up."

Anya snorts. "Bit ironic. Since Sy didn't step up. Fully."

Gretchen nods. "We gotta forgive him. Give him the benefit of the doubt. That's our major work to do this winter."

"I know." Then: "He was such a big man, physically. Strong and solid, I mean. And something about that made me assume he was fine. Here's how I think of him now: He was like a loosely held mold of sand, like those giant sand sculptures artists make on the edge of the ocean, and if I stuck my hand in too hard, he would simply crumble apart. So I didn't." Then she adds, "The one person Joe should have told was *you*. About Honey."

"Yes."

"He didn't want to lose you. He was in denial. Hoping for some other solution."

"Yes. That's what he told me."

"And you don't feel like you could give *him* the benefit of the doubt?"

"I could, actually. I can understand why he kept silent. I just don't want to be a mother. It comes down to that." The light from the TV flickers into the room as well, at odd angles and intervals and with a strange blue hue and all Gretchen can think to say is, "Next month, there will be two full moons. The second is the blue moon. I always wonder who named our mountain." Then she is crying. The hiccup of breath, the need to inhale—she has to stand up to breathe. Anya follows her, fast and startled, as if some whistle or shout has just burst through the air. Suddenly they are holding each other, Gretchen is sobbing, Anya rocks her back and forth, and when Anya slows up, Gretchen takes over, rocking, rocking.

They stay like that until something catches Gretchen's eye, something moving outside. She's trying to identify it. She keeps Anya tight in her arms, but her eyes wander across the landscape. It takes her a long time to realize it's a series of large slides of snow falling from the apple tree and from the roof; the wind must be picking up, or the depth of snow is at its break point. For a moment, though, she thought perhaps that it was the bear. Walking on all fours in the snow, swaying her head back and forth, stopping at the apple tree, sitting on her haunches and sharpening her claws, as if preparing for the battle to defend her world.

## Chapter Nineteen

# Moon's Solstice

The memorial was a surprise. Sergio and Ruben had been working on it for a month, and they got to Moon's early, with Angela there to approve its positioning and leveling, and they screwed hooks into the beams of the ceiling and attached two strands of rusted but strong thick chain, antique, from the Vreeland Ranch.

The plaque itself was solid and large, a thick slab of polished beetlekill, the blue stain running rivers through the light pine. Attached to it was a framed photo of Sy carrying a newborn calf in spring, snow all around, the sunlight haloing around his shoulder and blurring him to some extent, so that he looked both of this world and the next. Sergio had attached thin strips of tackboard to the frame, at the edges, so that everyone could add their own photos of Sy, or of the animals he'd helped, as well as slips of handmade paper, which Jess had made by blending newspaper and old drafts of her manuscript with dried flower petals and pine needles, happily ruining a blender, pouring the concoction onto screens and drying it. On these thick pieces of homemade paper, people were to write the names of animals Sy had saved in thick black marker.

This is the first thing everyone did as they walked in and were greeted. The snowstorm had ended just an hour ago, and so everyone was red-faced with the effort of shoveling out, or digging out their cars, or throwing sand and ice melt on the roads, or just the sheer cold. But every time the door dinged, there was a clatter of welcoming, and one table became covered with coats and gloves, and another with a few guitars and a violin, and meanwhile, new squares and rectangles of snow were left as everyone stomped their feet at the rubber mat. The tackboard got filled in too, with photos that everyone had been asked to bring, and with slips of paper. People stopped to scan the list as they took off gloves or drank their first beer.

PEACOCK, MALE.

TWO SOCKS, THE HORSE.

OH-BEETLE-BEETLE, CHICKEN NEARLY KILLED

BY THE MAMA BEAR

KOBE, THE AKITA.

PULLED DOZENS OF CALVES.

HE STITCHED UP MY ARM. BUT DON'T TELL THE LAW.

DON-QUIXOTE, THE DONKEY.

PUT DOWN MY HORSE WELL. A KIND KILLING IS A GIFT TOO.

MILKSHAKE, THE GUINEA PIG.

There was a cheerfulness and burble to the conversation, and open gossip about the New One, since the rumor had been roiling around like clouds since last week, the one about Joe's new blond-haired child named Honey. She'd moved in permanently, the story went, after her father's funeral, but none of them knew the whole story, except Lillie, who was refusing to say anything at the moment.

Beers were poured and drinks made and Angela and Korina

started bringing everything out to fill the big center table—chili and cornbread and cinnamon rolls. Lillie helped herself first—she was hungry for a real meal, having not gone into town recently—and as she ate, she overheard the fragments:

"She's seven, I heard," Ollie said.

"First grade next year, because she's a year behind," Celeste said.

"Maybe she's actually his child. You know, from some previous girlfriend," Korina said. "A baby that probably wasn't part of the plan."

"Wouldn't that be nice." That was from Angela, who was bringing out two new pitchers, one lemonade, one beer. "I mean, wouldn't that be nice, to have a plan?"

"No, it would not," said Violet, who, Lillie noticed, had cut her gray hair short and spiky, and had let Korina double-pierce her ears. "Having a plan sets you up for disappointment."

"We're all settling." This came from Ruben, who, Lillie knew, was referring to the fact that a new vet had expressed interest in buying the clinic, a woman ready to get away from the city and move with her partner to the mountain. This new vet had already said that Ruben was welcome to stay on as the vet tech, and everyone was relieved about this news, particularly Anya, who needed the sale of the clinic for financial reasons, and particularly everyone, who needed a vet and couldn't imagine life without Ruben.

The door dinged. It was Zach, who announced, "Earlier today, through the snow, I saw two bald eagles and a golden eagle eating a dead goose! It was a sight to see, I tell you!"

There was the start of a cheer, since no one really knew what to do with that piece of information, but then the door dinged again, and it was Antoinette with her grandkids, a big whoosh of cold air and color, and right after came Gretchen and Anya with her kids, and there was the flurry and chattering and the children ran off to the new pinball machine that Sergio had bought and put in the back, all proceeds to benefit the fire department.

"I have a pit bull," Lillie suddenly said. "I found him locked up. Anyone want him?"

Dandelion gasped, as Lillie knew she would. "Luce didn't take BW when he left?"

"No, left him in a crate. Good thing I went over to check. To see what the barking and howling was all about. You want him?"

"No," Dandelion said, but she was suddenly crying a bit, and Flannery went up and hugged her.

"Well, I don't want him eating my chickens. Or bothering the cats. But perhaps he won't. We'll see."

That's when Gris took a quiet moment to announce that she was moving into the old trailer, the one that had been occupied by Dandelion and Luce. This was because she needed her own space to read and daydream—it was exactly what she wanted.

Then several spoke of the lazuli bunting, which had made even the national papers, and Audubon magazine would be running a little story.

That made them speak of the radio story about the bears, which ended in a segment of Wyn huffing and grunting and crawling, backward, out of the bear den and quoting a line of poetry about refusing to go smoke's way, by which she meant never letting your life drift by, which caused Ollie to stand up, hold his beer, and quote T. S. Eliot, a poem about *water out of sunlight*, which caused Zach to stand and quote Elizabeth Bishop, the *shooting stars in your black hair*, which made Gretchen pause, and announce that next month there would be a blue moon, and that Walt Whitman used the moon to reflect on the inner lives of people, which are hard to get at. And did you know? Blue moons are created from the eleven extra days accumulated each calendar year, and it's said that the blue moon offers particular assistance to those who need it and ask, which she was doing on behalf of everyone on the mountain.

That caused Wendell to speak up about a phenomena called the Rayleigh scattering, and how Lady Tennyson wondered about the color blue, and how Lord Rayleigh had studied that question in Australia, and how things at a distance will always appear some shade of blue, an optical phenomenon. While he was talking, Lillie rolled her eyes and muttered about his scattered junk turning red from rust and went to the memorial to read what else had been put up.

SY TAUGHT ME TO FISH

SY TAUGHT ME THE NOISE OF CRANES

SY MADE US LATE FOR A HOUSE CALL BECAUSE HE WAS

WATCHING BLUEBIRDS.

From there, Lillie turned around and spoke up suddenly and in a nervous rush. "Joe's brother-in-law died! Of cancer! This happened soon after Sy died. This man, whose name was Tate, and who was a musician, was a single father, in Denver, because Joe's sister had already died in a car crash years ago. This child is Joe's niece. Joe, after much deliberation, adopted her. He didn't talk about it much because, well, we all know Joe. More of a listener than a talker! And because he wasn't sure it was gonna take, and why introduce something to this gossipy community if it wasn't worth the trouble?" Lillie looked around the room at the startled faces, particularly at Gretchen, who knew all of this already. "They'll be here soon. Her name is Honey, and she's going to need us. We're going to help her. We're all going to help each other a little bit more."

Everyone took a moment to absorb the fact that Lillie had spoken so much. Violet leaned over to steal Ollie's bread, and he raised his eyebrow, pretending annoyance. Jess looked at Ruben and then down at the ring on her finger. Korina said, "Plans are best kept quiet, anyway. They always change." Meanwhile, Flannery was looking out the window, and Dandelion went to touch her shoulder. Angela and Wyn had their heads ducked together, whispering something.

A blur of activity at the door meant that now the mountain would be complete. Joe and Honey. Everyone stood up to greet them, and Joe held Honey up in his arms. "I present Honey to you all!" and then there was the hubbub of hellos and introductions and someone's water glass spilled and coats were taken off and snow stamped from feet. There was the surprise of seeing Honey hoisted in the air like that, and folks wondered if she'd be scared or burst out crying, but she was laughing, having just been tickled. She had red cheeks and red snow boots and two red barrettes that flew up, along with her blond hair, when she reached the top of Joe's swing and started her descent. As soon as Joe set her down she shot toward Lillie, who gathered her up in her arms.

Lillie hugged Honey, whom she'd spent a lot of time with in the last week, as Joe worked on a back bedroom and installed a washing machine. Lillie had also started meeting with Anya, for therapy, at her own home, and Anya had explained about the *chemistry* of what might make Lillie so uncomfortable, about cortisol, about general anxiety disorder, which seemed so much worse after Sy, and about agoraphobia, which also seemed worse, and now she had a medication, which she'd only just started. But she felt now that she could be braver; she was going to *engage*.

Honey leaned backward into her. There would be a pattern to this, Lillie realized, just like there were two blue hours to every day, sunrise and sunset, an alpha and an omega, and the pattern held them all. Sometimes the pattern would weaken and loosen, but then it would be re-braided. She hugged the child and looked around. Noted the particular way in which Thayne rubbed Celeste's neck with one hand, the manner in which Gretchen greeted Joe kindly and handed him a beer, how Violet took Ollie's hand, how Jess hugged Ruben from behind, heard Honey shyly say hello and ask Zoë for the story of the bear. She saw Anya look at Sy's photo on the wall, and all the scraps of paper tacked around it, and then out the window, at the moon. No gunshots would ring out tonight, the bears were sleeping, and the full moon was going to bathe them in light just tinged with blue.

# Acknowledgments

Thank you to my readers and guides and keepers of the light: My agent, Jody Kahn, a gracious and tenacious soul. Dan Smetanka, an editor with an eye for the story under the story and the ability to call it forth. To the best of readers and friends: Laura Resau, Karye Cattrell, Kevin Coldiron, Todd Mitchell, Rick Bass, Rachel Maizes, Laura Katers, Mary Lea Dodd, Barbara Clark, Kurt Gutjahr, Mark Easter, Mary Dean, Jake Pritchett, and Eliana Pritchett. To Megan Fishmann and everyone at Counterpoint Press for doing beautiful work and caring about beautiful books. And to booksellers, librarians, and my readers: thank you.

*Thank you to the following journals and magazines for printing versions of these chapters:*

"County Road," *DoveTales*, 2016

"This Imaginary Me," *Split Infinitive*, 2014

"Recipe: I Am the Devil," *The Normal School*, 2011

"Plan B," *High Desert Journal*, 2011

"The Color of the Impression," *The Rocky Mountain News*, reprinted in the book *A Dozen on Denver*, Johnson Books, 2010

"Under the Apple Tree," *The Sun*, 2006, reprinted in the book *The Mysterious Life of the Heart: Writing from The Sun about Passion, Longing, and Love*, 2009

"Painting the Constellations," *The Normal School*, 2008

"Last Bid," *The Sun*, 2000

© Clayton Jenkins Studio

## ABOUT THE AUTHOR

LAURA PRITCHETT is the acclaimed author of *Stars Go Blue*, *Red Lightning*, *Hell's Bottom, Colorado*, and *Sky Bridge*, as well as several books of nonfiction. Her work has garnered several awards, including the PEN USA Award for Fiction, the WILLA, the High Plains Book Award, and others. Her work has appeared in *The New York Times*, *Salon*, *O, The Oprah Magazine*, *and Orion*. Learn more at www.laurapritchett.com.